HATRED ERUPTED LIKE A VOLCANO

Sam saw it coming and yelled her name. Too late. Without hesitation or warning she spit in Tayib's face. There was a gasp, Tayib's features darkened, his hand moved in a blur beneath his robe and emerged with a knife. Sam rushed forward but soldiers wrestled him back. Tracy was shouting, "Get your hands off."

Two of the *shaheen* pinned Katherine's arms. Tayib grabbed her hair, yanked her head back and brought the blade to her throat.

"No," Sam yelled. He rammed an elbow into one man's stomach, broke free and threw himself at Tayib. Something smashed the back of his head, jagged pinwheels of light, the room tilted and he was on his hands and knees. A drop of blood glistened and disappeared into the rug. Dead, he thought. We're all dead.

FLASH POINT

RICHARD AELLEN

HarperPaperbacks
A Division of HarperCollinsPublishers

This is a work of fiction. The characters, incidents, and
dialogues are products of the author's imagination and are
not to be construed as real. Any resemblance to actual
events or persons, living or dead, is entirely coincidental.

HarperPaperbacks *A Division of* HarperCollins*Publishers*
10 East 53rd Street, New York, N.Y. 10022

Copyright © 1991 by Richard Aellen
All rights reserved. No part of this book may be used or
reproduced in any manner whatsoever without written
permission of the publisher, except in the case of brief
quotations embodied in critical articles and reviews. For
information address Donald I. Fine, Inc., 128 East 36th
Street, New York, N.Y. 10016.

This book is published by arrangement with
Donald I. Fine, Inc.

Cover design and illustration by Designed to Print

First HarperPaperbacks printing: May 1992

Printed in the United States of America

HarperPaperbacks and colophon are trademarks of
HarperCollins*Publishers*

10 9 8 7 6 5 4 3 2 1

for M.N.
the happy defector

ONE

KATHERINE CAHILL'S CHILDREN WERE GIVEN A DEATH SENTENCE BY a man they never knew. Their fate was decided eight thousand miles from their Connecticut home on a moonlit night high in the mountains of Syria. The killer was chosen from five men who gathered in a courtyard outside a tent called the Garden of Heaven. Each man wore a white robe, the symbol of purity, with a yellow arm band identifying him as a *shaheen*, a martyr. Flanking them were thirty others, primarily men but a few women, devotees who hoped someday to become *shaheen* themselves. They knew of America but only their leader, Imad Tayib, had heard of Connecticut. None of them knew Katherine Cahill.

Imad Tayib spoke to them. He was not a tall man, perhaps five feet eight, but his voice was rich and authoritative. He spoke in Arabic, the language of poets, in which many words had multiple meanings and an accomplished speaker could make symphonies of speeches by the orchestration of his words.

1

Imad Tayib was such a speaker. He reminded them of their "great heritage," of their "noble past," and the "intolerable present." He enumerated the wrongs done them by Western nations and evoked a vision of a united Arab state "sweeping its enemies to destruction." Those closest to him could see the light reflected in his green eyes, unusual in an Arab and surely a sign of holiness.

Imad Tayib finished his exhortation and turned to the five martyrs. "Hear me, those who have chosen the ultimate glory. Tonight one of you will enter the Garden of Heaven."

"Allahu akbar," the five answered in near-unison. God is greatest.

Imad Tayib raised his right arm above his head. "One of you is chosen to be the hand of God."

"Allahu akbar."

"—the hand which has brought you the Book—"

"Allahu akbar."

"—the hand which will raise you to Paradise—"

"Allahu akbar."

"—the hand which slays the infidel—"

"Allahu akbar."

"—the hand of *jihad.*"

The young men began to chant, "Ji-had! Ji-had! Ji-had!" The crowd joined them, sending their voices up rock cliffs and echoing up the canyon. Imad Tayib walked toward the five devotees, his arm held high. He stopped before the first man, stared at him and moved on. He did this three times until he came to the fourth, a boy of nineteen. He touched the young man's forehead.

"Walid Hamri, you are chosen of God. Until to-

morrow when your shadow walks beneath your feet,
let earthly joy be yours."

Tayib took the young man by the hand, led him
to the tent, and drew open the flap. A translucent
gold and red curtain created a barrier beyond which
no one could see. The sound of a flute reached the
crowd. Imad Tayib turned to them.

"This man, your brother, is no longer Walid
Hamri. He is no longer the son of his father or the
child of his mother. Like the grains of sand that have
no name but which together make a nation, so shall
this man have no name but shall be called Beloved of
God." He turned to Hamri. "Enter now and taste the
one thousandth joy of Paradise."

Hamri stepped through the doorway. The four
men whose time had not yet come watched. Each had
passed through the Garden of Heaven once himself
during his initiation ceremony. They would not go
again until, like Hamri, they were chosen for a mission, but their memories remained vivid: abundant
food and wine, incense and music, the thick carpets
and silk pillows, and the girls with their scented oils,
glistening skin and pliant bodies—all this was only
one thousandth the joy of Paradise. And a prelude to
the death of three children.

BEFORE SHE opened her eyes, Katherine Cahill smelled
the coffee and heard the sound of giggles. Two of her
three children stood beside her bed. Nine-year-old
Allison held a cup of coffee near the pillow, while
six-year-old Joey leaned close and whispered in a
singsong voice, "Wake up, wake up."

Katherine freed her arms from beneath the covers and stretched. "Ummmm, what a nice surprise."

Joey tumbled into bed with her and reached for the television's remote control. Allison looked for something to put beneath the coffee cup so that it wouldn't stain the cherrywood side table.

"Here," Katherine said, handing her the copy of *Vanity Fair* she had been reading last night. Allison put the cup on it and crawled beneath her mother's arm. Katherine savored the smell of shampoo and sleepy childhood. The television came to life and the room echoed to the sound of cartoon voices. It was a silly way to spend a Saturday morning and Katherine loved it.

Jeff came into the room. "I just figured it out," he announced without preamble. "Tetras isn't random. Know how I know?"

He was talking about a video game.

"How?"

"Because the long rectangle is the easiest to place but it doesn't show up except once every twenty times. Actually once every twenty-one and a half. See, I counted . . ."

He showed her a piece of paper filled with numbers. Katherine didn't attempt to follow his explanation but pretended to listen and watched his face. He was eleven years old and filled with the serious enthusiasm of a child approaching puberty. He finished his explanation and pushed Joey's legs aside so he could sit down.

"Cut it out," Joey said.

"Shhh." Allison waved them to be silent.

"Cartoons are stupid," Jeff said.

"Then how come you're watching them?"

"I'm not, I'm just relaxing with mom."

"You can't see her if your eyes are glued to the tube."

They struggled to get closer to her. "Hey, hey," Katherine said. "If you make me spill this, nobody will watch TV in here."

"I made the coffee," Ali said, "you boys did nothing."

You boys. Katherine smiled inwardly at the inflection in Allison's voice, one she recognized as her own.

The phone rang. A familiar voice said, "Hi, it's me. Listen, I won't take too much of your time but . . ."

It was how he always started conversations: *I won't take too much of your time.* Glen Brandon had already taken twelve years of her life but now he worried about five minutes of her time. "I want to rearrange the holiday schedule with the kids."

Instantly she was on guard. "How?"

A burst of noise from the television obscured his answer. She put her hand over the receiver. "Turn it down." And then to Glen, "What did you say?"

"Is that the television?"

"The kids are here."

"In the bedroom?"

"Ali made coffee this morning. They served me breakfast in bed."

"I thought we decided the kids weren't to come into our bed."

"It's not ours any more, it's mine." Katherine kept her tone light, aware that although Allison's eyes were on the television, her attention was on the conversation.

"I know, but for the kids' sake I think consistency is important. Maria and I don't let them into our bed and I don't think you should encourage it, either."

"Why did you call, Glen?"

A pause. Allison turned and said, "Is that daddy?"

"Here, say hi." Katherine handed the phone to her daughter.

"Hi, daddy."

Glen's voice was small and too faint to be intelligible but Katherine recognized the booming tone of false good cheer. Or maybe it was sincere good cheer, Katherine could no longer tell. The divorce was over a year old but there were times when she felt she had never known Glen at all.

Allison returned the phone to her. "Daddy wants to talk to you. He wants to take us to Europe."

Glen had dropped the subject of the kids in the bedroom. His tone was affable and reassuring. "Maria and I are going to Italy in August. We want the kids to come."

"You have them in July."

"I know but we can trade. You keep them July and I'll take them August."

"Glen, they have camp in August. They're already signed up—"

"We can send them in July."

"If there's space available and if they don't mind changing plans and I don't mind changing plans—"

"There's space available. I already checked." When she said nothing, he pressed on. "Listen, everything's balled up at the office. Ron left for another firm and I'm the only one close enough to the Leland merger. I'm working nights and weekends and there's no way I can take the kids in July. It's a bitch but there it is. If you want to hold me to the letter of the law, then what can I do? I won't be able to see them this summer and that's it."

That's your problem, she wanted to say. But the kids were listening and she didn't want to argue. The truth was that she could rearrange her schedule easily enough. But, why was she *always* the one called on to make last minute changes?

"You'll have to ask the kids," she said.

"It's all right with you?"

"Whatever they want to do is all right with me."

"Thanks, Kat. Let me talk to Jeff."

She gave the phone to Jeff, who got off the bed and walked to the window, where he answered in monosyllables, "Uh huh, pretty good, I guess so." The divorce had been more difficult for him than the other two. Jeff adored his father who had left his family for another woman. The banality of it was depressing. Glen had fallen in love with his travel agent. When Katherine discovered the affair, Glen acted as if it were her fault. "You had to bring it up," he kept saying, "you had to ruin it." Now, watching Jeff's hunched back, his fingers toying with the cord of the phone, Katherine felt a stab of remorse.

Allison turned to her. "Are we going to Europe?"

"If you want to."

She hesitated. "The boys could go and I could stay with you."

Katherine gave her a hug. "I'll be fine. You go ahead."

Ali took the phone and when Katherine heard her announce, "Mom says okay," she felt a tug at the heart. Don't live through your kids, she told herself.

Let them have a good time in Italy. Imagine their excitement, the stories they'll bring back, the way they'll interrupt each other competing for attention. She smiled. They'd have fun and that's all that mattered.

TWO

WALID HAMRI WAS AFRAID HIS SUITCASE WOULD BLOW UP BEFORE he had a chance to check it aboard the aircraft. His contact in Rome had explained how the device operated, but all he remembered was the warning not to take the suitcase into the mountains or travel at altitudes above five thousand feet. In the taxi on the way to the airport, he flinched at every pothole. Rain battered the windshield and the taxi skidded as they swerved to avoid a motorscooter. An accidental death would be a catastrophe. Unless he gave his life in the service of *jihad*, he would not enter Paradise. He truly believed that. The taxi driver, noting his reaction, laughed and said something in Italian, which Hamri understood to be reassuring.

Keep calm, Hamri told himself. Any sign of nervousness might alert the security guards.

Fifteen minutes later he stood at the Alitalia check-in counter behind a family making a fuss about seat assignments. Come on, come on. Hamri's hand

9

was sweating. He gingerly placed the suitcase on the floor and wiped his hands on his pants. A little boy ahead of him stared. Hamri looked away and then back. The boy's eyes were still on him. Something was wrong, the child knew he had a bomb in the suitcase. He would tell the security men who would drag him away and torture him until he cried like a girl and then they would put him on trial—

Hamri remembered his disguise. He was wearing the turban of a Sikh and carried a false passport that identified him as a resident of New Delhi. That was what the boy was looking at, the turban.

"Next."

The family moved aside and Hamri stepped up to the counter. The agent's smile seemed genuine, probably glad to be rid of the complainers.

"Bags, *signore?*"

"Just one."

Hamri placed the suitcase on the scale. With a practiced motion the agent tagged it and lifted it to the conveyer belt. "Gate seven, Concourse A."

Hamri stared after the bag.

"Something else, *signore?*"

"No. *Grazie,*" he added, and moved away. It was his only Italian word.

In the terminal Hamri said a silent prayer as he approached the security gate. Earlier that morning he and his Italian contact had shared a pipe of hashish, but the euphoria had worn off and he could feel the tension. Relax, he thought as he placed his shoulder bag with its deliberately scuffed edges on the conveyer belt and stepped through the metal detector.

A security officer glanced at the X-ray machine

and turned to him. "Has this bag been out of your sight since you packed it?"

Hamri had been coached on what they would ask and how he should reply. He forced a smile and shook his head. "No."

"Has anyone given you a gift or a package?"

"No."

The security officer frowned slightly and opened the bag. Hamri's heart began to pound. The officer rummaged among the clothing, pulled out some magazines in Hindi, two apples and a sandwich wrapped in cellophane. He shoved the bag across the table without closing it and turned to the next person.

Another official gave a cursory glance to make sure the photo matched Hamri's face, then stamped his passport and waved him through. Now there was nothing left for Hamri to do. He had performed his prayers. Since his night in the Garden he had eaten only the fruits and vegetables that grew naturally from the earth. The flesh of no living thing had passed his lips. Filled with righteousness, Hamri boarded the plane.

KATHERINE CHOSE a red Chanel suit to wear to pick up the children. Before she left the house she draped a silk scarf over her shoulders and adjusted it carefully. The gold tones highlighted the light brown, almost amber, color of her eyes. She had an oval face framed by thick chestnut hair which was stylishly swept to one side. As a teenager she had worried that her nose was too small for the strong cheeks and full, wide mouth. Today her worries were of her children. They had been in Italy for two weeks and during that time

Iraq had invaded Kuwait, the United Nations had imposed sanctions, and American troops were on their way to Saudi Arabia. If the Middle East was going to erupt in war, she wanted her children safe at home.

Katherine left for the airport at three in the afternoon. Tony had offered to pick up the kids but Katherine wanted to get them herself. Tony was the chauffeur and gardener who lived in the carriage house. His wife Rachel was the housekeeper. Before she was divorced Katherine had employed a cook, but now she prepared the meals herself. It was not a matter of money. Katherine's trust fund provided her with an ample income. But meals were part of the family ritual that were more important to her now that Glen was gone.

Katherine and Glen had been divorced for fifteen months. She had passed all the anniversaries—the first Thanksgiving where Jeff took his father's place and sliced the turkey, the first Christmas without anyone to help wrap gifts, the first wedding anniversary to be ignored. She had adjusted to life as a single parent without too much self-pity, had given up those friends who treated her divorce as a communicable disease and devoted herself to filling the empty space in her children's lives. There were, she admitted, times she missed the presence of a man, the warmth and solidity of a friendly body, someone to park the car while she and the children stood in line for a movie. She missed those things but she was not man-crazy, which was why she was surprised at her own reaction when Jane Galloway had an affair.

Jane was a recent friend, a divorcée of seven months. She was flamboyant, brash and opinionated, which meant that people either enjoyed her or couldn't stand her. Katherine found her refreshing. They met three times a week at the country club, where they played tennis and had lunch. Because subtlety was lost on Jane, there were no taboo subjects. When the two got together, Katherine felt like they were sorority sisters sitting around a dorm room a little high on wine and newfound adulthood.

This morning Jane had been late for their tennis date. Katherine hit balls against the backboard until she was called to the phone. A voice sang, "Some enchanted evening . . ."

"Jane?"

"I know, I'm a false friend and lousy tennis partner but listen, just listen to this." There was a sound of water. Jane said in a low voice, "Know what it is?"

"Sounds like a shower."

"His name is Scott Ramsey, a real estate mogul, divorced with one little girl who he says looks more like me than her mother. We're getting married as soon as he stops wearing boxer shorts. Am I crazy or what?"

"You met someone?"

"Yesterday at MOMA," she said, referring to New York's Museum of Modern Art. "I should have called you—I would have called—but we've been in a trance all morning. Staring in each other's eyes. His are brown with gold flecks, and I've forgotten what mine are. I'm dizzy, absolutely dizzy."

"Where are you?"

"His place. I used my MCI card." In the background a man's voice called her name. "Coming," Jane called, and then in a low voice, "An exotic sea creature, that's what he is. A fairy godfather who's building his own house. If this works I'll have marble countertops in the kitchen and a skylight over the bed."

"When are you meeting his mother?"

"Remember the first time you did it in the shower? Never mind, he's wonderful. Wish me luck."

For the rest of the day Katherine had been oddly troubled. She found herself questioning Jane's behavior: was she being responsible? What about AIDS? Had they used condoms? The voice in her mind sounded like her mother's.

Now, as she joined the traffic on the Bruckner Expressway to Kennedy Airport, she tried to analyze her feelings. It wasn't jealousy, although the conversation had brought back memories of Glen and the heady days of infatuation. It wasn't betrayal. Maybe it was just the timing that bothered her. A divorce involved a recovery period, a time of safe anchorage before setting sail on the uncharted seas of dating. She had entered the harbor before Jane, but Jane was the first to leave. The timing was wrong.

Traffic slowed to a crawl. Now what? she thought as she braked to a stop. Cars stretched bumper to bumper for miles. The city was visible, the tops of its skyscrapers floating on a brown haze. She wondered if she would have enough time to shop Bloomingdale's as she had planned?

She used the car phone to call the airport to see if the plane would be late. The Alitalia agent assured her that Flight 67 was still on time. She turned on the radio to WNCN, the classical music station, and tried to relax.

● ● ●

IT HAD rained much of the day but the storm had passed and the russet hills of Siena lay somber and brown beneath a blanket of gray cloud. Olive-grower Gino Manelli rode his bike along a muddy path, the tail of his open raincoat slapping his knees. The explosion occurred six miles above him and ten miles southwest. Minutes later a descending ball of fire popped through the base of the low cloud and dropped behind a hill. A dull explosion and then another sound, like a cat, which ended abruptly as three objects struck the earth one after the other.

The bike slid from under him as Gino braked. He jumped clear and stood uncertainly, staring at the sky. From beyond the hill a plume of black smoke spread against the underside of the clouds. The wheel of the bicycle rasped to a stop. A suitcase lay embedded in the ground, clothing bursting out. Farther up the hill was a shiny piece of twisted metal. And the body of a girl. A young girl.

Gino scrambled over a low fence and went to her. Allison lay on her back, her right arm crushed beneath her, a glistening white bone jutting from the calf of one leg. Thick brown hair cradled her head. A trickle of blood from one ear was the only sign of internal injuries. One eye, burst red, stared vacantly at Gino.

"O Madonna," he whispered, and made the sign of the cross. He knelt and lifted her hand and felt for a pulse. And then, already shivering, he took off his jacket and covered her head. He ran back to the bike and pedaled quickly away. Nobody could survive such a crash, he knew, but maybe speed could make a miracle. If he called the police, the hospital, who could tell? As he reached the road, he remembered

the odd sound and realized what it was. A scream from the girl. A death cry.

I SUPPOSE they met Maria's parents, Katherine thought as she entered the terminal at JFK International Airport. The children's step-grandparents, that's what they would be. She imagined them as characters from a Fellini movie, aging trapeze artists who called the kids *bambini* or vintners who took them dancing barefoot on grapes. She tried to deflect a stab of jealousy.

At Gate 15 Katherine checked the monitor. Alitalia Flight 67 was listed as "Delayed." She went to the nearest check-in counter, where a group had gathered around a young woman in a maroon uniform with a gold scarf.

". . . changing the designation," the agent was saying. "If you'll follow me, please. Those waiting for Flight 67, this way."

Katherine caught up with the woman. "Excuse me, why is this plane late?"

"We have an announcement," the agent said. She quickened her pace. A man in a cardigan sweater said, "They changed it. Now it says 'See Ticket Agent.' "

Katherine took the agent's arm. "What's wrong? What's happened?"

The woman's head turned toward her and Katherine noticed two things: the nametag said Andrina and there were tears in her eyes. "It . . . it . . . ."

They had reached a private lounge where an Alitalia representative stood in the doorway. "Would those of you waiting for Alitalia Flight 67 step in here please?"

Someone cried out. Katherine turned to see a woman clutching a transistor radio to her ear who began repeating something in Italian.

"What's she saying?"

"The plane. Something happened . . ."

"Ladies and gentlemen, there has been an accident. If you will just step in here . . ."

Inside the lounge, taped music played an instrumental version of a Beatles tune. People were sobbing now as alarm spread like a chain reaction. Katherine's breathing was shallow and there was a roaring in her ears. She grabbed at the moment and tried to stop time. Uncertainty was hope.

"Ladies and gentlemen—"

No, please.

"—we've just had confirmation that—"

Not my children, not Jeff, not—

"—Flight 67 has crashed."

Screams and someone yelling, "Survivors. How many survivors?"

Don't ask, Katherine thought. She sensed the nightmare answer before it came.

"There are no survivors."

The roaring in her ears reached a crescendo. Jeff, Ali, and Joey. She took two brittle steps toward the couch and reached out. Someone grabbed her arm and helped her sit. She dug her fingernails into her forehead, oblivious to the screams and tears and questions that called for answers that held out hope for no one.

THREE

IMAD TAYIB MIGHT HAVE BECOME A DOCTOR. THAT WAS HIS ambition when his family moved from the country to the Shi'ite sector of Beirut. As a young man Tayib did menial work at a Red Crescent clinic during the day and attended English classes in the evening. Long before he could qualify for admission, he gathered application forms from a half-dozen medical schools in Britain and Canada. Then came the Israeli invasion of Lebanon, civil war, and the multinational peacekeeping force that brought the American battleship *New Jersey* and the random artillery shell that hit an apartment building.

The building collapsed onto the street where Tayib was passing. He was trapped in the rubble, his lower body pinched by jagged reinforcing rods. A broken gas line triggered an explosion and fire which shriveled his hair and seared his lungs. When the flames reached his legs, Tayib dragged himself free, screaming in pain as metal teeth ripped his body.

The medical technology Tayib admired could not repair the injury which left him impotent. He disappeared from his family and friends and made the pilgrimage to Mecca, where he prayed for a miracle to restore his body. None came.

Tayib stopped speaking, wandered in the desert. He became gaunt. One night, asleep under the stars, Allah sent him a dream. Alone in a vast desert he saw a horse and rider bearing down on him. The horse was a huge white Arabian stallion with blazing eyes. Its rider was wrapped in white robes and flowing *kaffiyeh,* headscarf, eyes invisible in the narrow opening of the garment. The rider carried a standard, the silver crescent of Islam, on a tall pole that he lowered like a lance. Tayib wanted to run but couldn't. His mouth opened but no sound came. As the lance plunged toward him, Tayib realized that the horse's hooves made no impression in the sand and he understood. Pulling open his robe, he bared his chest and in that moment of acceptance he became pure faith. The lance passed through his body and he was seized with a vision of an Arab nation united under Islam. The shell from the *New Jersey* had not been random but was guided by Allah's hand to turn him from error to the path of righteousness. He had been ordained. A man without children would father a united Arab nation. This was his vision, his calling, his revenge.

Tayib called his movement the *Rih Asfar,* Yellow Wind. He traveled throughout the region gaining converts, searching for a safe place from which he could train his disciples and send them to all corners of the land. One of his followers told him about the small Palestinian refugee camp in the Ansariyah mountains. It was a place of domed peaks and deep gorges cut into limestone cliffs pockmarked by caves. Perched on a promontory was the abandoned Castle Raqba, once manned by Crusaders to protect pilgrimage routes to Jerusalem. It was here that Imad Tayib established his headquarters.

The day after the crash of Alitalia Flight 67, Tayib finished his evening prayers at the mosque and crossed the grounds to the towerlike structure that had once been the castle keep. A squad of soldiers, his personal bodyguard, lived on the ground floor. Followed by four *shaheen,* Tayib climbed the narrow stairs to the radio transmitter on the top floor. Now that Hamri was gone, he would have to choose another martyr from among the recruits. Five martyrs to match the five pillars of Islam, the duties of every devout Muslim.

A fluorescent light provided harsh illumination to a room dominated by the controls of a radio transmitter. Tayib took his position at a low table in front of a microphone while the *shaheen* settled themselves around him. The equipment had been installed by the Rumanians during the Ceaucescu regime in payment for the assassination of a dissident living in London. Tayib was offered weapons or hard currency, but what he asked for was a powerful radio transmitter. His voice, he knew, was a more effective weapon than any gun. And tonight he had a new message to transmit.

"In the name of God I greet the faithful. Today soldiers of the *Rih Asfar* struck a blow against the forces of imperialism, atheism and Zionism. A loyal soldier has paid with his blood the price of our future and today sits in Paradise. The man known as Beloved of God has struck down Alitalia Flight 67. Let the evildoers tremble, there is no end to our struggle, there is no limit to the blood we will shed. For each one of us you kill, we will kill one hundred, one thousand, one hundred thousand. We fear no people, no army, no nation. We know one duty, which is to serve Allah. We know one triumph, which is the victory of Islam."

The voice rode the night air south to Damascus, to the refugee camps in Jordan, to the PLO training bases in the Bekaa Valley, to the Christian militia in Beirut, all the way to Jerusalem deep in the heartland of occupied Palestine, where the Jews would hear the sound of the future, the voice of Imad Tayib.

DAWN CAME. Katherine lay in bed staring out the window as the world took on color and form. Everything was the same: the tall oaks and maples bordering the yard, the balcony outside the window, the bedroom with its beige and cream wallpaper, the silver-topped jars on the dresser, the Matisse painting on the wall— everything the same yet so horribly different. The world lived, but Katherine had died.

The events of last night were a blur, scattered and disjointed impressions, the world seen through shards of broken glass. She didn't yet know the cause of the crash. Her brother Brian had come to the airport and brought her home, where Dr. Stravitz gave her a sedative. She lay in bed beneath extra blankets, fists clenched, legs drawn close to her chest while the world faded and with it the phone ringing and Brian's voice echoing down the hall, "No, I'm her brother . . ."

Katherine got up and wrapped herself in a robe. Passing the guest bedroom, she saw Brian asleep in his pale blue shirt with white collar and dark slacks with red suspenders. He lay on his back, arms akimbo, snoring slightly. He had found a hanger for his coat and his shoes were tucked neatly beneath the bed.

Katherine went downstairs and moved from room to room, not knowing what she was looking for, her thoughts in perpetual retreat until she saw her father's portrait in the library. The painting showed Jock Cahill cradling his favorite hunting rifle. He was dressed in a red plaid shirt and tan hunter's vest. She had been her father's favorite. When he died of a heart attack a few days short of his sixtieth birthday, she was devastated. But by then she was a mother. She had Jeff and then came Allison and Joey—

The doorbell rang. A young woman in a neat suit with carefully swept hair stood on the porch clutching a microphone. Behind her a man in a knit shirt and jeans balanced a video camera on his shoulder.

"Excuse me, you're Katherine Brandon?"

"I'm Katherine Cahill."

"Ravena Young, Channel 6 News. I know it's early, Ms. Cahill, but we saw the lights come on and we wanted to get your reaction to the Yellow Wind announcement. How do you feel about the men who killed your children?"

"What men?"

"Imad Tayib and the Yellow Wind organization." The young woman's eyes opened marginally wider. "You don't know?"

Before Katherine could answer, Brian appeared. He was barefoot and upset. "I *told* you people to leave us alone." He touched Katherine's arm. "Come on inside, I'll take care of this."

"But she said—"

"I know, I'll explain—"

Ravena stepped forward. "If we could just have a word or two."

Brian turned on her. "I told you people last night to stay off the grounds. This is private property and I'm ordering you to leave."

He guided Katherine into the house. Behind them Ravena called, "Ms. Cahill, do you have any reaction to the men who killed your children?"

Brian slammed the door and turned to her, his eyes bloodshot, a strand of hair sticking out from his head. "I'm sorry, I was going to tell you when you got up—"

"A bomb?"

"The State Department called late last night. An Arab group claimed responsibility—"

"Someone *killed* them?" She was trying to understand. Not an accident, not an act of God but a man-made catastrophe.

"It was some sort of retaliation for that terrorist they caught trying to bomb the Vatican."

She vaguely remembered the incident. The man had died in police custody when he jumped from a window. "What was his name?"

Brian shook his head. "Some Arab they killed."

"I mean the one who . . ." Bombed the plane. She couldn't say it. "My children. The man who took responsibility, what was his name?"

"Talib, something like that. It'll be on the news, in the papers . . ."

She moved past him and went outside. The news

team was in the circular driveway where Ravena, illuminated by a small, powerful light mounted on the camera, was talking into the microphone.

". . . here at the home of Katherine Cahill where the Flight 67 tragedy is all too real." Seeing Katherine, she continued quickly. "And here is Ms. Cahill, mother of the three—"

Katherine put a hand over the microphone. "Who took responsibility?"

Ravena tried to pull the microphone away. "Ms. Cahill, please—"

"What did you say his name was?"

Ravena stopped the tug of war for the mike and smiled tightly. "Please give me the microphone."

"What was his *name?*"

The cameraman's face appeared from behind the lens. "Imad Tayib."

"Thank you." Katherine walked back to the house while Ravena called after her, "If we could just get your reaction . . ."

She was too numb to react but she knew the name of death. The name of death was Imad Tayib.

DOUG LIVINGSTON lay between the legs of a SwissAir stewardess named Ursula. It was late morning in Damascus. The sheets and blankets had long since been kicked aside and lay crumpled on the floor. The remnants of breakfast were on a tray; empty orange juice glasses, plates smeared with pancakes and syrup, two half-filled cups of coffee grown cold.

"Hold still," Livingston said. He unwrapped two pats of butter and balanced one on each breast.

"What are you doing?"

"Don't move. See how long you can hold them there." His fingers traced a design down her stomach. She shivered. "It tickles."

"What about this?" His hands moved between her legs.

"Bastard," she whispered.

"Watch the butter."

Doug Livingston loved games. He was forty years old, with the build of a man ten years younger. Listed on the U.S. Embassy staff roster as a political affairs officer, he was actually the CIA's special projects officer in Damascus. Livingston's job was to recruit and infiltrate the terrorist groups based in Syria. His vocation was seduction. Safe seduction, as he thought of it. Unmarried and free of moral or logistical restraints, he chose his women carefully and never lied about his activity to his employer. The CIA could accommodate many forms of human weakness; the only unforgivable sin was lying.

Livingston's fingers found a sensitive spot. Ursula shuddered. A trickle of melted butter ran down her left breast and under her arm.

"Ah ah," he warned.

She gripped the bed, head thrown back, the underside of her lip glistening. Livingston savored her effort at control. He ran his thumb in small circles that sent silken flesh moving. Her legs twitched slightly.

"Not yet," he whispered.

With three fingers he entered her, pushed forward, rotating his hand. A convulsion, and Ursula's shoulders twisted. With a small cry she reached for the butter and smeared it on her breasts. Her lips pursed in mock dismay, she lifted her hands and showed him. "Too bad."

Livingston moved above her. She brought her hands to his face and rubbed his cheeks with butter.

"Lick your tits."

"You do it."

"I'll bite them."

"No."

"Then you do it."

She buried her chin but kept her eyes on him while her tongue darted unsuccessfully toward her nipple. She couldn't quite reach, so he moved his mouth to her breast and sucked hard. When he drew back, he blew across the dimpled skin.

"Again."

Now the nipple stood erect, and this time she was able to touch it with her tongue. He increased the tempo of his strokes—

His beeper sounded. Livingston quickened his pace, cursing the interruption. Whatever it was could wait, the whole world could wait. *Bip-bip-bip.* He moved quickly to climax and collapsed on top of her. They lay still, breathing heavily. Ursula toyed with his hair. Probably getting butter in it, Livingston thought irritably. He rolled away, grabbed the beeper and turned it off. In the air-conditioned room sweat felt like a cold shadow where their bodies had met. The sensual tide ebbed as he began speculating what might require his attention on a day off. He sat up and dialed a private number. Ursula curled close to him and ran her hand along his leg. The secretary answered, "Seven-oh-seven."

Livingston identified himself and a moment later

Jerry Riggs, the deputy chief of station, came on the line. "You want the good news or the bad?"

"Just tell me."

"The Alitalia crash last night. The bad news is that it was a bomb. The good news is we know who's responsible." Riggs paused dramatically, a characteristic Livingston found annoying.

"Who?"

"Your friend and mine, the Mountain Man himself."

"Tayib?"

"He just held one of his radio press conferences. Retaliation against the Italians for the death of the Vatican bomber. 'Let the world tremble' and all that."

"Any reaction?" He didn't need to say *from Washington*.

"Not yet."

But there would be, Livingston knew. "I'm on my way." He got up and grabbed his clothes.

"Hey," Ursula called out.

Livingston, buttoning his shirt, turned to look. Ursula crouched on her hands and knees in the center of the bed, her buttocks facing him, head canted against the sheets. She smiled as he approached. He took her ankles and yanked her legs straight. "You'll catch cold."

Outside the hotel, Livingston bypassed the first cab and got into the second, a precaution that had begun during his years in Beirut and was now habit. The cab rocketed down the street, horn bleating like an angry goat. Before going to the embassy, Livingston stopped at his apartment, where he shaved and put on a fresh shirt, one custom-tailored in London.

He arrived at the embassy forty-five minutes after

the phone call. There was a note waiting for him: the chief of station wanted to see him. He found John Berger in his office, which was predictably cold. Although the embassy was air-conditioned, an auxiliary window unit lowered the temperature to a level that everyone but Berger found uncomfortable. Some people said that the cold air reminded the chief of his boyhood home in Minnesota, while others maintained that he was overweight and hated to sweat. Berger greeted Livingston with an uncharacteristic smile that divided his face into two round cheeks. "Would you like a drink, Doug?"

The use of his first name was not a good sign; the two were not friends.

"No, thanks."

"That's right, you're a juice man. You want orange juice? I can send Lila."

"I already ate breakfast."

"Fine. To business. Why don't you shut the door?"

Livingston did, but the hospitality and sympathetic tone of voice didn't con him. He knew how the station chief and the permanent staff thought of him. Livingston had come to Damascus in the wake of Iraq's invasion of Kuwait. He was what they called a cowboy, a special-assignment man who reported directly to the Deputy Director of Plans in Washington. He used the local support staff—couriers, secretaries, code clerks—but gave nothing in return. He was a pariah, and Berger usually went out of his way to ignore him. Now suddenly they were on a first-name basis.

Berger settled back in his chair. "Just one question, Doug: how bad is it?"

"How bad is what?"

"What I mean is, how much did we know?"

"About the bombing? Nothing."

"Good. Because that's what I told the ambassador. We knew nothing about any bomb threat to American lives. If we *had* known, we would have red-flagged the information and sent it to Langley. The next question is, why didn't we know? But that's something they'll want to discuss with you in Washington. They want you back for consultation."

"Is that the rumor?"

"That's the fact, Doug."

With undisguised satisfaction Berger slid a piece of paper across the desk. Usually Livingston received his messages directly; that this one had been sent through Berger was both humiliating and ominous. The real message was clear: headquarters was displeased. Riggs was wrong, Livingston thought. There was no good news; there was only the bad news and the worse news.

FOUR

WHEN SHE WAS THIRTEEN, KATHERINE HAD BEEN A FINALIST IN the National Small Bore Target Championships. Using a custom designed .22 match rifle, she competed in a half-dozen different states until she reached the finals in Sacramento. Her interest in guns came partly from the family's arms-manufacturing business and partly from a desire to please her father. What she remembered most vividly was the pause before pulling the trigger.

"Focus," her father had called it. "You focus your attention and wait for the world to stop. Then you squeeze the trigger."

The world had stopped now, and Katherine's focus was on recovering the bodies of her children. She and her mother went to Siena, a picturesque town set among the red hills of Tuscany. During the summer of her freshman year at college, Katherine and two girl friends made an art tour of Europe. They had visited museums and made pilgrimages to sites made famous by great painters. Siena she remembered as a tranquil respite in an otherwise hectic summer. Now the streets were busy with police vehicles, army trucks and television news vans.

They were met by Leanne Rickover, a representative of the U.S. Consulate, whose wrinkled clothes and haggard looks testified to the strain she was under. She took them to the town hall, headquarters for the crash investigation, where Katherine was shown a small stack of Polaroid photographs. Here were the children of Flight 67: a girl with red hair and pigtails, a baby whose body had been flattened by the impact, a chubby boy who looked asleep, a teenager without a jaw—and then there was Joey. She closed her eyes.

"That's him," she whispered.

An Italian police officer gently took the photo from her.

"The boy's name?"

"Joey—Joseph Brandon."

The officer wrote the name on the back. Katherine forced herself to continue. Another little boy, then a baby whose waxy skin resembled that of a doll —and finally Allison. There was something wrong with her face, something a little lopsided. It took Katherine a moment to spot it. Although Ali's eyes were closed, one of them bulged slightly and the lid did not quite cover it. For some reason . . . she had no idea what . . . this minor imperfection bothered her more than a gaping wound.

"My daughter . . . Allison Brandon."

There were six more photographs of children but Jeff wasn't among them.

"Is this all? They must have been sitting together . . ."

"There's no rhyme or reason," Leanne said. They found one woman's purse five miles from her . . . from where they found her."

They checked the list for adults. Maria had been identified, but Glen was still missing. Katherine looked through the stack of adult male victims. Some were disfigured, but by now Katherine was blessedly numb to the mutilation. Glen was not among them. She returned the stack to the officer, who took it to a hollow-eyed couple that had arrived moments earlier.

Katherine said, "I want to see my children."

A temporary morgue had been set up in an unused warehouse. An army mortician dressed in green plastic coveralls met them in an outer office. He handed Katherine a face mask and, after she put it on, he dipped his fingers into a jar of Vicks VapoRub. *"Permesso, signora."* Menthol made her nostrils tingle.

Inside the warehouse, light filtered from dirty green skylights. The bodies lay in rows. They were covered with sheets of manila paper torn from a large roll. The arms were folded over the paper. Attached to each wrist was a tag with a number. The mortician led them to Joey, pulled the paper aside. Katherine barely stifled a groan. Even in sleep his features had always been active, fingers curling, lips twitching, eyes moving beneath the delicate lids. Now she saw only gray skin, an inanimate mask. She touched his cheek; the skin remained indented, like putty.

"All right," she whispered.

They went to Allison. Her denim jacket was stained with mud and Katherine thought automatically, We'll have to wash it. Allison, always so careful with her clothes, so fond of the latest style, so eager to wear makeup, so impatient to grow up, now lay among strangers, lifeless, demeaned by death. Katherine unhooked the amethyst necklace around her daughter's neck. It was a birthday present that Katherine had found at an antique shop. She gripped it tightly, seeking the warmth it must have held just forty-eight hours ago, lying so close to her daughter's heart.

All the hotels were full, but with Leanne Rickover's help they found a bed-and-breakfast inn run by an Italian couple with four children. Their hosts were sensitive to their needs, but the sound of the children's voices was too cruel a reminder to Katherine of her loss.

The next morning they learned that twenty-one bodies had burned so badly that the authorities were asking for dental records. Three of them were children. Filled with dread, Katherine called her dentist, who said he would send both Glen's and Jeff's records immediately.

Glen's records proved unnecessary. His body was found that afternoon. Katherine called his parents in Boston. She had always thought that the Brandons blamed her for the divorce, but at the end of the conversation Glen's father blurted out, "You should have worked it out, the two of you. We told him. But he was always so sure of himself and now, look. Now look." Katherine didn't know what to say. The conversation ended on a note of awkward civility.

Tragedy doesn't bring people together, she thought, it tears them farther apart. Certainly it did with her mother, whose constant attention and well-meaning solicitousness Katherine found suffocating. Grace Cahill, a nervous, stylish woman, was smaller than her daughter. Without cosmetic surgery she would have looked effortlessly young for her age; with it she looked determinedly so. Her method of dealing with tragedy was to avoid it by talking.

"Were you able to sleep, Katie? The starch they put in these sheets, it's like lying on sandpaper. Look at my elbows, they're rubbed raw. I'll have them changed. You have enough to endure without this."

To avoid eating with strangers Katherine and Grace had taken breakfast in the bedroom. The windows were open and a soft breeze moved in waves beneath muslin curtains. Grace noticed the breakfast tray. "Is that all you're going to eat? You didn't touch your eggs."

"I had some toast."

"You need protein. Eat some of this."

"I'm not hungry."

"Do you think I am? I force myself. That's what you have to do. Our bodies are vulnerable right now. Emotional distress lowers the resistance. You remember when Jack Reiner was fired, how June developed colon cysts? She's certain it was stress related and I believe her. Where are you going?"

Katherine was putting on her shoes. "Walking."

"Wait, I'll get dressed and go with you."

"I think I'll go alone."

Katherine saw the hurt in her mother's eyes. She had never been the little girl in pretty pink crinolines, the dainty daughter that her mother craved. She was her father's child, a tomboy more comfortable holding a tennis racquet or rifle than a tea cup. Besides, she couldn't stand being cooped all day waiting for a message to come.

It was two more days before they discovered

Jeff's body. During that time Katherine walked a great deal, out late at night and up before dawn. She saw the search teams leave at first light. They were Italian army soldiers, young men in good physical condition, who searched the fields and forests carrying plastic bags, clear for debris, black for bodies. Each morning they left with heads held high, voices strong, their steps brisk. They returned at dusk like old men, silent, shoulders hunched, feet heavy.

Katherine sought out the places where the wreckage landed. The tail section sat on a gently sloping hill, eerily intact and surrounded by popped rivets. A crane was loading it onto a flatbed truck. She asked a man who spoke English where they were taking it.

"To the air base at Livorno. They will put it together, all the pieces."

Why bother, Katherine wondered. They already knew the cause of the crash and who did it. Had the occupants been conscious during the long fall from thirty thousand feet? She imagined the horror of knowing death was coming at you, and shuddered.

Grace was waiting on the porch when she returned. She wore a stricken look.

"What is it, mom?" Even as she said it, she knew. "It's Jeff . . ."

"They found him. The dental records."

It was what she had feared, what she had tried to avoid thinking about while knowing she should prepare for it. Her stomach knotted. She forced herself to breathe. "I want to see him."

"Katie, you can't."

"I will."

"Don't. Don't put yourself through that."

She had to. She had to see them to know, not with her head but with her heart, that they were dead.

"I'll be all right, you stay here."

Grace grabbed her arm. "What they found is not Jeff. Why do you want to do this? Why do you want to put that image in your mind? Why?"

"Because it's all I have left."

The burn cases were kept in an ice skating rink. With the cotton mask pinching her cheek and the electric smell of Vicks VapoRub in her nostrils, Katherine walked down a row of bodies covered by sheets of plastic, some of them no more than lumps the size of a pillow. The mortician stopped beside a form roughly Jeff's size. She looked to him, he nodded. Katherine took the black plastic, hesitated, then lifted it.

The face was unrecognizable. She swallowed with difficulty. This is my boy, this is my boy. She reached out tentatively, as she had done with the other two, to touch his cheek, to say goodbye. Her hand faltered. This is my boy, this is Jeff. She tried again but the charred flesh was untouchable. She turned and ran out of the room.

Katherine's face mask lay on the blue-and-white tile floor of the bathroom, where she clutched the sink, tears stinging her eyes. This was the final indignity, not death but this, that her son's body, the flesh of her flesh, had been made alien to her touch. And this she could never forgive.

FIVE

Doug Livingston landed at Dulles Airport and took a taxi to an inconspicuous hotel in Arlington where visiting CIA officers stayed. The Washington Monument, bleached by summer haze, beckoned from across the Potomac. There had been a time when he would have gone to the city for dinner, but these days the capital depressed him. There were too many fatbellied tourists crowding the streets, too many homeless people living in cardboard boxes, too many black teenagers wearing cockeyed baseball caps, swaggering through red lights. Instead, he swam in the hotel pool and went to bed early.

The next day a mini-van with smoked windows picked him up and dropped him at an underground entrance at CIA headquarters in Langley. His meeting with the Director of the CIA was scheduled for 9:30, but Livingston arrived early so he could have a few minutes alone with his mentor, the Deputy Director of Plans, Bob Hatch.

"Are you wearing your shit-eating dentures?" Bob greeted him. He was a bear of a man, whose casual sarcasm disguised a furious ambition harnessed to an astute political sense. The two men had known each other since Livingston's first overseas assignment in Cairo, where Bob Hatch had been chief of station.

"Is it that bad?"

"Actually, no. Your punishment is the dark imagining of your soul. The truth is, you weren't brought to Washington to ride the barbed wire banister. Fearless leader has something else in mind, something so special it can come only from his honeyed lips. You will, of course, make the appropriate abject obeisance prior to your reprieve and express the usual boundless enthusiasm for your new assignment."

"Which is?"

"Inopportune for me to mention here in the land of a thousand ears. Come on." Hatch clapped him on the shoulder and led him to the hallway, where they ran into the Chief of Middle East, also on his way to the meeting. The CME was pompous and capable and an outspoken critic of the kind of cowboy operation Livingston was running.

"You look like shit this morning," Hatch told him happily.

The CME made a wry face. "I think the gene pool is deteriorating. My son called last night. He failed his bar exam."

"If he's really blind to the law, you can get him a job with us."

A secretary ushered them into the Director's office. A silver humidor sat on the desk between framed photographs of the Director's children and a cut glass inkwell. Tradition had it that the cigars foretold a man's fate; if offered one, a man could relax, but if the humidor remained closed, it was time to begin composing a resumé.

The Director had the patrician good looks expected of a man in his position: thick gray hair and features bracketed by a broad brow and wedge-shaped chin. Without getting up from his desk, he welcomed them in a nasal voice, apologized for having a cold and waved them to their seats. He opened the humidor and pushed it toward Livingston. "Cigar?"

Grateful for the good omen, Livingston took one. They were Cohiba cigars, Castro's brand, smuggled from Cuba, a subtle reminder that the agency operated in a world free from the constraints of the everyday citizen. After the lighting rituals were complete and the first tendrils of smoke hung in the air, the Director blew his nose and began.

"I suppose you expect a bashing. You expect it because you've got a man inside the Yellow Wind organization, and we should have had advance warning of the Alitalia disaster, and eighty-three American citizens should still be alive. Is that what you expect?"

Livingston ignored Hatch, who pursed his lips and nodded imperceptibly. "Something along those lines."

"Not going to happen. I'm not going to second-guess you, Doug. I'm not interested in recriminations. More to the point, the President is not interested in recriminations. For the record, we should have known. It's a lapse we don't want to repeat. You know it and I know it, and now let's move on. The question is, how do we respond to this atrocity? Do we make protests, threaten punishment and then do nothing? That's what we've done in the past and we've had no deterrence. This time we know who was responsible. We know it from his own lips and we intend to do something about it."

He held up a thin folder embossed with the CIA seal and labeled SECRET. "Operation Bright Justice. A plan to capture Imad Tayib and bring him to the United States to stand trial for murder."

Livingston was surprised. Like many senior officers, he had watched with dismay the gradual emasculation of the CIA. Mistakes made public resulted in a lessened prestige and increased Congressional interference, called oversight. Administrative ranks swelled but the number of case officers declined, as more and more information-gathering was performed by satellites and electronic intercepts. Computers grew fat on raw data but evaluation and analysis lagged far behind. Frustrated, Livingston had considered leaving the agency. Then came Iraq's invasion of Kuwait, the special assignment in Syria, and now this: a plan to capture Imad Tayib.

The Director tossed the folder to the table. "Not to leave the building. You can read it in the Situation Room when we're done here. Briefly, we are talking about an airborne assault on Raqba. Three choppers and a Delta Force snatch team. When Tayib makes his radio broadcast, he's got only a dozen soldiers inside the building with him. Seal the building and he's trapped."

"What about the recruits camped out in the courtyard?"

"They'll be immobilized by concussion bombs,

smoke grenades, tear gas, airborne suppression fire—
complete chaos, that's the goal."

"It's usually the outcome, never mind the goal,"
Hatch said.

The Director's eyebrow twitched in irritation.
"It's a Joint Chiefs show and we wouldn't be involved
except for one little detail. Raqba sits underneath the
missile umbrella controlled by a radar station on
Mount Kajar. Our brothers in uniform have asked us
to knock out that station long enough for the snatch.
Without the radar the missiles are blind and the choppers are safe. We're the asphalt crew. We pave the
way."

He got out another file and tossed it to the table.
This one was bordered in green. It was the 201 file for
one of Livingston's agents, a man known by the code
name LEGHORN, a courier who ran errands between
Tayib and the Yellow Wind office in Damascus.
"What do you think? Is this the man for the job?"

Livingston shook his head. "He's a Palestinian.
The Syrians wouldn't let him near the radar station."

"Doesn't have to get near it." The Director nodded to the Chief of Middle East, who from his briefcase took a map and laid it on the table. The DCI
continued, "The radar station gets its power from the
hydroelectric dam at Lake Afrin."

"Here," the CME said. He shifted the map toward
Livingston. The lake was a jagged finger of blue. A
power line marked in red ran from the dam to the
radar station three miles away. Between them was the
Castle Raqba outlined in yellow.

"You'll note there's a step-up transformer a quarter mile away from the castle."

"Here." The CME jabbed again with his finger.

"Tayib's power comes from a feeder line from the transformer. There's an access road—it looks like a footpath in the photos—that starts at the castle and dead-ends at the transformer." The CME traced it silently. "We want LEGHORN to sabotage the power line while Tayib is making his nightly broadcast."

"I don't know if he can do it."

The CME said, "He got us great photographs of the castle."

"The second time around. The first time he got scared and dumped the camera."

"He's a poodle," Hatch said. "We know that. How do we turn him into a wolf?"

"Or is there someone else you think would make a better candidate?" the Director asked.

For ten minutes the men discussed various possibilities within Tayib's organization, but for one reason or another none of them looked like a good candidate for recruitment. Finally a silence settled over the group. A sheen of sweat sat on the CME's upper lip. He removed the cigar from his mouth, smoke oozing as he spoke. "I don't see what's wrong with LEGHORN. He's got family at Raqba. That gives him an excuse to visit. He looks perfect on paper—"

"Except he's a poodle."

"You keep saying that," the CME said to Hatch. "What are you advocating? We tell the President to scrub the operation because our agent is a poodle?"

"I am *advocating* an analysis of his motivation. Is it ideology? Ego? Money? Big tits? Rosy red assholes? Maybe he wants a scholarship for his son to Harvard Law School. In short, how do we make sure he'll do what we want him to do?"

The Director said, "Doug, what's your feeling? How much control do we have over LEGHORN?"

"His ideology is only skin deep. I told him that, because the Soviets have run home with their rubles, we hold the key to Palestine. The American public will be sympathetic to a homeland once the radical elements in the PLO are discredited."

"You told him that was official policy?"

"No, my opinion."

"Does he believe you?"

"I don't think it matters. He's not much of an ideologue but he's an Arab, so he needs some kind of ideological linchpin to justify what he does."

"A linchpin." Hatch nodded. "I like that. We'll pull Tayib's linchpin."

The Director sneezed lustily and blew his nose. The CME said, "All right, if it's not ideology, what's our lever?"

"Ego and money in equal proportion," Livingston said. "He loves tradecraft—codes, dead drops, secret signals, any kind of hardware. When I sent him to get the photographs of Raqba, he didn't want to use an off-the-shelf Yashica. He wanted a *spy* camera. Something hidden in a cigarette lighter." This provoked smiles. "He's a low-level courier who sees himself as a hero. This mission will help build up that image. Aside from that, there's always the universal motivator—hard cash."

"No problem there. The budget on this one's unlimited."

"Not quite," the Director said quickly. "We were thinking roughly one hundred thousand. That should be enough."

"It'll be enough to motivate him, but I can't guarantee that once he's at Raqba he won't lose his nerve."

"The worst that can happen is that nothing will happen. Our AWACS monitor the station's radar signature. The mission begins only if the station goes down."

"One question," the CME said. "What's to prevent LEGHORN from accepting the payment and then selling us out to Tayib?"

Hatch said, "Ten percent down and the rest if he's successful."

"What if Tayib pays him off?"

"In what, camel turds?"

The Director said, "I'd like to hear what Doug has to say."

"LEGHORN is an Arab. He thinks like an Arab. If he admits any association with us, he'd be pork to Tayib, forever tainted. They'd call him a hero today and tomorrow put a bullet in his head. He might refuse the assignment, he might lose his nerve, but he's not going to turn. He's not that stupid."

When he left an hour later, Livingston had his mandate. For security reasons he would not attempt to recruit a more reliable candidate but concentrate on LEGHORN. Covert photographs would be taken. If blackmail became necessary, pictures of LEGHORN talking to an American CIA agent would be the man's death warrant. It was standard stuff: dollar bills in one hand and a man's testicles in the other.

SIX

THE FUNERAL WAS HELD AT ST. PAUL'S CHURCH. KATHERINE SAT in the front row with Grace and Brian and his family. She wore a black mourning dress decorated in French lace. Grace clutched her daughter's arm and periodically dabbed her eyes with a handkerchief. Katherine placed her hand over her mother's and listened dry-eyed.

"Jesus said, 'Suffer the little children to come unto me,' and surely there must be a special place in Heaven for those who join God in the fresh bloom of childhood. We cannot know why He called them early to His side, but we are uplifted and supported in the knowledge that Jeffrey, Allison, and Joey lie safely in God's arms."

The words brought no comfort to Katherine. She had never been a particularly religious person and church had always seemed more a social than spiritual occasion. To actually *need* the church was an admission of weakness. "A wonderful crutch if you

45

happen to be a cripple," her father had said, his voice pitched low in the confidential manner he reserved for her alone. During his life Jock Cahill inspired admiration in his friends, fear in his rivals, anxiety in his son, and adoration in his daughter.

"The test of our faith is not when our bodies are healthy, our loved ones safe, and life is rich with reward. The test comes when we are burdened with a tragedy so monstrous it threatens to drive charity from our hearts and undermines our faith in the Lord. Today our faith is put to that test and, as we open our hearts in prayer for Jeffrey, Allison, and Joseph, so we must not close our hearts to those who are responsible for this tragedy but must pray for the strength to forgive them so that God will—"

"No!" Katherine's voice rang throughout the church. Her mother touched her elbow as Katherine stood and crossed to the pulpit. She covered the microphone with one hand and spoke in a low voice. "Say one more word about forgiveness and I will walk out of this church and never come back." She paused a moment longer, then bent to kiss the Bible before returning, head bowed, to her seat.

Father Hanson saw the eyes of his congregation shift from Katherine back to him. The Cahills were a powerful family, an influential family. Katherine had served on the last fund-raising committee. He decided that it wasn't his job to create a breach within the parish. He would heal the congregation and let God heal Katherine Cahill's heart.

"Let us remember Jeffrey and Allison and Joey as they were in life, filled with light and laughter and hope . . ."

The children were buried in the family plot at the

town's oldest cemetery. The breeze was warm and smelled of freshly-cut grass. After a prayer, the coffins were lowered and Katherine moved forward and turned to face the mourners. She held three white roses.

"Jeff loved to invent things," she began with a shaky voice. "I think he was always searching for perfection. He has a whole drawer full of designs. Last month he wanted to put his ceiling on rollers so it would slide back at night and let him count satellites when he couldn't sleep." She lowered her eyes to the grave and said softly, "You lived a life rich in imagination, Jeff. Now live in God's imagination." She let the first rose fall and then moved to the next grave.

"Ali wanted to be so many things. Every year she dreamed of something different. In second grade it was a nurse, in third grade, an astronaut. In the fourth grade she wrote a paper and talked about becoming a ballerina. One sentence I remember . . . 'Sometimes I dream of jumping so high that I never come back to earth at all.' " Katherine's voice caught. She raised the white rose to her lips and whispered, "You have your wish, honey." She tossed it into the grave.

One of the mourners, a mother whose baby had begun to cry, tempted it to silence with a bottle. Katherine stood at the third grave and took a deep breath. "Joey loved to play hide and seek. When he was little, he had me put my hand over my eyes and said, 'Close your eyes.' If he saw me peeking, he'd say, 'Close your eyes wider.' " She paused. "Now it's your turn, Joey. Close your eyes very wide." She kissed the rose and released it. Then she turned and went back to the car. Family members passed by each grave with a handful of dirt. Katherine did not look back.

Family and friends gathered at the house. Katherine went upstairs to change clothes. As she approached Jeff's room, she heard the familiar sound of his Casio electric piano. She ran into the room and stopped. Brian's son, ten-year-old Ronny, stood at Jeff's desk, one finger poised over the piano key.

"What are you doing?"

"I was just looking . . ."

"This is Jeff's room, these are Jeff's toys. Don't you ever come in this room without permission, do you understand?"

Ronny nodded, his eyes wide with fear.

"These are *his* things!" she repeated more vehemently. The little boy was close to tears. "Go on, get out of here."

He ran from the room. Katherine turned off the Casio and looked around. Had the model of the Space Shuttle been there on the floor or had Ronny moved it? She picked it up, went to the closet and looked inside. Toys sat on shelves above his clothes. She couldn't remember where the Space Shuttle had been. The closet, the floor? Maybe Jeff's desk? Panic. His room, his toys, everything had to stay the same. The same . . .

"Katherine?" Brian stood in the doorway.

"Ronny was playing with Jeff's toys."

"I know. He came downstairs crying."

"He shouldn't have been in here," she said defensively.   "It's hard for them, the idea of permanence. This morning Laura asked if Ali would come back as a ghost."

"Tell him I'm sorry."

"You can tell him yourself later." Brian looked around the room. "If you need any help, you want me to contact a charity or be here to take care of all this . . ."

"All what?"

"The kids' things. When you decide what you want to do."

"I'm not doing anything. This is his room. I just don't want anybody touching it."

"Okay."

"I'm not crazy, Brian. I know Jeff's not coming back. But when I touch his things I want to know that his fingers held them last. That they're where he put them, where he wanted them. I don't want anybody else in here."

"Whatever you're comfortable with, that's all that counts." He paused. "Mom's in the kitchen. She's driving everyone crazy but it's keeping her busy. You want anything? Tea? Soup? Bloody Mary?"

"No. Thanks."

He took one last glance around the room. "You and I were lucky. Our world was safer."

He left. Katherine lay down on the bed and stared at the ceiling where twenty model airplanes hung suspended. From the back yard came the sound of children playing, chasing each other around the pool. One of the models caught her eye. It was an inflatable replica of a Boeing 747. Katherine stood on a trembling mattress and stretched to unhook it. The plane was blue and white and decorated with the Pan Am logo. A clear plastic nozzle was embedded in the bottom of the fuselage. She pulled out the nozzle, placed her lips where Jeff once placed his, and breathed the air from her son's body. It tasted of plastic. Sound-lessly, motionlessly, she cried.

THE PRESIDENT of Syria did not show his anger. Hafez al-Assad was a gaunt man whose thin gray hair lay uneasily across a high square brow. He stood at a window overlooking Damascus, his back ramrod straight, head hunched slightly forward. His eyelids were lowered so that it was difficult to tell where his gaze was directed or what he was feeling. It was an effect he had cultivated in his youth which had become second nature. It made his Minister of Foreign Affairs nervous as he gave his report.

"We have already had calls from the Italian and American ambassadors," the Minister said. "They demand Imad Tayib's extradition."

"Let them demand what they like," Assad said. "What can they do? Put us on a list of states that support terrorism?" It was a rhetorical question, since Syria was already on such a list.

"Unless Tayib is extradited, the Americans say they cannot normalize relations with us."

Assad smiled. The Americans had already come a long way toward normalizing relations in the wake of Iraq's invasion of Kuwait. In exchange for Syrian participation in Operation Desert Shield, they had sent military supplies to bolster Syria's defenses along its border with Iraq.

"The friend of my enemy is my enemy; the enemy of my enemy is my friend," Assad said, quoting an Arab proverb. "As long as Iraq remains a threat, the Americans will remain on our doorstep."

"Rostoff expressed concern."

"Does he ask us to extradite?"

"No, but you know the Russians. They say nothing until they get instructions from Moscow."

"And will they join the demand for extradition?"

"These days who can predict? They have many problems of their own and they want Western commerce and technology, which makes them more susceptible to American pressure."

There was a moment of silence. President Assad remembered how, as a boy, he had carried water from a well in two buckets attached to a stout pole across his shoulders. When both buckets contained the same amount of water, the task was simple, but let either one vary too greatly from the other and they became difficult to carry. For twenty years Assad had remained in power by balancing the two major powers, playing one against the other, just as he balanced the more intricate array of religious and ethnic groups inside his country. Now Imad Tayib was doing the same thing. In the shifting alliances and associations of the Arab world, Tayib had managed to weave an organization composed of many different threads. On one hand, he was carrying on an Islamic crusade and was perceived by many as a holy man, a messenger of God. On the other hand, his soldiers were Palestinian refugees made desperate and willing to give their lives for the struggle against Zionism. Tayib was popular, therefore powerful, therefore dangerous. Assad admired his skill but only for as long as it could be controlled. Now it was time to find out how much control he had left.

"Send word I want to talk to him. Arrange a meeting."

"Here or—?"

"Or what?"

"Tayib has said he will not come from the mountains until Jerusalem is in Muslim hands."

"I know what he says," the President snapped. "Now I want to know what he will do. Set up the meeting." He nodded his dismissal. When the Minister was gone, he leaned forward and rested his elbows on the railing, relieving the pressure on his back. Age, he thought with distaste. He would want a massage tonight.

SEVEN

KATHERINE SPENT LONG PERIODS STARING AT THE NEWSPAPER photograph of Imad Tayib. The photo appeared in numerous publications and was always the same one. Tayib's expression was not the angry glower of a fanatic but rather one of haughty suspicion. The full well-trimmed beard, narrow face and aquiline nose gave him more the aspect of a graduate student than a murderer. The eyes were eerily light in color, almost transparent, as if Katherine were looking right through the man. It was the black pupils that drew her attention, the center of a vortex, like looking down the barrel of a gun. The longer she studied the face, the more certain she became that this man, far from being insane, knew exactly what he was doing. She could almost believe he knew about Jeff and Allison and Joey . . .

Katherine looked away. It was the second week of September but already one of the trees in the back yard had begun to turn, a few pale yellow leaves appearing among the green. How long did it take a leaf to turn colors? Had the process begun the same day the children died? Lives extinguished before the season was over.

She turned back to the photograph. I won't let you do this. My children are not just a statistic, another notch on your scorecard of victims. You will know them, you will know their faces and their names and the terrible pain you caused. You will face your accusers. You will be brought to justice . . .

Katherine arranged a meeting with Charles Dorrit, head of the State Department's Office of Counterterrorism. She took the train from New York to Washington on an overcast day that matched her mood. At the State Department she signed in at the security desk and made her way past two gray-green plaques that listed the names of all American diplomats killed in the line of duty. The statesman's occupational hazard had become the common risk of being an American.

Charles Dorrit was a thin man with crewcut hair and thick-rimmed glasses perched on a large nose. He held out a chair for her, then took his place behind the desk. "First, Ms. Cahill, let me express my condolences for your loss. I say that both as an individual and a representative of the State Department. And let me assure you that the United States Government is doing everything in its power to cooperate with the Italian authorities to bring those responsible to justice."

"You mean Imad Tayib."

"If we can believe his radio broadcasts, yes."

"Has the Syrian government agreed to extradite him?"

"Not yet."

"Do you think they will?"

"I wish I could give you a concrete yes or no, but in this kind of situation all we can do is keep trying—"

"And if nothing happens?"

As if to emphasize his sincerity, Dorrit took off his glasses and placed them on the desk. "Ms. Cahill, I'll be honest with you. There's not a lot we can do. Syria is not a client state. Since the Iraqi invasion of Kuwait we've been repairing fences with Syria, but the relationship is still tenuous. We have to tread carefully—"

"Which means that if Syria doesn't extradite him we won't do anything?"

"Not at all. We'll keep trying every means at our disposal. My understanding is that we're talking to the Russians. They have more influence in Syria than we do."

"What do they say?"

"They're being very cooperative."

It was like talking to an answering machine: all available avenues were being pursued, the United States was asking for cooperation, the Administration was committed . . . Banalities sucked at her like quicksand. She tried a new approach. "What can you tell me about Imad Tayib?"

"There's not a lot to tell. Imad Tayib is not his real name, which makes him rather an enigma. His background is unknown, although from his accent we think he's from Lebanon. He surfaced about eight years ago spreading the usual mixture of fact and fiction and fury. Five years ago the Israelis tried to assassinate him in Tunis but he escaped. Since then he's moved his headquarters to the mountains in northern Syria."

"I know that much from the newspapers."

"Then you probably know as much about him as we do."

"Is he married?"

"Not that we're aware of."

"Then he has no children?"

"Again, we don't know of any. That may be a deliberate precaution on his part. A family would be a liability."

"How?"

"A terrorist who makes his business killing people invites reprisal. Arab families are very close and there's a legacy of frontier justice, an Old Testament kind of eye-for-an-eye mentality that demands violence be repaid in kind. A man without a family is less vulnerable."

"Can you let me see his file?"

Dorrit replaced his glasses. "We're a policy-making body, Ms. Cahill. We're not an intelligence-gathering organization."

"You don't have a file on Imad Tayib?"

"We have internal files on all suspected terrorists and their organizations."

"Then I'd like to look at your file on the Yellow Wind group."

"What good would that do?"

"Imad Tayib killed my children. I want to know who this man is and why he did what he did."

"The *why* is simple. People like Tayib are fanatics, motivated by hate. They have one myopic point of view of the world and that's all they see."

"I still would like to see the file."

"What I'm saying, Ms. Cahill, is that much of our information comes from classified sources. We have no brief to disseminate it."

She pulled out three photographs and put them on his desk. "Jeff, Allison, Joey. Would you be able to explain to them why the government that couldn't protect them is going to safeguard their killer's file?"

Dorrit kept his eyes on her. "That's emotional blackmail, Ms. Cahill."

"Can't you look at their faces?"

Dorrit glanced down, then back up. "I'll keep you informed of any new developments."

Katherine wanted to kick the desk and scream, *Look at my children, look what I've lost, talk to me.* Instead she put the photos back in her purse and said coldly, "Thank you for all your help."

Not his fault, she thought as she made her way out of the building, but still she was angry. If the government knew no more than the newspapers, then maybe the newspapers could help her. Most of the profiles of Tayib had quoted from an early interview given five years ago to a reporter from the *Washington Herald.* Katherine brought out one clipping and found the name of the reporter, F. Densmore. In the lobby she found a pay phone, called the newspaper and waited while a receptionist looked for the number.

"There's no Densmore on the editorial staff, m'am. Could he be in some other department?"

"He's a reporter. He did an interview with a terrorist five years ago."

The operator transferred her to Personnel, and Katherine explained who she was looking for. The woman on the other end of the line said, "Oh, she doesn't work here any longer."

"She?"

"Faye Densmore. That's who you want?"

"I think so. The article said F. Densmore."

"That was her byline."

"Can you tell me where she went or how I can reach her?"

"You can't. Faye Densmore died a year ago. At least a year."

"Has anyone else at the paper ever interviewed Imad Tayib?"

"I don't know. You'd have to ask someone on staff."

Katherine was transferred again, this time to the city room, where she spoke with a senior reporter named Paul Stafford. To the best of his knowledge Tayib had given only two interviews to Western journalists, one to a French reporter and one to Faye Densmore. "Both five or more years ago," Stafford told her. "Since he went to the mountains, Tayib has refused to meet Westerners."

"No one working there now has ever met him?"

"If they did they didn't write about it. You might try Sam Gaddis. He was the photographer during the interview."

"Does he work there?"

"He's freelance. Call Black Star, they'll put you in touch with him."

"Who?"

"It's a photo agency. Here, I've got their number."

Katherine wrote it down. Five minutes later she had the agency on the line.

"You want to buy the terrorist photo?" an impatient voice demanded.

"No, I just want to talk to Mr. Gaddis."

"You with a collection agency?"

"This is a personal matter."

"If it's not, don't tell him where you got the number. He doesn't need the headache, you know what I'm saying?"

"Yes."

"You can't get blood from a rock."

Katherine wrote down the telephone number without knowing what they were talking about. When she called the photographer, there was no answer. Of course not, she thought. It was a Friday, the man was working, maybe out of the country.

Rather than return to Connecticut, Katherine decided to spend the night. She had friends in Washington but didn't call them. Simple social interactions had become an enormous effort. Instead she checked into a hotel and, except for periodic unanswered phone calls to Sam Gaddis, sat in front of the television while her thoughts circled in an aimless holding pattern until finally she fell asleep.

IMAD TAYIB watched with contempt as his visitor hiked up his pants to be seated. Anman Kageesh, a special envoy from President Assad, wore Western clothing. He had made the journey from Damascus only to be kept waiting three hours before being escorted to an elaborate tent situated within the walls of a fort that had been built in the Middle Ages. Now, as he sat awkwardly on the single pillow provided, he pretended not to notice that Tayib sat more comfortably on two pillows. As they exchanged the elaborate Arabian greetings, Kageesh began the verbal sparring.

"I bring you greetings from His Excellency, the President." *Whose authority is greater than yours.*

"May the peace of God be with you." *Whose authority is greatest of all.*

"And the joys of your household doubled," replied Kageesh, knowing that Imad Tayib had no family.

"As it pleases the God who brought you safely to Raqba." *But not yet safely home.*

"And keeps you safe from foreign enemies." *With the aid of the Syrian Army.*

"And domestic, *inshallah.*"

Kageesh's smile tightened. The man's arrogance was beyond belief.

Formalities concluded, Imad Tayib had tea brought. They spoke of inconsequentials, of the crops in the village, of the poor quality of Soviet cement, of the recent rains. Finally Kageesh came to the point. "Imad Tayib, the President is concerned about the world's impression of our country. He is concerned about the difficulties created by an action you took with regard to the Italian jetliner. He wishes to discuss the matter with you. He wishes you to come to Damascus."

"The President knows that I have made a vow not to leave this place until I can walk the streets of Muslim Jerusalem."

"He does not ask you to come to Jerusalem but to Damascus."

"If it were in my power, I should be happy to comply. But I cannot."

"Surely you can make an exception for the man

who commands the army that insures your safety here in Raqba."

"My safety is a tiny bird in the hand of God."

"Then you have no reason to fear coming to Damascus."

The pale eyes fixed him. "Do you think I fear Damascus?"

Kageesh willed himself not to look aside. "Only God knows the secrets of the human heart."

Tayib leaned forward. "Then let us reveal them. Mahmoud!" A guard instantly appeared, his rifle at the ready.

"Is your gun loaded?"

"Yes, Imam."

"Step close."

Kageesh said carefully, "I am the personal envoy of the President."

Tayib reached into a bowl filled with the pits of peaches and plums. He held up a peach pit. "You see this? It is cracked and divided like the land of our birth." He held up a plum pit. "But this one is smooth and of even surface like the face of Heaven. I will mix the two in my hand and you will choose. Let God guide your hand, Kageesh, for he who is left holding this seed of Heaven shall Mahmoud place the barrel of his rifle against his forehead and pull the trigger."

Kageesh's eyes went to the guard, a young man barely old enough to grow a beard. Tayib said to him, "You understand, Mahmoud? If my guest draws the furrowed pit, then by God's will you must send me safely to Paradise. You understand?"

"This is foolishness," Kageesh said quickly.

Tayib ignored him, his eyes on the guard. "Do

you understand? You must kill me if I draw the smooth pit."

"Yes, Imam."

"And if our guest draws the smooth pit, you will send him to Paradise."

Kageesh felt a tingling sensation spread from his stomach. "Do you really threaten an envoy of the President?" he demanded.

Tayib turned to him. "With Paradise, if his faith is pure." He cupped his hands and rolled the pits between them.

Sweat trickled down Kageesh's ribs. He wished now he had refused this assignment. Mahmoud had closed his eyes, probably praying for his master's safety. Tayib held out closed fists.

"Choose, Kageesh. Let's see the strength of your faith."

Kageesh crossed his arms. "I am not playing games."

"Is your soul not ready for Paradise?"

"My soul is not your concern, but for my physical safety you will answer to the President."

"By your fear you know your soul is unworthy of Paradise. Through me God has given you a warning, return now to the faith of your forefathers before it is too late." With a quick flick of his wrists he tossed the pits over his shoulder, where they tapped against the side of the tent and dropped to the floor. "And tell the President next time to send a messenger whose faith is as strong as his words."

EIGHT

KATHERINE WAS AWAKE AT DAWN BUT SHE WAITED UNTIL EIGHT to call the photographer. A hoarse voice answered.

"What?"

"Sam Gaddis?"

"Who wants him?"

"My name is Katherine Cahill. Black Star gave me this number. Are you Mr. Gaddis?"

"You always call so early in the morning?"

"I'm sorry if I woke you up."

"You think I'm the paper boy? What time is it?"

"Eight o'clock."

"Not according to—oh shit."

"If this isn't a convenient time—"

"What's your name again?"

"Katherine Cahill. My children were—"

"Listen, Kate, they turned off my electricity. Let me call you back."

"I'm at the—" He hung up. Katherine dialed the number again but the line was busy. She tried twice more and then gave up and went downstairs to the dining room. She picked at her breakfast and searched the morning paper for follow-up stories on the Alitalia bombing. The news was dominated by United Nations efforts to end the Iraqi occupation of Kuwait. Her children had been forgotten.

At ten o'clock Katherine called Gaddis again but the line was still busy. Enough. She looked up the address in the phone book and took a taxi to a three-story brownstone on Q Street, a once-tawdry neighborhood now renovated so that the occasional trash-strewn yard and peeling facade was as out of place as a broken tooth in a bright smile. The Gaddis house hadn't quite made the transition. While the hand-carved front door gleamed with varnish, a crumpled beer can lay in a yard savaged by weeds and a stack of damp Chinese take-out menus lay huddled in a corner of the porch.

The brass nameplate was inscribed with two names: Sam Gaddis, Faye Densmore. They had been a couple. She pushed the doorbell and heard nothing. What was it Gaddis had said, the electricity was off? She knocked loudly. After a moment a woman's voice called, "Hello?"

Katherine stepped back and looked up. A woman with gray hair leaned out of the top floor window.

"My name is Katherine Cahill. Is Sam Gaddis here?"

The woman disappeared and a moment later a man with dark curly hair and lean, angular features appeared. "Yes?"

"Are you Sam Gaddis?"

"I don't know. Who are you?"

"I'm Katherine Cahill. I called you this morning."

"You didn't leave your number."

"I called back but the line was busy."

"Hold on."

He ducked out of sight, reappeared with a dark object the size of a tennis ball that he tossed into the yard. "When you come up, don't touch the banister."

Katherine recovered what turned out to be a blue sock rolled into a ball; inside it was a set of keys. I'm interrupting something, she thought as she entered the building. A narrow hallway ran along a plaster wall, parts of which had been chipped away to reveal the brick, to a dimly lit stairway. What had once been a living room was filled with boxes and lined with shelves knocked together from raw lumber and stacked with magazines. Two racing bikes were covered with white plaster dust.

What were these people living in? The wood stairs, dry and cracked, trembled beneath her feet. A woman's voice called, "Don't touch the banister, dear."

"I won't."

The woman who greeted her on the third floor was in her sixties and wore black tights and an over-size pink sweatshirt. "I'm Irene Gaddis, Sam's mother."

"Katherine Cahill."

"You haven't been here before?"

"No."

"There's a lovely elevator at the back of the house but it's broken. One of these days someone is going to fall on that stairway and break a leg."

Irene had a warm smile and dancing brown eyes.

She held open a plastic curtain and Katherine stepped into another world. The hallway was clean, the walls painted and hung with framed photographs. To the right she caught a glimpse of a large white-walled workroom dominated by a long table with blue file cabinets along one wall.

"Sam's folly," Irene was saying, "that's what we call it. He bought this house for Faye. Did he tell you about her?"

"I just called this morning."

Irene mouthed *oh,* glanced down the hallway, then took her elbow. "He's a wonderful man," she said in a low voice, "but he needs closure. Proceed slowly, dear, that's my advice."

Irene led the way to a small dining room and adjoining kitchen. An older man sat at a table, leaning forward on his elbows. ". . . not asking you to sign a lifetime contract, Sam. But life is change, inertia must be fought."

Sam Gaddis, dressed in a kimono and bare feet, was in the kitchen pouring coffee beans into a grinder. If he was listening, he gave no sign of it.

"That's enough now," Irene said. "Sam has a guest. This is Katherine Cahill. My husband, Mickey . . ."

"How do you do."

". . . and that's Sam."

Sam activated the grinder and the noise momentarily stopped all conversation. Mickey jumped up and pulled back a chair for Katherine. He was a stocky man with a rounded stomach. The two of them together, Mickey and Irene, reminded Katherine of two leprechauns. The grinding stopped. Sam said, "You want some coffee?"

"No, thank you." The table was cluttered with empty juice glasses, coffee cups and a white box opened to reveal four donuts. "I didn't mean to interrupt your breakfast."

"Don't apologize," Irene said. "He's been praying for an interruption, isn't that right, Sam? We're trying to convince him to come work in the studio. Gaddis Studios in Arlington. Do you live in Virginia?"

"I'm from Connecticut."

"Then you wouldn't know us. We're not national, not a franchise, only custom work. Mickey's great-grandfather took pictures of the Civil War. You've heard of Mathew Brady? Jeremiah Gaddis was his assistant. We like to say the Gaddis boys have Dektol in their blood."

"She doesn't know about Dektol," Mickey said.

"How do you know? Are you a photographer, dear?"

"No."

Mickey grunted. "You see? She came to see Sam and you're talking about Dektol in the blood."

Irene ignored him. "We think Sam should come work at the studio. He's a miracle in the darkroom—the eye of an artist and the hand of a surgeon. Sam worked his way through college doing custom printing—"

"Halfway through college," Mickey said.

"As much college as he finished, he worked his way doing custom color."

"Which is not *through* college."

"Will you let me tell the story?"

"No photographer ever got anything but ruined by college."

Katherine felt like she was in the eye of a storm

and being battered by words. She glanced toward the kitchen, where Sam was pouring a glass of orange juice, apparently oblivious to the conversation. Mickey tapped her arm. "So, Katherine, how long have you known my son?"

"I don't know him. I just came to see some photographs."

"An impartial observer, good, I have a question. Self-esteem comes through the application of a man's highest talent to the greatest challenge, you agree? Here we have a photographer, a man with a national reputation, who chooses, for his own reasons and for the time being, not to pursue a career as a photographer."

Irene said, "Except a few grip-and-grins."

"That's not a career. Second-rate work is corrosive to first-rate talent. Better he should be a garbage collector than take pictures of pigheaded politicians shaking hands with fat-assed financiers."

"It pays the rent," Sam said as he came into the room. He placed a glass of orange juice in front of Katherine. "I hope you like it warm."

"I feel like I'm intruding."

"You are."

"Sam!"

"It's a welcome intrusion."

Katherine said, "Why don't I come back later?"

"No need," Irene said. "We're on our way to an antique show. Sam is not going to change his mind, Mickey. Come on."

"Wait, I want to know what Katherine thinks. Granted, Sam should be shooting, but if he's not going to use that talent, he should fulfill his destiny by working in the darkroom. As an impartial observer let me pay you twenty dollars to tell him I'm right."

Irene grabbed her husband's arm. "Stop, Mickey. They have business."

Mickey allowed himself to be dragged to the door. Sam went with them and their voices echoed from the hall. "You're coming to dinner tomorrow?"

"I'll call you."

"Don't call, just come."

"Inertia, Sam. It must be fought."

"Goodbye, dad, goodbye, mom."

"These steps, someone's going to break a leg."

Katherine looked around. The room was like a museum. Displayed on the walls were artifacts from a dozen different cultures: a fertility goddess carved of wood from South America, a terra cotta relief from Asia, a beaded mask from Africa. It was the room of a man more at home away from home.

Katherine got up and inspected a photograph of a younger Sam Gaddis with his arm around a striking woman with jet black hair and fair skin. Sam wore jeans and had a camera dangling from his neck. The woman was dressed in a short-sleeved khaki shirt and wore a safari hat. The low sun gave their skins a bronze glow and their smiles were self-assured.

"That was taken at Petra," Sam said.

"Where's that?"

"Jordan."

"It looks beautiful."

"Because you don't feel the heat, hear the flies or see the Bedouin beggar selling post cards a few feet away."

"The woman with you is . . ."

"My wife."

"She's the one who interviewed Imad Tayib?"

"The only Westerner who ever got one."

Except for a Frenchman, Katherine remembered, but didn't say anything. Sam went to the window, picked up a bent clothes hanger attached to a length of string and lowered it. "Got to retrieve the key," he explained. "Like loft living."

"It doesn't lock automatically?"

"It's a new door, custom-designed not to fit. In wet weather the wood swells and only the dead bolt works."

He spoke with an undertone of sarcasm that seemed directed not toward Katherine but the world at large. With his pale legs bare beneath the kimono, he looked like a man in a bathrobe. A part of her—she had begun to think of it as the old part—would have felt uncomfortable in this situation. But the old part no longer seemed relevant. Sam Gaddis might be eccentric but what could he do? Throw off the kimono and expose himself?

Sam hauled the keys up and put them on the table. Katherine said, "I hope I didn't chase them away."

"Sharks couldn't chase my parents out of a swimming pool. Have a donut."

"No, thanks."

"Cigarette?" He flipped the top open and held out a box of Winstons. Katherine shook her head. Sam brought the box close to his mouth and with his other hand snapped a finger against the bottom of the box. A cigarette popped up. Sam caught it between his lips.

"Mr. Gaddis, I wanted to talk to you about the picture of Imad Tayib that's been in all the papers."

"It paid the electric bill this month. Maybe next month he'll sink a cruise ship and I can pay off the mortgage."

Katherine stiffened. "My children were on Flight 67."

About to light the cigarette, Sam paused. He saw the strain in Katherine's face, the lines around her eyes, the taut lips, the eyes made empty by her suffering. He recognized the stiff posture that spoke of the effort at control and the hunched shoulders ready to ward off blows already fallen. The flame on the lighter went out.

"You're handling it well," he said without apology. "Or does everybody tell you that?" He lit the cigarette and inhaled deeply.

"Mr. Gaddis, the reason I came to see you was to get some pictures of Imad Tayib."

"For publication?"

"For myself."

"The man killed your children, why would you want pictures of him?"

"I'm trying to understand what kind of a man he is. How he could destroy so many lives."

"You have more faith in photographs than I do."

"I thought you might tell me your impression of the man."

" 'Chin up, turn right, hold it right there.' It wasn't much of a conversation."

"But you were there when he was interviewed."

"Faye interviewed him and I was there."

"Well, what was your impression?"

My impression, Sam thought. He remembered the hectic exhilaration of life in Beirut, his admiration for Faye's skill in handling Tayib, his impatience because he had been eager to return to their room at the Hilton and make love. He remembered his delight in everything Faye did, the way she moved, the chances she took, the quick insights that leaped between them and made conversation unnecessary, the magic of their early years together . . .

Sam forced his mind back to Imad Tayib. "Tayib has an unshakeable sense of destiny that's both ludicrous and scary. He's one of those people who knows exactly why he was put on the earth and what he has to do to achieve his purpose. There are a lot of posers in the Arab world, imitation Saladins and would-be Mahdis, but most of them aren't smart enough or educated enough or disciplined enough or charismatic enough to command a following. Tayib is. There's a larger-than-life quality about him that world leaders pretend to have but only a few do. Good actors have it. Pick your favorite leading man and that's what it's like being in a room with Tayib. Except he's not playing a role, he *is* the role."

"He must be insane."

"If you want to think so."

"You don't agree?"

Stop looking for answers, Sam wanted to say. People die and you don't expect it, the world pulls the rug out from under you and there's no rhyme or reason to any of it. "I don't think it makes any difference what I think."

"What did your wife think?"

The question was deliberate. He felt a flicker of animosity toward this woman in her well-tailored outfit, her Cartier watch, Hermès scarf and unflinching gaze.

"Faye was attracted to strong men. That was her

weakness." He stood up. "Coffee's ready. Sure you don't want a cup?"

"All right."

They were silent, each aware of an emotional no-man's-land in the other. Sam returned with the coffee, sat down and dumped a spoonful of sugar into his cup. "If you want to dilute it," he said, pushing the sugar and half a pint of milk across the table.

Katherine took a sip. The coffee was strong and bitter. She added milk and sugar. Smoke curled toward her from the cigarette and she waved it away. Sam held up the cigarette. "Does this bother you?"

"That's all right, don't put it out."

"I wasn't going to." He took a drag and blew the smoke off to one side.

"Mr. Gaddis, do you have any other photographs of Imad Tayib?"

"Sure."

"Is there a way I could see them?"

"You want to see them now?"

"You have them here?"

"I have all my files here."

"If you wouldn't mind."

The tone of exaggerated civility which seemed to have evolved between them amused Sam. "I'd be delighted."

Five minutes later he returned with three contact sheets. They were thirty-six exposure rolls, six strips to a sheet. Katherine inspected them slowly. Tayib's expression varied only slightly. The last five shots were of Faye in what looked like a hotel room. In one picture she was typing. In another she was talking on the telephone, eyes on the camera but her expression distant. The last one showed her in front of the bathroom mirror with Sam behind her, camera to his eye. Faye was smiling, toothbrush in one hand, the man's shirt she wore open to reveal small full breasts.

"Your wife is in some of these but I'd like copies of the rest."

"Faye?"

She handed him the contact sheet. As he studied them, his expression became rapt and Katherine, embarrassed, turned her attention to her coffee.

"Another world," Sam murmured.

"How soon could I get them?" she asked, more brusquely than she intended.

The warmth in his eyes faded. "You want pictures to publish or for yourself?"

"For myself."

"Which ones?"

"All of them."

"All?"

"I'm willing to pay."

"I intended to charge. What size did you have in mind? Five by seven? Eight by ten?"

"Eight by ten."

"Cropped or full-frame?"

"It doesn't matter. Just what's here."

"That's three sheets, thirty-six shots each, less five of Faye. One hundred and three photos at ten dollars apiece is one thousand thirty dollars. You might want to cull them down to a more reasonable figure."

"Can I give you a check?"

"Have you got ID?" She looked up. "It's a joke."

Katherine nodded and took the checkbook from her purse. "How soon can I get them?"

"This is a slow month. You can pick them up Monday."

"I'm going home today. I'll add an extra ten dollars and you can send them Federal Express."

Fine, fine, fine, Sam thought. He resented efficient people who took their losses on the chin.

After Katherine was gone, he went into the darkroom and began printing. First he printed the photographs of Faye and inspected them while they were still in the wash. He stared at the last one, the private moment in the bathroom. It was one of his old shirts that she was wearing. The terrain of his hands beneath the wet photograph gave it a three dimensional quality. Faye stared at him twice, once as he took the photo and now as he held her in his hands. He slid a thumb along her breast and remembered the soft skin, the warm weight of her breasts against his palm, the give and push of flesh. The vivid memories brought a lightness in his stomach and a quickness in his pulse. You fucking bitch, he thought, as tears came.

NINE

THE IRAQI INVASION OF KUWAIT HAD SENT NERVOUS TREMORS through the expatriate communities of neighboring nations like Syria. Rumors flew and security was tightened at the oil rigs close to the Iraqi border. Whenever a military jet streaked along some distant horizon, the men instinctively glanced up from their work and looked east, the direction from which an attack would come. Those whose job required traveling from one rig to another no longer took shortcuts across the open desert. Caution was the order of the day for everyone except Mike Winn, who continued to travel his unorthodox routes alone and discovered the derailed freight train.

In the petroleum industry Mike was known as a Bit Man, a specialist in the drilling bits used in the search for oil. For twenty-eight days at a time he serviced the dozens of rigs spread across Syria's eastern desert. Then he flew home to Texas for twenty-eight days of normal life free of the heat, the desolation and

the strain of being a stranger in a very foreign land.
On this day he was on his way to Rig Number 7. He
drove an air-conditioned Land Rover with a spare can
of gas strapped to the rear fender, two spare tires
bolted to the roof and a carton of Boukien bottled
water in the back seat. The Land Rover belonged to Al
Furat, an oil consortium owned jointly by Dutch
Shell and the Syrian government. The portable cassette player was his own. The cab reverberated to the
music of one of the Beach Boys' *Greatest Hits.* "Everybody's gone surfing, surfing U.S.A."

"Everybody's gone crazy," Mike improvised,
"here in Syr-i-ay."

Tires thrummed over the bleached red earth
sending pebbles and small rocks clattering into the
wheel wells. The Land Rover topped one of the im-
perceptible ridges that seemed to materialize out of
shimmering air. A railroad bisected the shallow valley below, its silver tracks glistening in the sun. For a
moment Mike thought the train had stopped for some
reason; then he realized that the engine was missing.
Five of the cars had jumped the tracks and lay tumbled on their sides. They were flatbed cars stacked
high with wood crates, some of which had burst
open. The remaining cars were still upright.

A tingle of apprehension made its way up his
back. He drove forward, alert for any sign of life. The
broken shipping crates had disgorged a number of
fifty-gallon drums that lay at odd angles. And something else. The body of a man lying on the ground.

Mike stopped and rolled down the window. Heat
rolled into the cab. *"Marhaba,"* he called. Hello.
There was no answer. He drove slowly forward and
stopped near the body. At his approach a dark shape

detached itself and hopped away, a vulture with its wings spread for balance. Mike wished he had a gun. He slammed the door and the vulture took flight.

Leaving the motor running, Mike slowly approached the body. The victim, an Arab dressed in jeans and a work shirt, was dead. He lay on his back, one hand on his chest, the other at his face, as if trying to ward off his death. Mike's stomach tightened at the sight of the bloody eye sockets. He looked away. There were no signs of an ambush, no bullet holes, and other than the savaged eyes, no sign of injury.

"Hello," Mike yelled. *"Marhaba!"*

No sound except the cuff of his pants fluttering in the steady wind. He made a circuit of the cars looking for other victims but found no one. The cause of the crash was apparent; a rail had separated from the track bed. Mike inspected the crates. They were stenciled in three different languages—Arabic, English and French. The agent was Irskenian Shipping Company, the destination an Al Furat warehouse in Baghouz.

Not right, Mike thought. Baghouz was a small town on the Iraqi border. It had a seismic testing office but no active drilling. The contents of the barrels was listed as drilling mud but this, too, was wrong. Mike knew drilling mud. It was used at the rigs in copious quantities, kept in huge metal tanks and circulated down the shaft of the drill stem and back. One of the barrels was bent, the cover gaping, but there was no sign of escaping mud. He knelt, peered into the darkness and made out a jumble of gray canisters smashed into one another. The one closest to him had four colored bands, one yellow and three green.

Mike had spent two years in the army. These were grenades of some kind. Military hardware. Irskenian Shipping was dealing in contraband. Certain now that he was alone, Mike got his camera, a Canon automatic, and began taking pictures. Except for the click and whir of the motor advancing the film, everything was quiet. He took wide shots of the wreck from both directions, then photographed the crates and barrels, moving close to record the labels. He used a splintered two-by-four to pry open the lid so that he could get shots of the canisters. One yellow band and three green. Color coding.

He turned back to the body. The man apparently died of internal injuries because, outwardly, there were only a few scratches on his chest, where tiny beads of blood had dried to a dark brown. And the shirt torn in the accident. Or when he clawed at his—

One yellow, three green. It came back to him with a rush, the code for chemical agents. Poison gas.

Mike stepped back slowly, then turned and ran to the Land Rover, heart pounding, mouth dry. His fingers quivered as he turned the key in the ignition. The engine roared and the vulture that had perched on top of one of the crates took flight. Fighting panic, he drove quickly from the scene. "Shit," he whispered, "oh shit."

A new thought. The bird was alive, the crazy vulture. Sitting on the body when he arrived. Whatever had killed the trainman had dissipated. He would be all right. The ridge and the train were lost to sight. The familiar monotony of the landscape comforted him, as did the Beach Boys tape, which he now turned up loud.

He saw the shadow of the helicopter racing beside him before he heard the low wop-wop-wop under the music. It came into view ahead and to his left, a French Alouette painted camouflage with Syrian Army markings. Good—or was it? Normally the Syrians were protective of their oil installations and the foreigners who ran them. But they protected nobody who saw what shouldn't be seen. What *had* he seen? And did they know he had seen it?

Forcing a smile, Mike leaned forward and waved. *"Salaam,* boys." The helicopter flew closer. An officer in a black beret stood in the open doorway, one hand braced against the fuselage, motioning Mike to a stop.

"No, thanks," he said through gritted teeth. He held up the Al Furat card that was required to be on the dashboard of all oil-company vehicles. "Petro industry," he yelled, knowing they couldn't hear. "Official business, official car."

The officer disappeared and in his place stood a soldier with an automatic weapon. Mike was already slowing even before the burst of gunfire stitched the earth in front of him.

"Fucking ragheads," he yelled. "I'm *stopping.*"

But not without getting rid of the evidence. As he slowed to a stop, Mike lay the camera on his lap and kept his finger on the shutter, running the last few frames off until the camera automatically rewound.

The chopper circled once and then landed directly ahead of him. The officer jumped out, followed by two soldiers wearing black berets and holding automatic weapons. Mike kept a smile on his face but his hands were busy. He removed the film and tried to shove the canister up behind the dashboard. A bunch of wires and cables resisted him. The officer motioned him out of the cab. Me, Mike asked in pantomime while the hidden hand shoved and searched, trying to locate the little ledge near the speedometer —there!

The soldiers raised their guns. The officer motioned impatiently.

"Yeah, yeah," Mike muttered as he opened the door and stepped out to learn if he would live or die.

THE PHOTOGRAPHS of Imad Tayib arrived within a week of Katherine's meeting with Sam Gaddis. She lined them up, all one hundred and three, on the bookshelves in the library. The library had been Glen's office; now it was Katherine's war room. File cabinets which once held legal briefs and stock reports now contained information on the Alitalia disaster, on Imad Tayib, on the attempted bombing of the Vatican, on Syria and the P.L.O. Her mother was horrified.

"It's not healthy," Grace said. "You have to think about the rest of your life."

"Not until he's brought to justice."

There was no need any longer to specify who *he* was. Katherine's focus was on one man and one man only—Imad Tayib.

"Please come to Palm Springs with me."

"I'll be fine, mother."

Rachel and Tony, household staff, lived in the apartment above the garage and maintained the house. Katherine was relieved when her mother left. Meals were made, the silver polished, the grass cut, the pool cleaned—there was nothing for Grace to do.

Collecting information kept her busy for almost a month, but her mood changed at Halloween. Anticipating that the holidays would be difficult, she accepted her brother's invitation to come to dinner. Afterward she stayed to hand out candy while Brian and Leslie took the children trick-or-treating. Every time Katherine opened the door to another goblin, ghost or fairy princess, she imagined behind the mask Jeff or Allison or Joey. When the family returned, they found her in the guest bedroom, clutching photographs of her children and crying. She stayed the night and drove home the next day.

Katherine was aware of her growing despondency but felt incapable of doing anything about it. She spent long hours in each child's room arranging toys and folding clothes she had folded the day before. She cherished each photograph and culled through old homework assignments, fingering them with loving care. Rachel had orders to allow no one else into these three rooms.

Despair was like quicksand, sapping her energy, suffocating all chances for pleasure, making simple acts like brushing her teeth a burden. She left the house only to drive to the graveyard, where she went each day with three roses, one for each grave. She spent long hours sitting on a small marble bench while her mind replayed scenes from their childhood. The days grew short and the autumn leaves left skeletal branches clawing skyward.

One day a cold mist began to fall while Katherine was at the graveyard. She was wearing a fur coat but she still shivered. What if I just stay here, she thought? I could lie down, let the misery slip away. What would it be like, that moment her children had known when death took them?

She took off her coat, placed it between the

graves and lay down on her back. A lump beneath her hip; she shifted position and closed her eyes. The mist beat a fairy tattoo on her cheeks and eyelids. She reached out and imagined holding their hands just as she had so many times when they crossed a street. Their bodies lay a few feet away, souls distant by a heartbeat.

Something cold touched her wrist. With a cry she bolted upright. A black dog snorted in surprise and jumped away. It stood with wagging tail and lowered head, friendly yet wary. "Damn you." Her heart was racing and she felt foolish. The dog, some kind of Labrador, came forward and licked her face. She scrambled to her feet, put on her coat without shaking it, the beaded moisture turning her blouse damp and clammy. The dog followed her to the car. For some reason he made her furious. "Get out of here," she yelled. She scooped up gravel and threw it. The dog dashed off a few yards, then watched her uncertainly. Katherine got into the car and began to shiver. "Goddamn you," she whispered, "Goddamn you, goddamn you." Over and over, gloved hands gripping the steering wheel, thinking not of the dog but of Imad Tayib safely out of reach in Syria. Slowly she regained control, started the car and turned on the heater. If she was going to die, she would not be alone. A calm seemed to settle over her. She knew now what she had to do. Drops of water formed on the windshield and inched uncertainly downward. Katherine looked through them, beyond the invisible gray sky to the land where a murderer waited. "Your turn," she whispered. The world was helpless. She would kill Imad Tayib herself.

TEN

THE LAND OF MILK AND HONEY, MIKE WINN THOUGHT, IF YOU knew where to look. He stood on the pitching deck of a small ferry as it made its way across five miles of open ocean to Arwad, a tiny island off Syria's coast. He was on his way to see Sarkis Irskenian, the man whose name appeared on the shipping crates that had broken open when the train derailed. The man who, Mike was certain, wouldn't want his name in a newspaper linked to an account of the poison-gas shipment.

Mike's initial reaction after convincing the Syrian army that he was ignorant of the train wreck was to forget the entire incident. But as time passed his curiosity returned, particularly after he read a newspaper account that maintained the engineer had been crushed to death and the shipment was drilling mud. Somebody apparently had high-level contacts in the government. Or a lot of money to pay off the right people. It was the latter possibility that brought him to Arwad.

The ferry let him off at a pier crowded with fishing boats. A jumble of white houses rose in tiers to the highest part of the island, which was dominated by the ramparts of an ancient fort. Mike sent a boy to Irskenian's headquarters with a message: "Can we talk business?" Enclosed in the envelope were two photographs of the train wreck, one showing the broken gas canister, the other a picture of the corpse. While he waited for an answer, another kid tried to sell him a local souvenir, some piece of crap that looked like a jar of oil filled with colored plastic cords.

"What is that thing? What you got in there, colored worms?"

"Beautiful, okay?"

"You think this is beautiful?"

"Yes."

"Maybe to a worm or some kind of leech. Okay, here." He handed the boy five pounds and watched him run off. Arab kids were cute. It was only after they grew up and got angry with the world they weren't worth shit.

The messenger returned with word that Irskenian wanted Mike to come for lunch. At Irskenian's palatial home a tough-looking Arab whose shoulders started at his chin led him upstairs to a rooftop patio enclosed by a trellis covered with vines. Sarkis Irskenian sat at a table beneath a canopy billowing gently in the wind. He was a heavyset man with sad eyes and a glistening layer of black hair that looked like it had been treated with a grease gun.

"Welcome, my friend," he said in ponderous English. "I don't believe I know your name."

Mike introduced himself and sat down. A servant in a white *galabiya* brought food while the two men engaged in small talk: weather, work, world events. A snorting Pekingese dog paced back and forth, toenails clicking on a brightly colored tile floor. Occasionally the dog attempted to reach a piece of lamb Irskenian had dropped beside his chair, but when it came too close, Irskenian placed his foot beneath its stomach and tossed it a few feet away. He did it gently and the dog seemed to accept the rejection as a matter of course.

The meal ended and Irskenian said, "Let us discuss your photographs. May I ask how you got them?"

"Trade secrets."

"Dangerous secrets."

"Profitable secrets."

"Then you intend to make a profit from your visit here?"

"Unless you don't care if I send those photos to the nearest newspaper."

"I assume you have the negatives?"

"Hidden in a safe place along with a lot of other shots of the wreck. They all show the same thing: chemical and poison-gas canisters coming into the country illegally."

"Syria is a sovereign nation. We can buy such weapons wherever we like."

"If you bought them legitimately, you wouldn't be shipping them in drums labeled drilling mud. In fact, I'm willing to bet that if I start investigating I'll find out those projectiles were stolen from the U.S. Army. Where are you shipping them, Iraq?"

For the first time Irskenian's bland expression wavered. He glanced at the servant standing not far away. "Don't even suggest such things."

"Is it true?"

"No."

"Then where are they going? It's not to Al Furat. We don't use poison gas to look for oil."

"This is none of your business, Mr. Winn. I thought you had come to discuss business matters, not to make accusations."

You slime, Mike thought. You're selling American poison gas to use on American soldiers. "Maybe you'd like to buy my accusations."

"I am Armenian, a businessman. I have no country except the land of commerce. I prefer a peaceful land, one free of political persecution and mass hysteria. I have no army to repel an invader, only a modest income to safeguard the future of my family. Naturally I am concerned how much of my family's security must be sacrificed to maintain peace."

"The kind of peace you're talking about comes to, say, fifteen thousand American dollars."

"For which I receive the negatives of all photographs and copies of all prints."

"No way. As long as I'm working in Syria, I hold onto the negatives. What you buy is my silence. I don't tell the newspapers, I don't tell the government, I don't even tell my wife. If you're worried I'm going to come back next week and hit you up again, forget it. That's not the way I work, you can ask anybody. Mike Winn is good for his word."

Irskenian lifted the dog with his foot and lofted it

away, less gently this time. It landed and scrabbled to regain its balance. "How do I know you're good for your word?"

Mike shrugged. "If I'm not, you can kill me."

"*That* is true. If I cannot maintain the peace by mortgaging my family's future, then I must resort to war. Under the circumstances I think five thousand is a sufficient peace dividend."

They haggled and settled, as Mike expected, on ten thousand dollars. "A cashier's check," he said, "Payable at a Swiss bank."

"Always a Swiss bank. What is wrong with your own Citibank or Bank of America?"

"I like to spread my assets." Mike tossed a piece of cheese to the Pekingese.

"No, don't!" Irskenian's voice raised an octave. The dog picked up the cheese and chewed uncertainly. The servant, his white robes flying, chased the Pekingese to the far corner of the roof, where he fingered the cheese from its mouth.

"Cholesterol is not good for dogs," Irskenian said reprovingly.

"Neither is starvation."

"You make a mistake. That is a game we play. Askar would be unhappy if I allowed him his victory so easily."

The Pekingese had returned, sniffing and snorting around the spot where the cheese had landed. It was, Mike decided, as ugly as its owner. He also decided to turn over the photographs to the American government as soon as he got home. And as soon as the check was in the bank.

● ● ●

IT WAS said that members of the Penguin Club were masochists and those who watched them dash into the Connecticut River each Saturday morning were sadists. On this particular morning Katherine was the only spectator in attendance. She stood on the balcony of the White Duck Cafe, which overlooked the river and adjoined the clubhouse, a small wood structure that had once been an ice house.

Promptly at eight o'clock the president of the Penguin Club, clad in a black swatch of bathing suit, stepped outside and blew a whistle. Out came twenty men and women in bathing suits who rushed headlong toward the river chanting, "Bathwater! Bathwater! Bathwater!" It was a chilly November morning and their words burst forth on puffs of steam. Katherine grimaced and drew her coat close as they threw themselves into the water. Wait until the kids hear about—

Her incipient smile died. She had no kids.

Katherine watched until the man she had come to see spotted her. Darryl Sikes was in his sixties. He was a gunsmith who had worked at Cahill Arms for as long as Katherine could remember. She had been assigned to Darryl's department during her sixteenth year when she followed Cahill family tradition and worked one summer in the factory. Darryl waded ashore and jogged over to her. He was a tall, stooped man whose skin was creased in the shallow arcs born of gravity and age. The gray hair on his chest glistened wetly. "You saw the splash-in?"

"You're all crazy."

He smiled. "I'll be with you in a few minutes."

"Take your time."

"Go inside and get a table. I don't want you catching cold."

"Me? Look at your skin, Darryl, you look like a plucked chicken."

"Unless you're numb, it's no fun," Darryl said, quoting the Penguin Club motto. He jogged back and joined the others. Katherine stood for a moment longer, caught by their laughter and the memory of happier times, then went inside and ordered a hot apple cider. Ten minutes later Darryl joined her. He wore a sweater now, his hair wet and freshly combed, his face glowing with good health. He ordered an iced coffee.

Katherine said, "I hope you're not doing that to impress me."

Darryl turned to the waiter. "What's the official Penguin Club drink?"

"Iced coffee."

"See?"

They spent a few minutes speaking of Darryl's family, his wife and children. Then he asked how she was doing and Katherine said, "People tell me I'm doing pretty well."

"Brian's been worried, I know that. He said you stopped coming over to dinner. You hardly go out of the house any more. Frankly, that's why I wanted you to meet me here."

"Did you tell Brian?"

"You asked me not to."

"I need a favor, Darryl, but I want your word that, whether you say yes or no, you'll keep this private."

His bushy eyebrows shot up. "Unless it's something immoral or illegal."

"What if it's both?"

"Then I can't promise."

Katherine looked away. A young couple leaned close to one another at the next table. Darryl reached for her hand but she drew back. "I have all the sympathy I need, Darryl. I have more than I need. What I need is a friend, someone I can trust implicitly. Will you be that friend or not?"

"Of course." His tone sounded paternal, almost patronizing.

"Not *of course.* I'm not sixteen now and I don't need you to tell me to wear eye goggles around the lathe. I've been to the bottom of the pit and back. I've listened to advice, I've read the books, I know the stages of grief, I know what sympathy can and can't do. I don't need a moral arbiter, Darryl. I need someone I can trust with a confidence. Can you do that for me or not?"

The bushy gray eyebrows were almost touching. He looked at her with uneasy respect. "All right. Ask anything you want. I don't guarantee I can help, but it will go no farther than the two of us."

Katherine pulled out a Mont Blanc pen the size of a cigar and laid it on the desk. "I need you to turn this into a gun. A barrel, some sort of trigger, a single shot of the most lethal round available. It can't look like a gun and the pen has to function. Is it possible? Will you do it?"

He squinted first at the pen and then at her. "What's this for?"

She held his gaze and told the lie. "A bounty hunter. A man who is going to rid the world of a plague."

"You're talking about the man who killed your children."

"That's right."

"Katherine, there are better ways. Extradition. The legal process—"

"*What* legal process?" Katherine told him about the trip to Washington and how little hope there was for Imad Tayib's extradition. "There's only one way to do it and that's send someone to execute him."

"Who is he?"

"I can't tell you his name. That's part of the agreement."

"How in hell did you find a man like this?"

"I put an ad in one of those mercenary magazines. Come on, Darryl, what about the pen? Will you design it for me?"

"You're talking about murder—"

"Tayib killed Jeff, he killed Ali, he killed Joey. He admitted it, he *boasted* about it. It's not murder, it's justice."

Darryl drained the coffee, held up the glass and shook the ice. "Have you ever been swimming when there's ice in the river?"

"No."

He placed the glass on the table. "Most people think it sounds terrible. Most people haven't experienced it so they don't really know. I haven't experienced what you've been through and I thank God for it." Darryl picked up the pen and inspected it. "He'll have to be close to the target. Very close."

OPERATION BRIGHT JUSTICE proceeded in utmost secrecy. In Fort Bragg, North Carolina, U.S. Army carpenters built a replica of Tayib's headquarters out of frame and plywood. The fifty-foot-square structure rose three stories high and included a stairway to the roof bordered by a three-foot-high rampart. Once it was finished, another crew laid out a perimeter made of used tires that encompassed almost three acres. Within the perimeter the position of other buildings was marked by poles and outlined in blue plastic ribbon. Army tents were set up in the open area between them. None of the construction workers knew that the tower duplicated Tayib's headquarters building, the tents were those of the Yellow Wind recruits, and the perimeter of tires outlined the exterior walls of the castle.

Four five-man teams were chosen from the army's Special Operations Detachment known as the Delta Force. For greater security the men were given information in stages. At first they knew only the broad parameters of their mission: "an airborne extraction of a human resource from a hostile environment." When they were issued black battle dress they knew the mission would take place at night. Because of Iraq's invasion of Kuwait they assumed they would be sent to the Middle East. Some men speculated that their job would be to rescue Americans caught in the U.S. Embassy in Kuwait City. Others argued that Bright Justice was a plan to kidnap the Iraqi leader himself. Some thought it might be a mission to rescue hostages still held in Lebanon.

The man in charge of Bright Justice was Major Chuck Layton, a wiry Oklahoma farm boy. The major was given four priorities: the first three were to leave no Americans behind; no captives, no bodies, no one. There was to be no repeat of the Desert One fiasco, in which United States forces bungled the attempted rescue of Americans held hostage in Iran. Layton's fourth priority was the mission's objective: bring back Imad Tayib.

The men familiarized themselves with every inch of the building until they were able to run, literally, blindfolded from one room to the other calling out their position: *"East wall. Window six. Stairway alpha."* Next came a walk-through of the operation, one team entering from the roof, the other from the ground floor, teams meeting at the radio room after subduing mock defenders. They would use a stun gun on Tayib, hustle him to the roof and into a quick-snap harness from which he could be hoisted aboard the helicopter. One man wore a white armband and was designated the Target. The first walk-through took ten minutes. They would do better, Layton knew. Five minutes from first shot to last, that was his goal. Five minutes to send an Arab terrorist on a one-way trip to the States.

ELEVEN

MIKE WINN WAS KIDNAPPED BEFORE HE HAD A CHANCE TO LEAVE Syria. The incident was witnessed by half a dozen people, including Mike's counterpart, an Englishman named Peter Wickam. Every month one man returned home while the other took his place. They met halfway between Damascus and the oil fields at a tiny town situated on cracked and rocky plains. The town was little more than fifty cinderblock homes, a gas station, barber shop and coffee house. Mike and Peter ate lunch on a concrete patio sheltered from the sun by a corrugated metal roof.

According to Peter's later account, Mike was nervous during lunch and eager to get moving, but this was normal. The outgoing man was always in a bigger hurry to return home than the arriving partner was to begin his stint in the desert. After reviewing the status of the drilling sites, they flipped a coin to see who would buy lunch. They hadn't noticed the white Peugeot station wagon that had arrived during their meal, or its occupants, four Arab men in casual Western dress.

While Peter paid the bill, Mike went to his car. The Peugeot had parked in such a way that he had to detour around it. Peter heard Mike yell, turned and saw two men wrestling Mike into the Peugeot. He ran to help, but a third man emerged and sprayed the ground with automatic rifle fire. Peter dived behind a low wall and heard the slam of the doors and skid of gravel. When he looked again, the car was racing away.

Mike's wallet lay on the ground. Inside it was a cashier's check for ten thousand dollars. The town's only policeman had no car; his engine had blown up the week before. Long before someone alerted an army base fifty miles away, Mike Winn and his abductors had disappeared.

FAWZI ASHRAF, twenty-nine-years-old and desperate for admiration, did not know that his CIA code name was LEGHORN. He would not have wanted to know. He already had the uncomfortable feeling when Imad Tayib looked at him that the initials CIA were branded on his forehead. Praying that his nervousness did not show, he kissed Tayib's hand and embraced him in the Arab fashion. Tayib stepped back and held him at arm's length.

"You are sweating, Fawzi. Isn't our mountain air cooler than Damascus?"

"A headache, Imam. I have a cold." To prove it Fawzi opened a container of Bayer aspirin.

"Let me have it," Tayib said.

"Here, you can have two."

Tayib's hand remained outstretched. "The bottle."

Puzzled, Fawzi gave it to him. Tayib said, "A headache is the sign of resistance to Allah's will. Live in accord with His plan and your mind remains serene. You spend too much time in the city."

"You are right, Imam."

They sat on cushions and drank coffee. Tayib's initial admiration for the daring kidnapping of Mike Winn had turned to disdain when no one came forward to take responsibility for the heroic act. His compatriots were too comfortable living in Damascus, too afraid of alienating the Syrian government, which coddled the Western oil companies and their employees. Perhaps fear had turned the lion's heart to that of a rabbit. When the formalities were concluded, Tayib asked for the latest news of the kidnapping.

"No one takes responsibility," Fawzi said, "but there is a rumor that the license plates on the kidnappers' car were Lebanese."

"Privately what is being said?"

"Nothing. Abu Shapour has been in touch with the other groups but all disclaim it. There is one piece of news: a ten thousand dollar cashier's check was found in the American's wallet."

"For what purpose was the money?"

"Again, no one knows."

Later that evening Tayib walked along the parapets of the castle. From this fortress Christian invaders had been repelled from Arab lands a thousand years ago. Now the enemy had returned with a weapon more subtle and effective than sword and cannon—its culture. Tayib took out the Bayer aspirin container with its fancy label and threw it high into the air, where it flickered in the sunlight, disappeared in shadow and cracked into the rocks of the canyon.

Why take a hostage if you had not the courage to proclaim it? Tayib went to the cistern and drew water to cleanse himself for prayer. First he washed his face, hands and feet, then rinsed his mouth and released the water through his nostrils. He knelt facing Mecca, placed both hands on the ground and leaned forward until his forehead touched stones still warm from the sun. Tayib prayed for guidance, and Allah sent him an idea that made him smile. Here was a way to drive the rabbit from its burrow.

That night in his radio broadcast Tayib baited his trap. "Five days ago an American oil man was kidnapped. Ten thousand dollars was found upon him, an obscene amount of money that would feed a Palestinian village for a year. Where did the money come from? There is only one answer. The American Mike Winn is a CIA agent. The money was in payment for his spying activities on behalf of the CIA and its secret Zionist partner, the Mossad. His cynical masquerade as an oil worker had been uncovered and we see him for what he is, a wolf in sheep's skin. Because he has confessed to his crimes, his life has been spared. Mike Winn will be returned to his home and family when the Palestinian people return to their homes in a free Palestine. Let the Western powers know that, as our homeland is stolen from us, so shall we steal their husbands and sons and brothers who come to enslave our men and plunder our lands."

Good, Tayib thought when the broadcast was over. Now let those responsible for the kidnapping come forward or know themselves as cowards.

• • •

TAYIB'S ANNOUNCEMENT sent a wave of concern through the American intelligence community. Had Tayib learned of Bright Justice and taken an American hostage to insure his own safety? Doug Livingston flew to Geneva for a meeting with Bob Hatch. The two men walked along a lakeside park bordering the Quai Gustav-Ador, while autumn leaves skipped across the pavement. In the harbor a plume of water rose high into the air, dissolved into spray and bowed before the wind as it fell, Geneva's trademark symbol, as elegant and cold as the city itself.

"It's the new Berlin," Hatch said, gesturing to the ornate facades of banks and retail shops. "The city of secrets. In the hotel this morning I overheard two Iranian generals, civilian clothes, talking about some fire-control system they came to buy. Walk softly and carry a fat wallet, that's the motto of this country."

"Is that the device?" Livingston indicated the portable cassette tape player that Hatch carried. It was a Sony Sportsman made of yellow plastic with round black speakers. Inside the unit was an explosive charge that would cut the power line to the radar station.

"The *Asfar* Avenger, is what I call it. Not to be deployed without authorization from the Kahuna himself. As of yesterday Bright Justice is on hold."

"Why?"

"Because as racist and chauvinistic as it sounds, the American public would consider it a bad bargain if we sacrificed an American oilman for an Arab terrorist. We are concerned about the Mike Winn abduction. Notice I use the imperial *we*—I'm speaking officially now."

Livingston was annoyed. At the embassy he had already endured the snide comments and pitying looks of those who thought he had again failed to predict a terrorist attack by the Yellow Wind.

"Tayib doesn't have Winn."

"We would like further assurances."

"LEGHORN was there. Tayib was pumping him for news. Nobody in Raqba knew a thing. What more can I say?"

"Has LEGHORN turned?"

"What?"

"It came up at the last meeting. What if LEGHORN told Tayib? What better way to protect himself . . ."

Livingston was shaking his head.

"Why not?"

"I told them before, LEGHORN might pee in his pants, he might lose his nerve, but he isn't going to turn. He's squeezing his guts dry to do what he does for us. He hasn't got the strength or intelligence to double."

"You're sure about that?"

"I'll stake my career on it."

Hatch smiled. "We all will. As Benjamin Franklin said to Nathan Hale on the eve of the American Revolution, 'We shall all hang together or we shall assuredly hang separately.'"

A kid on a skateboard, long hair flying from beneath a headband, careened toward them. Hatch braced himself, then relaxed as the skateboarder zipped past. "That's an American cultural phenomenon isn't it? No wonder the world despises us."

"What about Bright Justice? Is it compromised?"

"Delayed, hardly compromised. But it would be reassuring to know what Tayib is doing. Why is he taking credit for a kidnapping he didn't commit?"

"Power. Prestige. There's only a certain amount of money coming from countries like Iran and Libya to support organizations like the Yellow Wind. Tayib's had a high profile ever since the Alitalia bombing, he doesn't want to lose the position. If nobody claims responsibility he'll take the credit and the glory that goes with it."

"Sounds reasonable. Or unreasonable enough to seem reasonable to an Arab."

"Can you convince the Director?"

"I could have convinced him without meeting you but I thought we should speak freely, face to face. I've made lunch reservations at that fondue restaurant where we ate last time. You can background me on Damascus and I'll show you how to operate the little Avenger here. A yellow Sony for the Yellow Wind— just a little color coordinated destruction."

JANE GALLOWAY had coaxed Katherine into resuming tennis. They played three times a week, Jane with her ungainly flamboyant style, Katherine more precise, controlled. The cold weather made it easy to schedule the courts, but Katherine found it difficult to concentrate; a stray thought or sound or smell could distract her from her game and the ball would flash past.

One windy day they played quite early, and as they walked across the parking lot, Jane said, "Listen, Scott and I are having a few friends over and we'd like you to come."

"Who's Scott?"

"The man I've been dating for the past couple of months."

"Sorry." Katherine was carrying her sweatshirt. Chilly, she draped it over her shoulders. Jane in her skimpy tennis skirt seemed oblivious to the cold.

"Anyway, Scott has this friend from college. I met him, the man's a charmer. Looks good, got a nice laugh, doesn't take himself too seriously, makes a good living. Will you stop shaking your head every time I try to get you into circulation?"

"I don't feel like socializing."

"He's a man. You just stand there with your eyes open and he'll think you're listening." When Katherine didn't respond, she said, "So maybe you won't like him, at least you'll be there to laugh at my jokes. Not everybody appreciates my sense of humor like you do. At least you used to. Nowadays I say something funny and you look at me like I've got dental floss on my chin." Katherine smiled. "There, thank God I haven't lost my touch. I figure I'm not the smartest or sexiest woman in town but at least I'm funny."

Katherine took out her keys as they reached her car. "What size is Laurie? Ten or twelve?"

"She's a ten, why?"

Katherine opened the trunk and pulled out a wide, flat box. "I bought this for Ali on the last day. A skirt and blouse for school. I forgot it was in here until the car was cleaned. It should fit Laurie."

"Just take it back for credit."

"I don't want to deal with it. If you don't want it, give it away, okay?"

"Well, thanks," Jane tucked the box awkwardly

under one arm. "I hate all this. Everything that happened to you. It scares me."

It scared a lot of people, Katherine thought, remembering those who had stopped communicating after the disaster. "Listen, I won't be playing tennis for a while."

"Oh, yes, you will. You need the exercise."

"I'm getting exercise. I've got a trainer who comes every morning."

"A trainer? You mean one of those body-builders with huge muscles and skimpy shorts?"

"She's a woman."

Jane's grin faded. "And she doesn't badger you to go to parties or talk all the time trying to cheer you up."

Katherine put her hand on her arm. "I can't be much of a friend right now. I've got nothing left to give."

"Have I ever asked?"

"No. That's why you'll give me a little time."

She got into the car. Jane leaned down to the window. "You're not going to slit your wrists or anything?" She said it lightly but her eyes were clouded with worry.

"I gave up that idea weeks ago."

She started the car and Jane stepped back. "I'll consider that a promise."

Katherine had hired a trainer to design a regimen that would give her the strength and stamina she would need to confront Imad Tayib. Her plans were vague but at some level she realized she might have to sacrifice her own life to end his. First, she would need a reason to meet him, a compelling one.

The answer came that night while she was riding

a stationary bicycle and watching the news. Imad Tayib had taken responsibility for the Mike Winn kidnapping, and here was an interview with Mike's wife, Tracy. The reporters had caught up with her in front of her house in Dallas. After the usual questions one reporter asked, "If you could get a message to Imad Tayib, what would you tell him?"

"I would just beg him not to hurt Mike and to send him home, because my husband, he never hurt anybody in his life."

"Mrs. Winn, what is your response to reports that your husband was carrying a cashier's check drawn on a Swiss bank for one million dollars?"

"Where'd you get that?"

"Is it true?"

"No, it is not."

"Then there's no cashier's check?"

"There's a cashier's check but no way is it a million dollars."

"Half a million?"

"That's nobody's business but mine and Mike's. If you people will excuse me."

She started toward her front door and another reporter called, "Is it true your husband was once caught trying to smuggle religious relics out of Syria?"

Tracy Winn's answer was a raised middle finger as she disappeared into the house.

Katherine got Mike Winn's number from the information operator and moments later Tracy's oddly familiar voice answered. "Winn residence."

"Mrs. Winn, my name is Katherine Cahill. I read about your husband in the newspapers. I'd like to help you."

"Who is this?"

"Katherine Cahill. My children were on Alitalia Flight 67."

"Cahill?" she said slowly. "The one who . . . your whole family was on that airplane. You're that one?"

"That's right. I'd like to talk to you about getting your husband back."

"Get him back how?"

"I'd rather talk to you in person. Can I come see you tomorrow around three o'clock?"

"Sure, if you want." Tracy gave her the address and said, "You need directions? Where are you now?"

"I'll be coming from the airport."

"You're not in Dallas?"

"No, I'm at home."

"Where's that?"

"Connecticut."

"You're not coming all the way out here just to see me?"

"It's important that we talk."

"We can talk on the phone, it'd be cheaper."

"I'll see you tomorrow at three, Mrs. Winn."

Katherine hung up before the girl could protest. You are going to be my Trojan horse, she thought, my chance for a face-to-face meeting with Imad Tayib.

TWELVE

KATHERINE ARRIVED IN DALLAS THE NEXT DAY AT NOON. SHE rented a car at the airport and drove to the Winn residence in a development called Driftwood Estates. Rambling ranch-style homes sat among circular streets, guarded by lawns groomed as carefully as a golf course. Each house had an oversize mailbox, some of them with cute labels. The one at the end of the Winn driveway read "Mike's Mansion." In the side yard a twenty-foot Donzi speedboat sat on a trailer covered with a plastic tarpaulin.

Katherine rang the doorbell and from inside the house dogs began to bark. She heard Tracy's voice as the door opened. "Hush now, hush now, you two. Go on out of here."

Tracy Winn was smaller than she looked on television, no more than five feet, with a figure too ripe for such a tiny frame. She wore a short red skirt, oversize white sweater with a pocket watch on a chain dangling around her neck. "Ms. Cahill? Come on in."

The two dogs followed them to a living room with an exposed beam ceiling and flagstone fireplace. Sliding glass doors led to a lawn, where a sprinkler sent a staccato spray of water in a slow circle. One of the dogs, a red setter, pushed at Katherine's hand while the wire-haired terrier jumped onto a chair.

"Get off of there, Dusty." Tracy swatted him and the dog jumped down. "If they bother you, just give them a whack. That's Rusty and this here is Dusty, on account of their colors. They keep me company during the long months Mike is gone. Don't you, boys? Those thirty dirty days, huh? Are you my good boys?" The dogs surged toward her face, licking and pawing. "All right, enough." Tracy clapped her hands and the dogs moved away.

"Here, sit down, Ms. Cahill. What can I get you? Beer, lemonade?"

"Nothing, thanks."

Katherine ignored the dog hair on the couch. Tracy sat in an oversize chair and tucked one leg beneath her like a teenager. She was blond but the true color of her hair was visible in the light brown eyebrows. "So how was your flight?"

"Fine." How can I start this, Katherine wondered? She had tried a dozen different approaches on the plane and now she was nervous. She didn't entirely trust what she was doing.

"You should have been here earlier," Tracy said. "I had this jackass from the FBI show up. One of those guys with porcupine hair and aviator glasses—you know how they look. I think they've got some school somewhere that puts their heads in a mold so they all look the same. And this guy, he starts asking these questions: Does Mike know any Palestinians?

How about Israelis? What are his political beliefs? Who are his friends? What does he do in his spare time? And I say, 'Why are you asking all this stuff?' and he says, 'It's just routine,' so I told him, 'Mike is on call twenty-four hours a day at the rigs, and when he comes home he likes to forget all about it. If you want to ask questions, why don't you ask the people who kidnapped him?' I mean I love my U.S. of A. but sometimes I think the people running it are straight out of the circus.''

Katherine nodded. If the government had spent half the effort getting Imad Tayib extradited that they seemed to be spending investigating Mike Winn, the kidnapping might never have happened.

Tracy tossed her head and flipped her hair back. "Look at me going on about my problem. At least I got a chance to get Mike back. I'd die if I lost my kids the way you did.''

"Do you have any children?''

"Not until Mike gets a job in the States. No child of mine is growing up with only a part-time daddy.''

"Have you had any word from your husband?''

"You mean like a ransom note?''

"Any word at all.''

"Only somebody from the State Department called yesterday, and then that FBI fellow this morning. They're full of questions but they don't have any answers. The State Department won't even say for sure that Imad Tayib is the one that kidnapped Mike, even though he already admitted it.''

"They don't think Tayib has your husband?''

"They don't know what they think. These are people who couldn't give hope to a saint.''

Now, Katherine thought. Do it. "How would you like to go to Syria and get Mike back?"

"I'd like to go over with the Seventh Army and a nuclear bomb."

"What if you could meet with Imad Tayib and offer to ransom your husband?"

"Ms. Cahill, everything you see around here is in Mike's name and most of it's owed to the bank. The way we live is, be happy today, the Devil takes tomorrow. And now it looks like the Devil did."

"What I'm suggesting is that we go together to meet with Imad Tayib. I'll pay all expenses and put up a million dollars for his release."

Tracy's expression became very serious. "Ms. Cahill, you better think what you're saying."

"I've already thought about it. A lot. That's why I'm here."

"You don't hardly know me."

"I know what you're going through and I want to help." Not a lie, she thought. I can help free Mike Winn and then kill Tayib . . .

Tracy was shaking her head. "I'm sorry, Ms. Cahill, I appreciate the offer, really, but I can't take money that doesn't belong to me."

"Not even as a favor?"

"It's no favor to take somebody's money. I learned that a long time ago."

"You've *got* to let me help you."

"Why?"

Katherine hesitated. Should she tell the truth? No, there was no predicting how the girl would react. Tracy seemed the type who wore her emotions on her sleeve. There had to be some other way to convince her.

"Tracy, can I ask how old you are?"

"Twenty last May."

"Jeff was eleven, Ali was nine. You're closer in age to them than you are to me. When I go to bed at night I lie awake thinking what I might have done differently. I wish I could turn back the clock and warn them not to take that flight. When I wake up in the morning I don't want to open my eyes. There's no reason to get up, no reason for anything. I have enough money—more than enough money—to last the rest of my life. None of it can bring back Jeff or Ali or Joey, but at least it might bring back Mike. If you take the money you give *me* hope. You give me a reason to open my eyes, a reason to face the day. That's the favor I ask."

Tracy's eyes glistened with tears. "All right, if you still feel the same way tomorrow—"

"I *will*. I guarantee it, Tracy."

"Then . . . all right, we'll do it. But I want to keep track of every penny."

Dizziness came over Katherine. She blinked, braced herself.

"Ms. Cahill, are you all right?"

"I'm fine, just a little faint."

"You want some water or something?"

"Please."

Tracy jumped up and ran to the kitchen. Katherine let out a deep breath. Something had changed, something deep in her makeup had shifted, moved into the shadows. What have I done? She cast about, searching for it, the absent tree in the forest.

Tracy returned. "We don't have any fancy stuff, plain old tap water. I got some aspirin in the bathroom."

"This is fine."

Shame was missing, that's what it was. She had just deceived this girl and felt no shame at all.

IT WAS the darkroom chemicals that convinced Sam Gaddis that it was time to resurrect his career. He had given in to his parents' urging and returned to dark-room work at the studio. When he went to bed at night, the smell of the processing chemicals remained in his nose, a constant reminder that he had come full circle from darkroom rat to hot shooter and back again. Occasionally he stayed for dinner with his parents, but more often he spent the evening at a local bar, where successive bottles of beer dulled the anger that had stalked him since Faye's death.

The smell of the chemicals was the smell of time lost. Sam knew it was time to rebuild his career but lacked the will to do it until he saw an article in the *Herald:* Katherine Cahill and Tracy Winn were going to Syria to negotiate with Imad Tayib for the release of Mike Winn. Like mixing vinegar and baking soda, Sam thought, as he tried to imagine Katherine Cahill and Imad Tayib together. For the first time since Faye's death he felt a stirring of the old desire, the need to be where the action was.

He made an appointment with Lulu Yost, the pic-ture editor of the *Washington Herald.* From her office on the third floor Lulu was in contact with photogra-phers on assignments all over the world. She was an oversize woman with an oversize personality. Lulu had no family—no personal life at all, some said—but her office was witness to a fondness for cats; a photo-graph of fuzzy-faced kittens stared down from the calendar, a three-foot porcelain cat sat in the corner and the coffee cup featured a Garfield cartoon. When Sam arrived, Lulu's eyes did a quick inventory. She sat like a pyramid, elbows planted on the desk.

"Sam, I have five minutes. What's up?"

"I'm fine, Lulu, how are you?"

"Busy, but you said it was important."

"I'm back. I want an assignment."

"I gave you an assignment. You blew it."

"That was last year. I thought it would be good to start with a clean slate."

She shook her head. "My policy is like God's—you don't come back to life after you're dead, and you don't come back to me after you screw up."

Her reference to death was not coincidental, Sam thought. After Faye's death he had taken assignments before he was ready. He was drinking back then, he didn't care, he showed up late, didn't show up at all.

"You want the apology on my knees or can I give it standing up?"

"Go somewhere else, Sam. You don't need to work here."

"She worked here. It's like my home."

"She who? Faye is gone. This is a newspaper. You can't just say *she* and expect the world to know who you're talking about."

"You knew who I meant."

"I liked Faye. Doesn't mean I have an assignment for you."

"What about this one?" Sam put the clipping about Katherine Cahill and Tracy Winn on the desk. Lulu glanced at it.

"No one's assigned, we get it off the wire."

"Send me. I can do words and pictures."

"So can a lot of people."

"I know the players. I've met Katherine Cahill and Imad Tayib."

"Whoopie-doopie."

"Come on, Lulu, this is a circulation builder. A close-up of Katherine Cahill's face when she meets Imad Tayib and you'll need the rest of the rain forest for newsprint."

"Like I said, we'll get it off the wire."

"Not if it's an exclusive."

Lulu gave him a sharp look. "Is that what we're talking about?"

"First rights with a twenty-four-hour hold."

"These women, they agreed?"

"We're finalizing it tomorrow."

"Then come see me tomorrow."

"A fully funded assignment for an exclusive. Do we have a deal?"

"I'll need to clear it with the Mahues. And if you want to do words you better talk to Bernie."

"I'd like to know you're in my corner first."

"Don't talk like a politician, it makes my teeth hurt."

"How's Tinkerbell?"

Lulu's expression automatically softened. "She had a litter three weeks ago. If you want a kitten, there's a sign-up sheet right there." She pointed to the back of the door.

Sam stood up. "I'd love to but I'll be in Syria, won't I?"

"I think you're blowing wind on this one, Sam."

"Tie down your desk, Lulu."

The phone rang and she grabbed it. "Yost." A

pause. "Tell him to hold." She glanced up. Sam was at the door.

"Sam, you remember what Thomas Wolfe said?"

"Yeah, too much."

He closed the door without waiting for a response. You can't go home again, that's what Lulu meant. But she had it wrong. The Middle East had never been home, just the place he'd been the happiest. And lost the love of his life.

THIRTEEN

KATHERINE DRAFTED A WILL DIVIDING ALL HER SHARES IN Cahill Enterprises between her brother's children and assigned the remainder of her assets equally among the families who lost loved ones in the Alitalia crash. She bought a condominium, put the house up for sale, and discharged the staff after paying them each six months' salary. There were tearful farewells but the tears were not Katherine's.

Friends offered to help her move. Katherine was polite, appreciative and firm in her refusal. She called a moving company. Some of the furniture went to the condominium, while the rest was packed and put into storage. Only the three children's bedrooms remained untouched. When everything else was gone, Katherine told the men to take the contents of these rooms—all the toys and clothing—and dump them into the empty swimming pool.

The supervisor was puzzled. "What do you aim to do with this stuff, Ms. Cahill?"

"That's not your concern."

She sounded cold, she knew, but any hesitation and her resolve might fail. On her way downstairs a vaguely familiar voice echoed through the house. "Anybody home?"

She found Sam Gaddis standing in the open front doorway. In slacks and a sportcoat he looked more substantial than the last time she had seen him.

"I could have called but why break the tradition? Did I catch you at a bad time?"

"I don't know. Why are you—?"

"I wanted to talk to you in person. It won't take long."

Katherine led him through the living room, now barren of furniture, to a library vacant of books. There was a bar with four stools at one end of the room. "This is the only place left to sit," Katherine said. "I'd offer you something to drink but I'm afraid there's nothing here."

"Who plays the piano?"

"Ali and I—" She hesitated. "I do. How did you know about the piano?"

"Three indentations in the living room rug about the size of a baby grand."

"You're very perceptive."

"I'm a photographer. The world seen through a viewfinder."

"What brings you here, Mr. Gaddis?"

"I read in the papers you're going to Syria."

"With Tracy Winn. We plan to ransom her husband."

"Have you been in contact with Imad Tayib?"

"I sent a telegram to the Yellow Wind office in Damascus telling them we're coming."

"Abu Shapour."

"What?"

"The man who runs the Damascus office. His name is Abu Shapour. At least he was the one in charge when I was there. Did you get an answer?"

"No, but I didn't expect one. That's why we're going in person."

"How would you like a guide? Someone who knows the country, understands the people, speaks Arabic *and* has met Imad Tayib?"

"Are you volunteering?"

"You'll need a man with you in Syria."

"Because it's too dangerous for women to travel alone?"

"No, not really. In Damascus there's less danger walking the streets at midnight than talking politics at noon. But you *will* need a man for credibility. A woman's status in Syria falls roughly between a goat and a camel."

"Thank you," she said dryly.

Sam spread his hands. "Don't kill the messenger for bringing bad news."

"What you're saying is you want a job."

"No, I have a job, an assignment from the *Washington Herald.* What I want is exclusive rights to your story—photos and interviews—for as long as it takes to ransom Mike Winn."

"I thought you weren't taking pictures any more."

"Things change. The sun rises and the sun sets. You put your house up for sale and I'm back in the photo game." Sam's attention was drawn to the back yard where a workman emptied a box of toys into the pool. "Can I ask the obvious question?"

"My children's belongings."

"You're going to drown them?"

After a long moment she said, "How did your wife die, Mr. Gaddis?"

"She killed herself, Ms. Cahill."

"Is that—?"

"What?"

"I'm not sure if you're trying to shock me or telling the truth."

"I'm telling the truth."

"I'm sorry."

"Why? It was her choice. People ask, I tell them, suddenly they're sorry, they don't want to hear it. Faye lived her life on her own terms. When she couldn't have it anymore she opted out." And left me behind. He thrust the thought aside before it found expression in his eyes.

"What made her opt out?"

Sam looked toward the ceiling. "Faye was in a car accident in Lebanon. It left her paralyzed below the neck. After eighteen months of physical therapy she learned to use her left hand well enough to feed herself. She fed herself sleeping pills one night while I was chipping plaster in the living room. I woke up the next morning and she was gone."

Who was driving the car, Katherine almost asked, but she guessed the answer. Her initial negative reaction to Sam's offer faded. It *would* be good to have someone who knew the territory, someone she could trust.

"I'll talk to Tracy about your proposal. Where are you staying?"

He gave her the number of a friend in New York City and she agreed to call him that evening. Katherine watched from the window as Sam left. He lit a cigarette as soon as he was outside the house and drove away in a blue van. The van had a hydraulic lift. For a wheelchair, she realized . . .

The workmen finished emptying the rooms and Katherine paid them. After they were gone she went to the garage and got four cans of charcoal lighter. These she emptied one at a time into the pool, forcing herself to see only a jumble of shapes and colors, refusing to recognize Jeff's computer games or Ali's beaded purse or Joey's super-heroes tumbled upside down in courageous poses. Her hands trembled when she lit the match. The fumes ignited with a *whomp* and the heat forced her back. She watched numbly as dark sinuous smoke rose above the house and flames turned the last evidence of three small lives to ash.

I'M JUST a physical guy, Doug Livingston thought. His lips were sore from a night of lovemaking and the girl's scent hovered about him. She was a teacher at the American School, a girl with an adventuresome spirit who liked to kid him about his work and make fun of his elaborate denials. Livingston didn't mind. If the initials CIA had certain aphrodisiac qualities he was willing to make the most of it.

Livingston was sitting in his car at the top of Mt. Qassioun. To the west a mountain range marked the border with Lebanon. To the east the arid plains of the interior faded into a hazy sky. From this vantage point he could look down on the road, which looped across the steep and rocky face of Mt. Qassioun, past the tea and coffee shops perched along the cliffs above the city of Damascus. In the evening the sons and daughters of wealth and privilege would come up here to park and party but now the parking lot was empty.

A tiny Citroen struggled up the mountain, disappeared from view and a few minutes later joined him. Fawzi Ashraf, code-named LEGHORN, made a point of backing the car into its parking space. In case he has to make a fast getaway, Livingston thought derisively. Fawzi came forward and shook his hand.

"Hello my friend, how are you?"

"Fine, yourself?"

"My burdens are forgotten in the pleasure of our meeting."

"And your family is well?"

"As Allah has decreed it."

Fawzi wore loose pants and a flashy fitted shirt with the top buttons undone. He climbed into Livingston's car, from which they could watch the road below. The CIA man lifted the yellow Sony Sportsman from the back seat. In an earlier meeting he had briefed Fawzi on his assignment. Now all that was left was to demonstrate the Sony. Fawzi struck a pose, one arm draped over the back of the seat, as he listened.

"It's a factory radio-cassette player with detachable speakers. All the controls operate normally. On-off switch, AM and FM selector, here's the tuner, the preset selector—"

As he mentioned each control Fawzi nodded and repeated the words like an echo. "Volume control, yes . . . Dolby sound . . ."

Shut up and listen, Livingston felt like saying, but his job was to build the poodle's confidence, not diminish it. "You probably know all this but—"

"I have used these machines before."

"All right, then, here's how you set the charge. Hold out your arm."

"My arm?"

"Just stick it out."

Fawzi complied and Livingston placed the two speakers back-to-back on each side of his arm. When they touched him, Fawzi flinched. He laughed nervously. "It will not go off now?"

"It's not armed."

"But the explosive is inside of these."

"That's right. Pretend your arm is the power line and this is how you position the speakers. Back-to-back and then tape them securely into place."

"And then what?"

"You see the two switches here for the cassette? You have to depress them both if you want to record."

"One is a safety switch. I know how it works."

"If the machine is turned on it works the same way it always did. You can record a radio show, use the microphone, whatever you want. But if the buttons are depressed and you turn the machine *off*, what happens is that a timer inside will detonate the explosive. It's preset for seven twenty-five at night."

Fawzi's eyes widened. *"This* evening?"

"If you armed it." Livingston said patiently. "It's like an alarm clock. You set it any time twenty-four hours before you want it to go off."

"Ah. You mean if the play-record buttons are pressed to the 'on' position and the machine itself is turned to the 'off' position."

"That's right."

"One more thing," Fawzi said importantly. "I

think it is necessary to have a cassette in the recorder, otherwise the play-record buttons will not operate."

No shit, Livingston thought, but pretended ignorance while Fawzi removed the cassette tape and tried the buttons. They wouldn't work. "You see?" he said. "I have used these before."

"Good. When will you go to Raqba?"

"In the next few days, I think. I will let you know."

They reviewed details of the plan. Fawzi was worried that his relatives might be hurt in the attack. Livingston tried to reassure him. "Your uncle lives in the village outside the castle, right?"

"Yes."

"Then don't worry. The attack will concentrate on the castle itself. Nobody wants civilians hurt."

"Still, I think it is a good idea if I bring them to Damascus for their safety."

"*No.* You endanger them more if you do that. After the attack it's going to seem too convenient if your relatives aren't there. Tayib's people will figure it out and you'll all be dead, you, your uncle, his family. My friend, believe me, you must not change your routine on this visit. Your safety and your family's depend on it."

Fawzi still looked worried. "I could not forgive myself if something bad happened . . ."

What a poodle, Livingston thought. He pulled out the ten-thousand-dollar down payment and watched Fawzi's courage return. He spent another five minutes inflating the agent's ego and gave him a gold Cross pen for luck. Fawzi proceeded to embrace Livingston and call him "my brother." He swore to fulfill his mission and cover them both with glory. Livingston, quickly removing himself from the embrace, would believe it when he saw it.

The CIA man then drove back to the embassy wishing there had been time to recruit someone stronger for the mission. When he arrived at his office, he found a VIP advisory on his desk. Advisories were sent to all departments whenever a notable American, usually a politician, came to Syria. In this case there would be two visitors, Katherine Cahill and Tracy Winn. They would arrive Tuesday and they wanted to meet with Imad Tayib. There was no mention in the advisory of Sam Gaddis. Livingston popped a Certs breath mint into his mouth and began to consider ways that two women unfamiliar with Damascus could be delayed on their way to Raqba.

KATHERINE CAHILL and Darryl Sikes sat at a test bench in the soundproof target range at the Cahill Arms factory. There were a number of firing stations with overhead pulleys to position the targets. A sign on the wall reminded all employees to wear hearing protectors whenever live ammunition was in use. When she was a teenager, Katherine had spent many hours in this room practicing for competitions.

"I'm still not sure I should give you this," Daryll said.

"I'd feel more secure with a weapon."

"What about your mercenary?"

"He can't go in until we get Mike Winn back. If that's impossible, I may be able to leave Mike the weapon. Either way I'd like the option."

"Don't make me regret this," Daryll said. He

placed the Mont Blanc pen on the table. "It's a little heavier than normal but not as bad as you'd have in an all-metal barrel. Since you're not worried about cylinder-wall degradation, I used a metal insert in a graphite shell. It won't show up in a metal detector."

"The top comes off when it's fired?"

"Right. You hold it like a flashlight and aim it like this. There's zero accuracy, it's virtually a contact weapon."

"Where's the trigger?"

"Here. This part of the top unscrews to fill the pen. Or it did. Now it cocks the hammer like so." He rotated the upper part of the top and pulled it back half an inch. A small metal tongue popped out and clicked into position. "The shooter's thumb rests here. To fire, press down." There was a snap and the metal tongue disappeared.

"What kind of round?"

Darryl pulled out a .22-caliber bullet with a starburst pattern cut into the tip. "Twenty-grain disintegration round, a soft-tissue cartridge only. Make sure whoever uses it knows the limitations."

Katherine nodded. A low-velocity expanding round meant she had to place the bullet through the ribs to the heart or through the eye to the brain. Hit a bone and Imad Tayib would kill her before he bothered to bandage the wound.

"I want to test fire. I have to be able to demonstrate how it works."

"Not with this, the top will disintegrate. I've got a practice prototype." Darryl brought out a rough metal replica of the pen in which no attempt had been made to conceal the barrel. "With this you can use over-the-counter .22 shorts. Good to practice the grip and test angle of fire."

He dismantled the piece, showed her the firing mechanism and how to load it. Katherine opened a plastic bag and brought out a piece of molded styrofoam in the shape of a human head. She put it on a stool about fifteen feet from the target wall. Holding the flared base of the neck secure with one hand, she positioned the gun with the other. The styrofoam features were rounded and stylized; there was no detail to the empty eyes.

"Clear on the left, clear on the right," she murmured automatically.

"Clear on the firing range." Darryl finished. His words were lost in the sharp crack. The barrel jumped and the styrofoam head flipped out of her fingers and bounced to the floor. Darryl picked it up. There was a tiny hole where the pupil would be, which made the eye look more realistic. The back of the head behind the left ear was missing or hung in chunks; other pieces had bounced off the wall and scattered on the floor.

Darryl said, "Lethal, if you're close enough."

"How long will it take you to load the Mont Blanc?"

"Say ten minutes."

"I'll wait here."

"It's more comfortable in my office."

Katherine saw the concern in his eyes and wondered how much he guessed. She put a hand on his cheek. "It's all right, Darryl. I'll be fine."

While he was gone, she practiced with the metal prototype, reloading it again and again, testing different positions, aiming carefully, making adjustments, noting the results. She didn't bother with earplugs. By the time Darryl returned, her ears were ringing and styrofoam pieces littered the floor.

FOURTEEN

THE FLIGHT TO DAMASCUS HAD A DIFFERENT MEANING FOR EACH of them. Tracy Winn had never traveled outside the United States. For her the trip was an adventure. Having grown up without money, she assumed that, backed by Katherine Cahill's funds, Mike's safe return was almost certain.

Sam wore his shooting outfit: jeans, khaki shirt, Greek captain's hat and a canvas camera bag slung over his shoulder. For him the trip evoked bittersweet memory; the last time he had been in Damascus was with Faye. To keep himself busy he took pictures of Katherine and Tracy at the airport. He didn't expect to use the pictures but wanted to get the women feeling comfortable before the camera.

Katherine was calm as she watched her purse go through the metal detector. The single bullet shouldn't show up hidden inside a metal tube of lipstick. No alarm bells rang and the impassive expression of the security guard monitoring the video screen didn't change. She felt strangely serene, as if this trip and the meeting with Imad Tayib were destined and no longer alterable by anything she might do or say. *I have a gun in my purse*—even if she spoke the words, it wouldn't matter. Nothing could change things now, she felt.

The twelve-hour flight was made in two legs with a stop in Frankfurt. The two women rode First Class while Sam, constrained by the *Herald* budget, sat in the smoking section of Economy. Katherine had a window seat but she switched with Tracy when the girl kept leaning across to look out. Tracy seemed in high spirits, animated and talkative. After the meal, when the stewardess brought a dessert menu, she took one look and said, "Don't I feel like the fool. I didn't know we'd be in First Class so look what I brought." She pulled from her purse a piece of cake wrapped in cellophane. "Carrot cake. I always make it for Mike because he hates airplane food so much. If you don't want yours maybe I'll give it all to Sam."

"Me?"

"I made us each a piece. You, me, and the photographer."

"He can have mine." Don't make me like you, she thought as Tracy squeezed past. I can't do it. I made a promise and I'm going to keep it. She took out a cassette recorder, inserted an Arabic language tape, and listened to the language of the man she meant to kill.

They landed in Damascus late in the afternoon. When the women stopped inside the terminal to wait for Sam, an American in a yellow dress shirt and black slacks approached them. "Katherine Cahill? Tracy Winn? My name is Jerry Riggs, Deputy Public

Affairs Officer at the embassy." He flashed an identification card. "If you'll follow me I'll get you through the red tape and drive you to your hotel."

"We've got someone with us." As she spoke Sam appeared. "This man."

"There are three of you?"

"I'm the bodyguard."

Jerry gave him a quick once-over and smiled when he was satisfied it was a joke. He escorted them to the currency desk, where they exchanged a mandatory one hundred dollars for an artificially low number of Syrian pounds. Skirting a barnlike room crowded with people filling out immigration forms, they went directly to a small cubicle, where two men in uniform interrupted their conversation long enough to stamp their passports.

"Why the VIP treatment?" Sam asked.

"The consul would like you to stop by the embassy on the way to the hotel."

"Let's check in first," Katherine said.

"This will only take a few minutes. You'll still get to the hotel sooner than if I hadn't been here."

THE LIMOUSINE rocked and swayed over the bumpy road to the city. Damascus reflected the color of its surroundings, brown and gray, as if raised from the arid plains that surrounded it. The American Embassy was located in the Malki district, an area of large homes built during the French colonial era. The multistory building bristled with communications antennae and was surrounded by a fifteen-foot-high concrete wall. After they were given temporary ID badges, Riggs led them to the officer of the consul,

Edward Jurman. Katherine and Tracy entered first, and Jurman rose from behind his desk to greet them. He was a bald, neatly dressed man with a somewhat harried look.

"Ms. Cahill, Mrs. Winn, I'm Edward Jurman. This is Doug Livingston, one of our political analysts."

The CIA man rose from a chair near the wall. "Welcome to Dama—" He stopped when he saw Sam. Katherine said, "This is Sam Gaddis. He's traveling with us."

Her words trailed off as she realized from Sam's fixed stare that the two men knew one another. The CIA man said, "Hello, Sam."

"You two know each other?"

"That's right," Sam said. He stepped forward and hit Livingston in the mouth, knocking him back across Jurman's desk. A memo box, a brass beer mug, pens and papers scattered to the floor.

"What the hell—"

Riggs grabbed him but Sam hadn't pressed his attack. Livingston got to his feet as Jurman pressed a button for help.

"It's over," Sam said to Riggs. "Hands off."

Riggs looked at Livingston, whose lip was bleeding. "Sir?"

"Get him out of here."

"Wait." Katherine turned to Sam. "What's this all about?"

"Something I promised I'd do the next time I saw him."

"Why?"

Before he could answer, the door abruptly opened and two Marines, guns drawn, rushed into the room. Jurman pointed to Sam. "This man, escort him out of the building."

Riggs released him to the Marines but Sam's gaze was fixed on Livingston. "She's dead, Livingston, in case you give a shit."

"Come with us, sir."

"Yeah, yeah." Sam pulled one arm free as they marched him out.

"Just a *minute*," Katherine said. "Where are you taking him?"

"Out of the building."

"Sam, wait for us at the gate."

Jurman picked up a pair of broken eyeglasses while Livingston dabbed his mouth with a handkerchief. Riggs said in a low voice, "You want some ice or something?"

"It's a cut lip, Jerry. I'll live." His voice shook with anger.

Jurman said, "Can I ask what that was all about?"

Livingston lowered the handkerchief. "I knew Gaddis in Beirut. He was having marital and drinking problems. I was one of the people he blamed for his troubles. The man is unstable."

Jurman said, "I'm sorry, ladies, I had no idea Mr. Gaddis was traveling with you."

"Why did you want to see us?"

"Sit down, please. We don't usually welcome people this way."

"We'd like to get to the hotel."

"Then I'll be brief. Basically I'm here to offer you the services of the consulate and ask exactly what your plans are."

"We're going to see a man called Abu Shapour here in Damascus and see if he can arrange a meeting with Imad Tayib. If not, we'll go to Raqba and meet with Tayib there."

Jurman squinted as if trying to make out a distant object. "I would be less than candid if I did not tell you that your plan has substantial negative political implications. Since the invasion of Kuwait the American government has taken a leading role in the Middle East, as I'm sure you know. Our Syrian support is tenuous and it could be jeopardized by any public confrontation with Imad Tayib."

Tracy shook her head. "You got your job and we got ours. All we want is to get Mike back."

"Much as I admire your courage, I think you would be well-advised to let your State Department handle this."

Katherine said, "The way you've handled Imad Tayib's extradition for the murder of my children?"

The consul stiffened and Livingston said, "What Mr. Jurman means is that the area you're talking about visiting is nominally under Syrian army control, but actually the only authority at Raqba is the Yellow Wind soldiers. Any attempt by the Syrian government to take control from Imad Tayib might precipitate a civil war."

"That's got nothing to do with us."

"It might if Imad Tayib took you hostage."

"He won't," Tracy said. "According to Sam, Tayib would lose face if he took women hostages."

"I wouldn't put much faith in anything Sam Gaddis has to say. You just saw how unstable he is."

"He seemed fine until he got here."

"How many drinks did he have on the plane?"

There was a pause. Katherine filled it. "What did you say your job was, Mr. Livingston?"

"I'm a political analyst."

Jurman intervened. "I think we got off to a bad start here, Ms. Cahill. Our job is to aid and protect American citizens. My advice is a good-faith attempt to do just that. Of course, you are free to pursue your own course of action and we will help in any way we can. In return I ask that you keep us informed of your plans and let us know when you leave Damascus. It will make our job easier and protect you."

He gave them his card and they left with Jerry Riggs. As soon as the door closed, the consul's pleasant expression withered. He said to Livingston, "Don't ever ask me to do something like this again."

"You did fine, sir."

"I don't know what I did, that's the problem." Jurman picked up his broken glasses and inspected them.

"I can have those replaced in a week."

"So can I, Mr. Livingston. If you'll excuse me, I have a real job to attend to."

Livingston went to the door. His lip had stopped bleeding but it lay thick against his teeth. "You will let me know their plans?"

"Yes, yes."

Feeling like a damn schoolboy banished from the principal's office, Livingston left.

SAM WASN'T outside the embassy. Katherine questioned the Syrian security guards whose post was a red-and-white-striped booth on the sidewalk in front of the main gate. One of them pointed. "The man with the camera bag, yes, he went that way."

"In a car?"

"No, just walking."

Tracy said, "That man has a real temper on him."

Probably at the hotel, Katherine thought. Jerry Riggs drove them to the Sheraton, which was situated on spacious grounds outside the center of the city and only a mile from the brooding presence of Mt. Qassioun, a rocky, dome-shaped mountain overlooking Damascus. While Katherine talked to the registration clerk, Tracy looked around. Sunlight flickered through brass chain-mail curtains across a lobby of white marble with interlocking maroon bands. A man in traditional Arab dress, white robe and headscarf, sat on a low couch in front of a charcoal brazier with two brass coffee urns in front of him. Tracy touched Katherine's elbow and nodded. "Look."

Noting her interest, the desk clerk said, "You are invited to have a cup of coffee with Mahmoud. Our traditional welcome."

"He works here?"

"Mahmoud is part of our hospitality staff."

When the clerk went to get their keys, Tracy whispered, "You want to have a cup?"

She shook her head. "Sam's not here."

"Well, he can't be lost, right? He's lived here before. Probably just takes more time to walk."

Katherine wasn't so sure. She remembered the pictures in Sam's house of the dark-haired woman with the reckless smile, and how disembodied his voice became when he talked about her. Livingston was right about one thing: when it came to his wife, Sam Gaddis was unstable.

● ● ●

SAM WALKED the familiar streets without any destination in mind. The CIA man's face floated before him, not shocked as he had been moments ago, but with the smug expression Sam remembered from Beirut. *She doesn't want to be owned by anybody.* Don't tell me about my wife, he thought angrily.

He hadn't intended to stop at the Meridien Hotel —in fact, he had promised himself he would stay away from the old haunts—but he needed a drink, and the Meridien was on the way to the Sheraton. The bar had the feel of a Monte Carlo casino and was a popular gathering place for newsmen. Spotting someone he recognized, Sam walked up behind him and slapped Skip Robinson on the back. "Buy a man a drink?"

"Sneaky Sam, hey, I thought you drowned in Panama."

"I heard you were killed in the Congo."

It was the usual routine, the journalist's equivalent of a ghetto high-five. Skip pulled out a chair and introduced him to the others. "Who are you with, Sam?"

"A special for the *Washington Herald.*"

"The Unity Conference?"

"No way. That why you're here?"

"Arab solutions to Arab problems. Assad is hosting a bunch of representatives up at the big palace."

"Here's the Arab solution to Arab problems." Sam made a gun of his hand and pointed his index finger at his temple. There was laughter, more drinks, gossip and the warm glow of alcohol easing the tension, dulling the turmoil inside, lifting him on clouds of good-hearted camaraderie.

Skip was staying in the hotel. At midnight, when

he went to get his key, Sam was with him. With alcoholic belligerence Sam thought, why should I go to the Sheraton? The Meridien was the place to be. Here was where he and Faye stayed. Room 702 with a balcony overlooking the city. Hadn't they hauled their bed outside one night to make love? Didn't this give him lifetime rights to Room 702?

The desk clerk, a snooty Arab who spoke with a terrible French accent, didn't think so. "That room is occupied, *monsieur*. We have other rooms."

"No, that's my room."

Skip scratched his stomach. "You can stay with me."

"There, see? I can stay with him."

"As you please, *monsieur.*"

"I please your mother," Sam said in Arabic. The man colored.

"Come on," Skip said. He pulled Sam to the elevator, but when they got to the fifth floor, Sam had a change of heart.

"I'm not sleeping in your goddam bathtub, Skip. I want my own room."

"Got your cards?"

"The *Herald*, sure, I got Visa, Mastercard, whatever the hell it is."

"The *Herald*, that's right."

"Screw it."

"Hey, Arab solutions." He pointed a finger at his temple. They fell back laughing and the elevator door separated them as it closed. Fucking Arab solutions. Sam pushed the button and rode up to the seventh floor. He arrived at Room 702 and began searching his pockets for the key. No key. He remembered now, supposed to be at the Sheraton, the Mike Winn story.

Somebody else in this room. He straightened his shoulders, straightened his hat and knocked on the door.

"Monsieur. Un bomba." Was that the right word? He shouted it louder and then switched to English.

"Bomb threat! *Le bombe, au secours.* Wake up in there."

He beat on the door again. Someone opened it marginally. A heavyset man in red silk pajamas peered out. "I beg your pardon?"

"We have a bomb threat, sir. Please move quickly to the lobby."

"What?"

"Is there anyone with you?"

"No, but—"

Sam stepped back. "Come quickly, please. There is a bomb in the room below you."

"My things."

"No time, sir! Now!"

The man jumped from the room as if poked from behind. "Quickly, quickly," Sam urged him past. Then he stepped into the room and slammed the door. He turned on the light. It was the same beige furniture, the same silver-and-blue bedspread pulled back from the unmade bed, the same sliding glass door that opened onto the balcony.

The former occupant was pounding on the door. "Quiet," Sam shouted. "People are trying to sleep."

He moved onto the balcony. The city lay bathed in patchy moonlight beneath scattered dark clouds rimmed in silver. An eerie wail came from some distant quarter, followed by another and another. It was the call to prayer, echoing across the city from loudspeakers hidden among the minarets of a hundred mosques. The lilting voices rose and fell, intermingled and drifted through the streets in changing chorus. Sam sat with his back against the wall and remembered the mattress on this balcony when he and Faye had joined their voices in passion with those raised in public prayer. He was on his back and she straddled him, her black hair and eyes blending with the night, disappearing, leaving only the white mask of her face and lips moving in ecstasy . . .

Sam closed his eyes, aroused by the memory. Footsteps and voices. The night manager entered with three security guards. Sam could have gone quietly, but the prayers were dying now, and he wanted to stay until they finished. Or maybe he just wanted to hit someone or be hit himself until the pain disappeared beneath the kicks and blows that left him curled on his side trying to protect his face and neck while the rest of his body absorbed the punishment. Faye. The blows rained down but he hardly felt them.

FIFTEEN

KATHERINE SLEPT DEEPLY FOR A FEW HOURS AND THEN WOKE UP to the sound of prayers. She turned on the light and checked the time. It was after midnight. She was talking on the phone to the front desk, when there was a hesitant knock on the door to the adjoining room and Tracy's voice, "You awake?"

Katherine let her in. Tracy's hair was mussed from sleep and she wore a wrinkled oversize T-shirt with a cartoon of a man in a hardhat, an oil rig in the background. The caption read "Drillers Do It Deeper."

"You hear that? Somebody out there is in trouble."

"I think it's the call to prayer."

"What do they think, God's hard of hearing?" Tracy crossed to the window and looked out. "Mike, he's out there somewhere. Could be right across the street and we'd never know it."

"I just talked to the front desk. Sam never showed up."

"You think we should call the police?"

"He's supposed to know his way around . . ."

For the rest of the night Katherine slept fitfully, waking now and then to stare at the alarm clock on the nightstand and the objects beside it: photographs of each of her children and the Mont Blanc pen. Dawn came and still no Sam. Katherine called the consulate and spoke to Edward Jurman. The man sounded tired. "Yes, I know," he said. "I'm looking at a report right here. Sam Gaddis was arrested last night at the Meridien Hotel."

"Arrested? What for?"

"He broke into a room and assaulted members of the hotel staff who tried to remove him. That's the official version. We'll find out more this afternoon."

"I don't believe it."

"Evidently he was drunk."

How many drinks did he have on the plane? Wasn't that what Livingston asked? Katherine's apprehension turned to anger. Less than twenty-four hours in Damascus and already Sam's lack of control could be jeopardizing their mission.

She went to Tracy's room and found her in jeans and a halter top applying eye makeup while listening to a music tape on a cassette recorder. When Katherine told her about Sam, she said, "We got to get him out of there."

"The consulate will get him out unless the Syrian government expels him from the country."

"Expels him? But we need him."

Katherine shook her head. "No we don't. We can't depend on him."

"But we can't speak the lingo and we don't know how to find Tayib."

"We'll find someone."

The lobby of the Sheraton was designed to make it convenient for Europeans and wealthy Arabs to spend Western currency. In addition to gift and candy shops, there was a foreign exchange desk and an office of Syria's rental agency, Europcar. Katherine arranged for an English-speaking driver to meet them with a Mercedes 190. The driver's name was Mustafa Murwan, a round-shouldered man with bright eyes and a fold of skin below his neck that wobbled like a chicken's when he spoke.

"Lovely ladies, you have the best, forget the rest. Where do you wish to go? A tour of the city?"

Katherine explained what they had in mind and gave him the address of the Yellow Wind headquarters. "Is it far?"

"Not so far. The day is beautiful. I have a car, the lowest fares, the fastest driver."

Mustafa kept up a running commentary, pointing out various parks and memorials until they entered the older section of the city where streets were crooked, crowded and narrow. The pace became a series of leaps and crawls accompanied by much honking. Twice they stopped to ask directions before arriving at a residential neighborhood that looked so dilapidated Katherine wondered if they had the wrong address. Mustafa waved aside the piece of paper. "This is good, this is good."

They got out and followed Mustafa, who marched through the narrow doorway without holding the door for Katherine or Tracy. The Yellow Wind office was a small room whose plain walls were

adorned with signs in flowing Arabic script and a
faded poster of the late Ayatollah Khomeini. A long
table against one wall was stacked with fliers. At the
end of the room four men were gathered around a
copying machine the size of a dishwasher. One of
them, evidently a mechanic, sat on the floor, surrounded by parts and tools. The others crouched or
stood in a semicircle. They stopped talking when the
women entered. Mustafa moved forward quickly, his
hands clasped together as he spoke. The oldest man
responded brusquely. He was short and round and
wore thick glasses. Like the others, he had a dark
beard but there was an aura of authority about him
that made Katherine suspect this was Abu Shapour.
Mustafa continued talking, sweeping his hand toward
them. Shapour made a couple of responses that
seemed to Katherine barely civil, then turned and began speaking to the others.

"What's happening?"

"They're discussing whether or not to speak to
you."

The decision was made quickly. Shapour said
something to Mustafa, who turned with an apologetic
smile. "I am sorry. Abu Shapour does not wish to talk
with you."

"Did he get my telegram? Does he know why
we're here?"

"Yes, he knows. He does not wish to speak."

"We don't want to speak with him, we want to
talk to Imad Tayib."

Mustafa translated. "Imad Tayib has nothing to
say to Westerners."

"What about fifty bucks?" Tracy demanded. "Ask
this guy if he'll talk for a little Western money. I

mean, if you want to," she added with an apologetic look at Katherine.

Shapour made a staccato response accompanied by a gesture of dismissal. Mustafa turned. "We must go."

"What'd he say that time?" Tracy put her hands on her hips.

"He is not interested in your money," Mustafa said carefully.

"Is that what he said?"

"It is the meaning, if not the exact words."

"What were the exact words?"

"He said that he eliminates himself upon your money."

"He does what?"

"He makes shit upon the money."

"Oh, yeah? You tell him to bend over and I'll stick that fifty bucks so far up his ass he can count it with his tonsils."

"Tracy," Katherine said quickly, "I think the man understands English. Is that right, Mr. Shapour? Do you speak English?"

"I hope you do," Tracy said, "because that way—"

Katherine grabbed her arm. "Let the man speak."

Shapour spit on the floor and turned his back. Mustafa said, "It is better we should go."

Katherine took Tracy's arm. "Come on."

"You're letting this guy insult us and kick us out?"

"Let's talk outside."

As soon as they were in the street Tracy said, "He knows where Mike is, I got me a feeling about that man."

"If he does, it won't help any calling him names."

"He started it, treating us like some kind of trash that blowed in off the street. You don't get anywhere taking shit from people. I learned that a long time ago. The only way people respect you is if you stand up and fight for your rights."

A taxi, blaring its horn, pulled to a stop and Sam got out. His shirt was torn, his hat was missing and he sported a black eye and swollen nose. Katherine's smile died on her lips. Why welcome a man who had caused so much worry and trouble? Sam pulled a camera from his bag. "Hold it, ladies. Back up, back to the entrance."

"It's not a wedding, Mr. Gaddis." Katherine marched past him to the car.

"What's that mean?"

"You're supposed to be a news photographer. And you're supposed to help us, not create problems."

As Tracy passed Sam she said, "You look like homemade dogshit."

"You should try it from this side."

Sam followed them to the car and slid into the passenger seat. He said, *"Marhaba"* to Mustafa, who responded in Arabic.

Katherine said, "Are you looking for a ride, Mr. Gaddis?"

"Whither thou goest, I go. Your lives are my career, your wish my command."

The car leaped forward and Mustafa said, "Now we will make a tour of Damascus. I will show you everything, the Hamadieh Souk, Hadrian's temple, the tomb of Saladin, the Bab Sharqi, you will enjoy it."

"Take us back to the hotel. That's where you want to go this time, isn't it, Mr. Gaddis?"

"Yesterday I was *Sam*."

"Yesterday you didn't look like a prizefighter and smell like a bum."

Mustafa said, "Omayyad Mosque, it is most beautiful. You like to see it?"

"The Sheraton."

Tracy said, "So what does the other guy look like?"

"There were three of them and their boots are scuffed."

"Where'd you go yesterday? What happened?"

Sam gave them an abbreviated version. Tracy listened with pleasure but Katherine remained cool. "We need to talk," she said, when Sam asked about the next day's plans. Tracy told him about the abortive meeting with Shapour, then stopped in midsentence, when a gold-paneled building caught her eye.

"Is that the Cham Palace?"

"Very nice hotel," Mustafa said.

"Wait, stop a minute. That's where the office is. I promised Larry I'd check and see if he heard any news about Mike."

They pulled up to the curb. Katherine said, "Who's Larry?"

"Mike's boss."

"Photo op," Sam said as he got out of the car. " 'Distraught Wife Pleads for Information.' "

Tracy turned to Katherine. "You mind, or should I do it later?"

Katherine glanced at the hotel. High above the garish gold panels was a revolving rooftop restaurant. "Go ahead and see if he's there. We'll wait for you." She turned to Sam. "Mr. Gaddis, we need to talk."

"Shoot first and talk later, the motto of Marines and the *Herald*."

"No. We leave for Raqba tomorrow. If you want to come with us, we have to talk now."

Tracy looked uncertainly from one to the other. "Go ahead," Katherine told her. When she was gone, Sam said, "All right, what's the problem?"

Mustafa, smiling, leaned toward them. Katherine looked around. "Let's go over there."

They crossed the street to a small park ringed in flowers and dominated by a huge statue of President Assad, head hunched forward, hands outspread as if giving a benediction to the city. Katherine faced Sam with her arms crossed. "I think you owe us an explanation."

"I got beat up."

"You got drunk."

A lopsided smile forced its way out. "It would have hurt more sober."

"Mr. Livingston says you're unstable."

The smile died. "What else did he say?"

"That you had marital problems when he knew you and you drink too much."

"He was fucking my wife. How's that for a marital problem?"

She refused to be shocked by either the language or its tone. "It's no reason to hit a man."

"I didn't have a gun."

"You told me your wife committed suicide."

"I didn't tell you why. Faye had a special appetite for life. She'd look you in the eye and want to know who you were and what you thought. She really loved life, all of it, not just what she could see from a hospital bed or touch from a wheelchair. Suicide? Yeah, technically. But the car wreck killed her, sure as if she'd bled to death on the highway." He lit a cigarette with a quick, angry movement.

Katherine said, "Why do you blame Livingston?"

Sam hesitated, then let it out. *"Because* he had an affair with Faye. That's why she was on the road that night. She spent the night with him and left early to get to Tel Aviv the next morning."

"Then you weren't—?"

"What?"

"In the car?"

"I was in Tel Aviv. We were doing a photo story on an Israeli general."

"You were working together?"

"Yes."

"While she was seeing another man?"

"We were in love, okay?" The words came in an angry rush. "She was infatuated with all the hocus-pocus CIA bullshit. It was nothing. I understood it, I understood her. I wasn't about to let a Livingston screw us up. There was only one lasting thing in Faye's life and that was what *we* had together."

Katherine couldn't imagine staying with someone who was having an affair . . . her own marriage ended when she found out about Maria.

"All right, Mr. Gaddis. Why don't we just erase the last twenty-four hours and begin again? But this time I think it's fair to ask that you refrain from drinking until we reach Imad Tayib."

"I'm forty-two years old, Ms. Cahill. I hate to be

called by my last name and I've already got a mother. But if you promise to call me Sam, I promise not to let things get out of hand again."

She allowed a rare smile as they went to the hotel lobby to wait for Tracy.

THE FIVE children held Cousin Fawzi in high esteem. Fawzi held an important job in Damascus and always brought presents when he came to Raqba. This time he brought a shawl, sunglasses, a cap, a harmonica and, for the youngest boy, a metal robot. The robot was especially popular. It made sounds as it walked and its eyes flickered red. Every ten steps it stopped to fire a space gun and make a new noise. The children played with it constantly and on the second day the batteries began to fail. When the oldest boy, eight-year-old Naif, brought his friend to see it, he found the robot stopped in mid-stride.

"Its eyes are red," he said, "like the *shaitan*."

"I want to see it."

Naif turned it off and back on. The robot took another half step and stopped.

"The battery's gone."

"You have more?"

"No."

"Then what good is your gift if it does not work?"

"It does work. I can show you."

Naif had already taken a secret look into Fawzi's bag. Usually there was something of interest from the world beyond the mountains—a pen or a new bottle of cologne or a folding comb. This time there was a yellow radio cassette player. Naif had found it the day before and could barely contain his excitement. All night he waited impatiently for Fawzi to bring out the machine and boast of it. When the loudspeakers on the mosque broadcast Imad Tayib's nightly message, Naif could scarcely keep himself from blurting out the secret. *There is another way we could listen.* But Fawzi gave no hint that he had a radio. Now the boy said to his friend, "Promise not to tell and I will show you a secret."

The others were gone and his mother was preparing dinner outside on the dirt patio. Naif carefully separated the clothing and lifted the radio. His friend's eyes filled with admiration. "Let's play it."

"No, my mother might hear."

The boys took turns pushing the buttons and running their hands over the smooth plastic. When they had finished admiring it, Naif opened the compartment, took out the batteries, and tried to use them on the robot. They were the wrong size.

"I want to see it walk."

"I will ask Cousin Fawzi to bring more batteries the next time. The eyes are red, though, you can see."

His mother called him. Naif replaced the batteries in the radio but in his haste he put them in backward, reversing the polarity.

The explosion blinded him even as the first disintegrating pieces struck his chest and noise and darkness obliterated his world.

Fawzi was with his other men, sipping Arabic coffee and smoking the *nargileh,* the water pipe, when the explosion sounded. A plume of white smoke rose from the center of the village. The conversation with the men had relaxed him so much that it wasn't until he arrived at his uncle's house that he realized what had happened.

The *radio.*

Naif lay dying on his mother's lap, while his friend wandered in a daze, blood seeping from a clump of tissue and bone that had once been a hand. Someone grabbed the boy and applied a tourniquet. Fawzi was horrified. Hadn't Livingston told him that the clock was set only for seven twenty-five? And that only by pressing the right buttons it could be armed?

The tin roof of the house had been blown off and one wall collapsed. The family's meager belongings lay spread over the ground. And something else. Pieces of yellow plastic. Fawzi's hands began to tingle and his mouth went dry. Wait, he thought. No one knows the radio was in my bag. I never showed it to anyone. I am as surprised as the next person.

As if to prove it, he ran forward and comforted one of his uncle's children, a little girl who was crying. She had a small cut on her cheek. Fawzi held her and dabbed the blood with his handkerchief. The recruits and soldiers came running from the castle. Orders were given, squads mobilized to search the village and block all exits. Fawzi was glad that he hadn't tried to run.

He was still on his knees with the little girl when a hush spread through the group. The neighbor boy was bandaged now. He stared at Fawzi while one of the soldiers, a major, leaned close to talk to him. The boy nodded. As the major stood up, one of his men approached with a piece of yellow plastic. People turned toward Fawzi. The lingering smell of the explosive made him want to gag.

SIXTEEN

TROUBLE IN PARADISE, TRACY THOUGHT WHEN SHE LEFT Katherine and Sam outside the Cham Palace Hotel. A drunken brawl and a night in jail didn't seem like such a big deal, but it was Katherine's money, so she called the shots. Tracy made her way through an inward-looking lobby dominated by a massive atrium, where ivy and hanging ferns overflowed the balconies in a cascade of green. Like many Western companies, Wright-Morris found it convenient to have an office in one of the city's three five-star hotels, where there were overseas operators, telex machines, FAX facilities and a twenty-four-hour staff.

She took an elevator to the third floor, where Larry Probst, the director of operations, greeted her warmly. He had a crewcut that made his ears stick out and his neatly buttoned sports coat couldn't hide a middle-age paunch. As she stepped past him into the office, Larry's gaze slid down her body.

"Here, sit down. You want something to drink?

151

I've got soft drinks, Perrier, beer, wine, just say the word."

"That's all right, I got people waiting."

"A Coke then? You look like a Coca-Cola girl to me."

Larry the Loser, that's what Mike called him. Now she knew why. He opened a miniature refrigerator tucked behind the door. "Sorry the place is such a mess but I don't get many visitors."

If there was a mess Tracy couldn't see it. There was a file cabinet, a couch, a table stacked with the last few issues of the *International Herald,* and tacked to one wall a huge map of Syria with colored pins to indicate the oil rigs Wright-Morris serviced.

"Here you are," Larry said. He leaned over her with the Coke and looked down her blouse. Then he moved behind the desk and made a show of squeezing juice from a withered lime into a glass of Perrier.

"The water here is terrible. They say it stains your teeth and rots your gut." His grin revealed teeth that Tracy thought proved his point.

"Listen, Mr. Probst—"

"Call me Larry."

"Okay, *Larry,* I just want to find out if you heard anything more about Mike."

"Not about him but I do have a letter for him. It came the other day but I knew you were on the way so I saved it."

He pulled a pale blue envelope from a drawer and handed it to her. In careful block letters it was addressed to "Supervisor of Mr. Mike Winn." Tracy took out a sheet of cheap stationery embossed with a crown and the name Emir Restaurant in both English and Arabic.

Dear Honorable Sir:

Peace upon your house. I am Izzet Kerribar, owner and proprietor of Emir Restaurant in Dier Ezzur. I can inform you that your Employee Mr. Mike Winn has not paid rent of 300 Syrian pounds for this month. The Police have told me he is kidnapped. My question is if his company, Wright-Morris, will pay his rent? The Apartment is a river outlook and the belongings of Mr. Mike Winn are one Expensive Stereo system, one television with many Video Tapes, and much Attractive Furniture in the Arab style. Because he is a good Tenant I would regret the sale of these goods. If you wish to save them please return the 300 Syrian pounds before my hand is removed from their protection.

Your Devoted Servant, etc.
Izzet Kerribar

Tracy finished reading and looked up, puzzled. "This isn't the company apartment on Choukatari Street?"

"Looks like Mike has his own apartment."

"But why?"

"Maybe he wanted something better." He was watching her closely, jiggling the ice in the glass, which he held with his little finger extended. "Do you still plan to go to Raqba?"

"Tomorrow."

"You're one brave woman," he said. "Mike is lucky to have you for a wife."

Tracy stood up. "Yeah, well, if you hear anything else just leave word at the Sheraton."

"Do you like Arab food? I know a good restaurant, the Al Shallal. Why don't we have dinner tonight? Give us a chance to talk over options, put our heads together, see if we can come up with a plan to get Mike back."

Tracy could sense the man trying to keep his eyes above her chin. "No, thanks, my partner and me have other plans."

Larry the Loser, she thought. Mike was right. In the lobby she was surprised to find Katherine and Sam sitting on a leather couch drinking coffee, a map of Syria spread on a low table in front of them.

"I'm sorry I took so long."

Katherine said, "We were just going over the route to Raqba."

"Does that mean . . . ?"

They both stared at her. "Mean what?" Katherine said.

It's too much for me, Tracy thought, remembering the frosty atmosphere when she left them. She shrugged. "Is Dier Ezzur on the way to Raqba?"

"Same general direction but I wouldn't call it on the way," Sam said. "Why?"

She told them about the letter. "I'd like to settle this bill one way or the other."

"Why don't you just send a check?"

"This old boy might have read about Mike and sent this letter to get money out of Wright-Morris. Just like people sue insurance companies."

Sam turned to Katherine, "How'd somebody this young learn to be so cynical?"

Tracy said, "People play the angles, that's just how it is. You got to watch out."

"If it's a matter of money," Katherine said, "I'll cover it—"

"It's not money, it's the principle of the thing."

"Forget it," Sam said. "If we get Mike back he'll take care of it. If not, we can stop at Dier Ezzur on the way back. Meanwhile there's a few things we have to do today, right, Katherine?"

She frowned slightly at his prodding, then turned to Tracy. "Maybe you and I can go shopping and pick up some clothes . . . suitable for the mountains."

"What do you need?"

They were both looking at her. Katherine said carefully, "Not for me. Sam brought up the point and I think it's valid . . . outside the cities Muslim values are pretty conservative. We don't want to offend people whose help we may need, so—"

"She means your jeans are too tight, your sleeves are too short, and what you're wearing under that top isn't enough to cover the details. It's nothing personal." He stood up. "Ladies, I'll meet you back at the hotel."

IMAD TAYIB was familiar with torture. He knew that pain was not a goal but a process by which the mind's apprehension of horror might be turned back on itself and increased a thousandfold. He would render the traitor Fawzi Ashraf so filled with terror that he would betray family, friends, even his religion to avoid it.

During the first half hour Imad Tayib was absent and Major Yazdi handled the questioning. Who was he working for? No one. Where had he gotten the radio? A man in the souk had sold it to him. Liar. They hit him. When Tayib finally appeared, Fawzi dropped to his knees and begged. "You are a man of the holy vision. Believe me, I am innocent of wrongdoing."

"Stand up."

The guards pulled Fawzi to his feet. Tayib slowly reached out. Fawzi's chin lowered as his eyes followed the outstretched hand that came to rest on his chest. "Traitor to your people," Tayib intoned, "your heart is an empty vessel."

"By merciful Allah, it's not true."

"He of the Hundred Names may grant you mercy but at Raqba you will find only justice."

Tayib led the way to a flight of steps cut into the hillside, the entrance to a huge reservoir built into the mountain. All the rain that fell within the castle walls was routed here through an ancient system of pipes and culverts. The reservoir looked like a giant ballroom filled with water and carved out of rock. Long shafts of sunlight angled downward from four square openings in an arched roof and bounced off the water's dark surface.

They took Fawzi to a landing at the water's edge, where two *shaheen* waited with a plank ten-feet-long and two-feet-wide. The air was damp and voices echoed in sepulchral tones. Fawzi was stripped and tied face-up to the plank. A dark bruise mottled one cheek and angry welts were visible on his chest. Fawzi's eyes were wide and his skin dimpled with goosebumps.

"Please," he whispered hoarsely as they lowered him to his back.

Tayib said, "You believe you have the strength of a man but you have not. A man's strength is founded on faith. Have you adopted the faith of your enemy?

Are you Israeli? Have you the faith of the misguided Hebrew? Or have you only the faith in yourself?"

"I am innocent, I swear—"

"As a man may choke on food, so may he drown in lies. Fawzi Ashraf, if you can remain one minute beneath the water without choking on your lies, I shall believe you and set you free."

Free? Fawzi grabbed at the word and held it close. The wood scraped as soldiers shoved the forward half of the plank over the water, where it sat like a teeter-totter, the fulcrum beneath his hips.

Tayib said, "Let no water pass your lips for one minute and you walk from here a free man. Do you understand?"

"Yes."

"Then fill your lungs with truth."

Fawzi took a deep breath and closed his eyes. The guards raised the foot of the plank; water slid over the back of his head, into his ears and covered his face. One minute, he thought. I can do this. Yes, I can do it . . .

And then he felt the fingers close around his testicles and he knew. A voice in his mind screamed *no.* The grip tightened slightly. He strained against the ropes and tried to lift his face. The fingers hesitated and then, like an eagle's claw, clamped tight and twisted. The scream burst out of him. He heard it muffled beneath the water and then his lungs grabbed for air and water surged down his throat and shot up his nose. His eyes bulged, his body bucked. By the time they raised him his stomach was heaving and he was gagging. The *shaheen* turned him face down and forced the water from his lungs. He coughed and retched, but the scream of pain lay trapped in his brain. They turned him on his back. Imad Tayib kicked him gently in the temple three times, then paused. "Will you speak the truth?"

"Yes."

"Who do you work for?"

"Americans . . ."

An angry murmur from those around him. Tayib nodded. "You will tell the world. Bring him."

They untied Fawzi and dragged him to Tayib's headquarters which was built into the castle wall at a point overlooking a deep canyon. Fawzi had no doubt he was a dead man once he broadcast his confession. He did not want to imagine the horrors Tayib would inflict before the end. This gave him a kind of desperate courage when he saw a possible opportunity for escape. The stairways were so narrow that they marched single file, guards ahead and behind him. At the top floor there was a moment when the first guard turned to take his arm. Fawzi shoved the man aside and raced up the final stairway to the roof.

Footsteps pounding behind him. He burst onto the roof—but there was no ladder, no fire escape, no way down. He leaped onto the three-foot-high parapet and ran along it looking for a rope, something, anything. Guards burst onto the roof and came running toward him. Something extended from one of the windows below him. An air conditioner, the only one at Raqba, used to keep the valuable electrical equipment cool. If he could drop to the air conditioner and get in through the window . . .

He scrambled over the edge, scraping his chest, and hung by his fingertips. He looked down. The unit was still four feet from his toes, and a terribly small target. The guards grabbed at him, and Fawzi let go.

Fingernails scraped the back of his hand as he slid down the wall. One foot struck the air conditioner, the unit twisted, pulled from the window, then held. His foot slipped and the metal corner stabbed him in the stomach as he wrapped his arms around the conditioner. It sagged beneath his weight. Fawzi reached for the edge of the window. If he could crawl inside—

The supports gave way. Clutching the air conditioner tight to his chest, Fawzi fell backward beyond the castle wall, into the gorge. His last thought was how peculiar his bare legs looked, kicking at the clouds.

THAT NIGHT at the embassy Doug Livingston sat in the communications office with the door closed. Through the glass partition of the translation booth he could see Nancy Aziz, the interpreter. She wore earphones, and on the table beside her was a cup of coffee grown cold. Nancy's attention was on a book she was reading, one of her innumerable romance novels. She was Lebanese, overweight and glum. If she was curious about why Livingston had called her to do a simultaneous translation of Imad Tayib's diatribe, she didn't show it.

As the hour approached, Livingston switched on the transmitter. Frowning at the intrusion, Nancy reached out and lowered the volume without moving her eyes from the book. Livingston was nervous. He sucked on a Certs breath mint, rolling it back and forth over his teeth. Dusk fell and the radio remained silent. Was tonight the night? Had Fawzi done his job?

The radio crackled to life and Imad Tayib's strident voice filled the headphones. Without moving, Nancy Aziz closed her eyes and began a simultaneous translation that reached Livingston a few seconds after the words in Arabic.

"Today an agent of the Western and Israeli provocateurs launched a cowardly attack on the village of Raqba. One house was destroyed, one child murdered and many innocent civilians injured. We see from this attack the true intent of the American and Israeli terrorists, which is the genocide of the Palestinian people."

Livingston sat upright. An attack on the village? What craziness was this? You fucking poodle, he thought. He was already imagining the tongue-lashing he would give Fawzi—

"The traitor has paid the price of his betrayal. Let all men know that he who comes to the mountain a friend shall be exalted but he who comes as an enemy shall be cast into Hell."

There was more, all in the same vein, all on the same theme but without any further specifics. Livingston tried to take it in. Fawzi had been caught? Killed? Had he given away anything? How much did he know?

Livingston flicked off the radio and took off the headphones. Tomorrow the official translation would arrive on his desk; he didn't need Tayib's voice in his ear tonight. He tried to make some sense of the disaster. Tayib called it an attack on the village. That meant either Fawzi lied or had been killed in the explosion. Either way Bright Justice was still a secret, or so he hoped. But that was small consolation.

I knew he was weak, Livingston thought bitterly. We should have recruited someone stronger. For a moment he had the wild notion of going to Raqba himself. No, foolish. His CIA affiliation was known to Imad Tayib. He needed someone with a plausible reason to see Tayib and . . . Jesus, could it work? He made a mental list of reasons why it wouldn't but still his excitement grew.

The room was quiet now except for the rattle of the shrinking breath mint sliding across his teeth.

SEVENTEEN

THE PHONE WOKE KATHERINE. AS SHE FUMBLED FOR IT SHE glanced at the clock on the nightstand; it was after midnight. "Hello?"

"Ms. Cahill, don't speak my name. Just tell me if you recognize my voice."

"What?"

"It's urgent that we talk. Take a moment and collect your thoughts. You know who this is? Think."

"A man with a bruised lip."

A beat. "Are you alone?"

"Yes."

"I'm in the lobby, I'm on my way up."

"Wait, I'll come down."

"That wouldn't be a good idea. We need privacy."

Katherine turned on the light and put on a robe. Her eye fell on the Mont Blanc gun-pen and she put it in a drawer before Livingston's soft but firm knock.

"I'm sorry about this," he said as he slid into the room.

"What is it?"

He crossed to the window. There were two sets of curtains, one which matched the decor of the room, and behind it, a heavy fabric opaque enough to block the morning sun. Livingston pulled the second curtain, then turned on the television. Since none of the stations broadcast after midnight, the room filled with static. Watching him, Katherine felt like she was part of a Hollywood thriller, except the tension in his face was all too real.

Livingston sat down on the couch. He put a cassette tape recorder on the low coffee table and motioned her to join him. She took a seat in an adjacent chair. "If you're going to tape our conversation, I'd first like to know why."

Livingston shifted his position closer to her and turned the recorder to "Play." Classical music joined the television's grating noise.

"Keep your voice low, please. The Syrians aren't real sophisticated when it comes to electronic surveillance, but the government owns fifty-one percent of this hotel and it's possible this is one of the wired rooms. Before I tell you why I came, I need your promise that whatever is said here you will keep in absolute confidence. The safety of a number of people, including myself, will depend on it."

"Are you trying to frighten or impress me?"

"I'm trying to alert you to a real danger. Do I have your promise?"

"If you don't trust my judgment, Mr. Livingston, don't tell me."

Livingston hesitated only a moment, then nodded. "All right, how would you like to see Imad Tayib returned to the United States to face trial for the bombing of Flight 67?"

"Are you saying there is such a plan?"

"There is, if you're willing to be part of it." And then he proceeded to brief her on Operation Bright Justice. As she listened, Katherine was caught up in conflicting emotions . . . excited at the prospect of bringing Imad Tayib to trial, and struck by the irony of the situation. Having made her own plans, now she was being asked to participate in exactly the kind of mission she had given up all hope of the government ever pursuing.

"So that would be your job," he concluded. "To disrupt power to the radar station long enough for an airborne assault team to enter and leave the area undetected. I can give you everything you need—explosives, a detonator and timing device. Understand, I'm not asking you to risk your life. If you can't find the opportunity, if it seems too dangerous, don't try it."

And Tayib gets away with murder, she thought. Livingston was watching her closely.

"Something like this must have taken weeks or months to prepare. You couldn't know I'd be here right now."

"That's true. I had an agent in Tayib's organization. He was killed by some kind of foul-up before he could fulfill his part of the mission. It will take months to find and recruit someone else. By then the political situation may have changed, word of the operation may have leaked, the decision-makers in Washington may have changed their mind—I guess I don't have to tell you how hard it is to get a commitment from our elected representatives." His smile implied a shared disdain of politicians and Katherine felt she was being manipulated. "I think I need a drink."

She started to her feet but Livingston jumped up. "I'll get it. You take a minute, think things over. What would you like?"

"See if there's cognac. The key to the liquor cabinet is on the dresser."

Why am I hesitating? Katherine wondered. Here was an opportunity to show Tayib for the murderer he was, place him on the witness stand in open court, force him to look at their photographs, Jeff, Allison, Joey, and see them not as faceless statistics but real people. She realized suddenly that her reluctance didn't stem from fear but the desire to see Tayib dead. Had she really become so fixed on killing?

Livingston's plan was better, and for another reason. She couldn't kill Tayib if it meant Mike Winn's death. This was something that had been bothering her since the trip began. At first Mike and Tracy had been names to her, conveniences, ways of meeting Tayib. Now she saw them as allies, friends even, and knew she couldn't put their lives at risk by killing Tayib. Operation Bright Justice gave her a new option.

Livingston returned with the drinks. He had poured himself a cognac to match hers. "It's a lot to hit you up with all at once, I know."

She shook her head. "You know, these people at the State Department never gave me any hope, never even suggested there might be a plan—"

"Ms. Cahill, there were eighty-three American victims on that plane. That's about how many minutes this operation would be a secret if the relatives were told about it."

She knew he had a point but it didn't make her feel any better about being kept in the dark. She sipped her cognac and said, "I'm not an explosives expert. You'll have to teach me."

"You'll do it?"

"I'll try."

In a gesture as incongruous as it was unexpected, he reached across the table and shook her hand. "You're doing the country a great service."

She pulled her hand away and a baffled expression flashed across his face. My God, Katherine thought, he thinks this is patriotism.

Livingston recovered quickly. "I'll need forty-eight hours to get the explosives and detonator and show you how to use it."

"We plan to leave tomorrow."

"Make an excuse. Get sick or something. Just don't tell your friends about this. The girl I doubt can keep a secret, and Gaddis, well, he's a case history right out of Freud." His attitude irritated her. Deliberately she said, "He told me you had an affair with his wife."

"It takes two to tango. Sam never understood that. He didn't want to see her part in it. How'd she die? Slit her wrists?" Katherine looked up sharply. "What? Am I right?"

"An overdose. How did you know she committed suicide?"

"She was the most selfish woman I ever knew. Exciting, a wicked body, but if she couldn't have what she wanted . . . Sam, he loved her like a puppy. You know how suffocating that can be."

No, but I'm sure you do, she thought. There was no sign that Livingston felt any responsibility for his part in Faye's death. She turned the conversation back to Bright Justice. They arranged a meeting in two days at a shop in the Hamadieh Souk. Livingston gave her a business card with the name and address on one side and a map on the back.

"If you have to call me for any reason, dial the embassy prefix and then 707, like the airplane. Don't write it down. Ask for Adam."

"Is that your code?"

"No, Ms. Cahill, that's *your* code. I'll know who's calling."

"Is all this subterfuge really necessary?"

"Not for me. The Syrians know what I do. But the success of failure of Bright Justice now depends on you."

THE NEXT morning Sam was gingerly maneuvering the razor around the cuts on his cheek when someone knocked on the door. It was Tracy. "You better come. Katherine's sick."

She wore a dark green jumpsuit that even Sam, whose interest in fashion was marginal, recognized as awful. "Pretty snazzy," he said as they walked down the hall.

"What's that?"

"I haven't seen an outfit like that since the May Day Parade in Moscow."

She wagged a finger at him. "There's a reason your face looks like it does."

They found Katherine sitting in bed in a robe. "Dysentery," she told them. "It usually runs its course in a day or two but I'm not comfortable traveling. I'm sorry . . ."

"We're not leaving today?" Tracy said.

"I'm not, but yesterday you talked about going to Dier Ezzur to see about Mike's apartment. Why don't you do that, you and Sam? I can fly to Aleppo on Friday and meet you there."

"Where's Aleppo?"

"City up north about two hours from Raqba," Sam said.

"Will you be okay here alone?"

"I'm not going to be much company for the next couple of days. Go ahead."

"I like it," Sam said. " 'Wife Tracks Husband's Final Movements.' We can get some shots where Mike was kidnapped."

"Don't talk like that," Tracy said. "You make it sound like he's dead."

FOR SAM it was a relief to get out of the city. They drove a Mercedes 190 with air conditioning. As soon as they reached the highway, he handed Tracy a list of Arabic names. "See the top one? Yell if you see a sign with that on it."

"I don't read Syrian."

"Arabic."

She shoved the paper back at him. "You do it, you're the driver."

"Okay, but don't blame me if we end up in Istanbul."

"How close is that to where we're going?"

Sam turned to see if she was serious. "Istanbul is in Turkey."

"Well, I *am* sorry but not everybody knows that."

She turned her attention outside, where the landscape became progressively more bleak the farther they went from Damascus. Irrigated fields lay outlined by hard, dry earth, and the low ridges looked like they were carved from rock. Sam pulled out his Pearlcorder, turned it on and put it on the dashboard. "So how did you meet Mike?"

"What are you doing?"

"Interviewing you. How'd you meet?"

"On purpose, I'll tell you that. My daddy, he never had nothing and kept moving from one job to another. We never stayed in one town long enough to get in the phone book. I made up my mind I'd marry me somebody solid, so I got a job in this bar where the guys working the oil rigs came in. I knew they made good money, so that's where I set my trap."

"And Mike was the target of opportunity?"

"What? Oh, right." Tracy smiled at the memory. "Yeah, he was with some buddies and this one guy is giving me shit. He keeps trying to get a tape measure around me like I was some kind of prize calf. Mike sees I'm having trouble—I didn't know his name then —but he comes over and says, 'Leave the girl alone,' and this guy says 'She your wife or something?' and Mike goes, 'Maybe she is,' and the guy says, 'Well, I don't see no ring on her finger,' and Mike holds up his hand and says, 'See *this* ring?' Mike hits him and lays his cheek open like a ripe banana. We heard later it took twenty stitches to get his face back together and even then the lips didn't match."

"Mike's a real romantic."

Tracy's grin disappeared. "What's the matter with you? You ask a question, I give you an answer, you make a joke. Just because you got left in the lurch is no reason to get smart about other people."

"I got what?"

"Never mind."

"Left in the lurch? What's that supposed to mean?" Tracy lifted her chin and looked out the window. Sam turned off the tape recorder. "Just how did I get left in the lurch?"

"Your wife and everything. Only Katherine said not to mention it in case you go haywire."

"She told you about Faye?"

"I asked her about it."

"Next time ask me, okay?"

Sam shoved a tape into the cassette player and turned up the sound. Three hours later they reached the town of Palmyra where Roman ruins dotted the landscape and tall victory columns stood in rows marching toward the vanished city.

"My God," Tracy said, "who put all them here?"

"The Romans. Used to be a huge trading center."

"Out here in the middle of nowhere?"

"Not nowhere—there's water. See the oasis?" He pointed to a depression where the tops of squat palm trees were visible.

Tracy nodded. "Places like this is where Mike gets the goodies."

"What goodies?"

"Well, see, his job takes him all out over the desert and he says there's ruins from Roman and Greek times and you find all kinds of relics. He gets them home in company containers like dirt samples and there's this guy in Dallas who sells them to museums."

"You mean he steals antiquities?"

"Steals? There's nobody living in these places except nomads and they're the ones that find most of the stuff. Mike just buys it at rock-bottom prices and doubles or triples his money on the resale. He's smart that way. They got you beat in this world unless you play the angles, that's what Mike says."

"Sounds like a real philosopher."

"Listen, Mr. Wiseguy, he never spent a night in jail like some people I know."

They passed a Karnak bus that had stopped so tourists could have their pictures taken sitting on a tired-eyed camel. Sam slowed and drove off the road onto the hard-packed earth.

"Where are you going?"

"Something to tell the folks about back home." He slowed to a stop only inches from two weathered columns supporting a stone arch. When he opened the door the heat was like a wall. Tracy followed reluctantly. Sam climbed onto the trunk and held his hand out to her. She stared at him. "Has this heat eaten your brain out?"

"Come on up. I want to show you something."

"I don't need no help."

She slipped off her sandals and joined him. Sam positioned her next to the column. "Now touch it."

"Touch what?"

"The column. Touch it as high as you can."

Tracy did. "Now what."

"You are the first person to touch that spot in two-thousand-eight-hundred and fifty-two years."

"So?"

"So think of it. The last person who had his fingers on that spot was the stone mason checking to see if his work was smooth."

"Jesus." She hopped down and got back into the car. Standing on the roof, Sam wondered what he was doing. He hadn't intended to go to the Meridien and he hadn't planned to stop here. When it happened with Faye it had been a magic moment. Now he felt like a damn fool.

Tracy's hand appeared above the roof. "Can I have the keys?"

"No."

Before climbing down he placed his hand on the spot he thought Faye might have touched. The stone was warm but he had no sense of the craftsman who formed it and no sense of Faye at all.

He returned to the car and they drove to the ramshackle restaurant where Mike was kidnapped. Sam interviewed the owner, Mr. Ghazala, who waved his arms like a conductor when he told about the attack. Tracy batted away a persistent fly and listened with growing impatience. "What's he saying?"

"Later."

She made an elaborate show of filing her fingernails until Sam wanted pictures of the two of them in the parking area where Mike's car had been. Mr. Ghazala had one of his children bring him a brush and a small hand-mirror. Once satisfied with his hair, he slapped his neck with cologne and straightened his shirt.

"What's he think," Tracy said, "you're taking a picture of the way he smells?"

"Probably out of consideration for you. Don't scowl." She forced a grin. "Don't grin."

"Well, what?"

"Look worried about Mike."

"I *am* worried about him."

"Mr. Ghazala says Mike was right where you're

standing when the men grabbed him. He tried to fight, maybe got hit in the stomach—"

"They hit him?"

Click. He kept talking, moving, shooting. "He's not sure. Mike tried to shove his way free, hit one guy who let him go but the other still had his arm. That's when he lost his wallet. Somebody came out of the car with a rifle and started shooting." Click. The fear and upset registered on Tracy's face. Ghazala smiling, smoothed his hair, smiled some more. Sam embellished the story, Tracy reacted, Sam got his shots.

EIGHTEEN

THE EMIR RESTAURANT WAS LOCATED JUST BEYOND THE CENTER of town on the banks of the Euphrates River. A rusted metal arch led to a cracked concrete patio, where tables were covered with discolored plastic and the yellow webbing sagged from frame chairs. A row of lightbulbs strung above the patio only added to the sense of seediness. Fifty feet away the river moved sluggishly around a low-lying island choked with reeds.

A boy in a *galabiya* appeared, and with an irresolute wave invited them to sit. Sam asked for Izzet Kerribar, and moments later the proprietor appeared. He had heavy jowls and was dressed in a Turkish costume that included a worn red fez and embroidered vest. Kerribar's taciturn features became radiant when he discovered they had come to pay Mike's bill.

"Mr. Mike is a fine man," he said in stilted English. "I have trust he will return, even when my friends say, 'You must sell his things for your rental money,' but this I refused."

"What things?" Tracy asked.

"He has very fine stereo equipment. Sony, Panasonic, Grundig. And a chair which lifts the legs when you push with the shoulders. I like it too much."

"Let's see it."

Kerribar led the way up a flight of chipped concrete exterior stairs to a small landing. With a guilty smile he knocked twice on the door. Tracy exchanged a look with Sam. "If he rented this place," she said in a low voice, "I'm not paying for it."

Kerribar looked hurt. "No, no, I follow Mr. Mike's instructions."

From inside a woman's voice called in Arabic, "Who is it?"

"I have the wife of Mr. Mike and a friend come to pay the rent."

The door was opened by a young woman dressed in a *galabiya* decorated in yellow, green and purple.

"Salaam aleikum," Kerribar greeted her.

"Waleikum a salaam," she repeated automatically, her eyes on the newcomers.

Tracy put her hands on her hips. "Thought you said you weren't renting this to no one else."

"I have not."

"Who's this? A ghost?"

"Her name is Malan. She belongs to Mr. Mike."

"She what?"

"She lives here."

"What are you saying? She's his mistress?"

Izzet looked horrified. "No, no. She is his wife."

A moment of stunned silence. Malan dropped to

one knee, took Tracy's hand and began speaking in Arabic. Tracy yanked her hand away. "What's she doing?"

Sam was still too surprised to speak, but Kerribar said, "She offers greetings and obedience to Mr. Mike's first wife."

"His *first* wife!"

"She asks for news of Mr. Mike."

"This . . . girl is not his wife."

"Yes," said Kerribar, all innocence. "I believe it is so."

"Bull fucking shit." She turned to the girl, who now stood up, confused. "You get out of this apartment right now. Go on, get."

She pointed down the steps. Malan, eyes filled with apprehension, stepped back as Tracy grabbed her and tried to force her out the door.

"Hey, hey." Sam moved forward. Malan dropped to the floor and tried to escape between Tracy's knees.

"No, you don't," Tracy yelled. Sam grabbed her as she made a swipe at the girl, pulling her headscarf off. For the first time it was apparent how young she was. Taking advantage of their surprise, Malan sprinted into the bedroom and slammed the door.

Tracy shook free of Sam and faced him. "I want her out of here. You see how young she is? Jailbait. I've seen her kind before. I know what she's after." She turned to Kerribar, who stood grinning in the doorway. "You think it's funny?"

"Girls fighting, yes, I like it."

"Well, let's see how you like no rent payment and the police on your ass for running a house of prostitution."

"No, no prostitution here."

"Just little Miss Round Heels in there."

Sam said, "How do you know she's not his wife?"

"Don't get smart. Mike's no saint but he wouldn't marry what he could buy for a quarter on a Friday night."

"When was the last time you saw a whorehouse in Syria?"

"Soon as I set foot in this doorway."

Sam looked around. Kerribar was right about one thing, the apartment was well furnished. There was a stack of black stereo equipment in one corner, a floor to ceiling video library, and dark walls hung with bronze metalwork. Overlapping Oriental carpets covered the floor.

"Nice place."

Tracy spotted a photo of Malan and Mike standing beside a Land Rover somewhere in the desert. She picked it up and threw it at the bedroom door. There was an answering wail from inside. Kerribar came forward with hands raised. "No, No, Mrs. Mike, you must have respect."

Tracy turned to Sam. "Tell him to get her out of here."

"She lives here."

"No more. It's my rent money and I'm staying here tonight and I don't fancy a pajama party. I want her gone, I want her out of here and I don't care how he does it." She glanced at her watch. "It's quarter after six. I'm going downstairs to get a Coke. If she's not gone in one hour I'm stripping this place down to the bare floors and he's not getting one single penny of his back rent." She pointed at Kerribar. "You know English, so you know what I'm saying." She looked with disgust toward the bedroom, then marched out of the apartment.

The two men looked at one another. From the bedroom came quiet sobbing. Kerribar lowered his voice. "The other wife is better. Not so much problems."

Sam questioned him and learned that Malan was from a Bedouin family, Kerribar didn't know which tribe. The girl kept to herself and spent long hours walking the banks of the Euphrates when Mike wasn't there. Shortly after Mike's disappearance the police came and spoke to her and then searched the apartment.

"They filled two boxes and took them away. They asked if Mr. Mike has given me a gift or left a package in my care. Thanks be to Allah it was my friend Jasfar in charge of the search. Otherwise they would throw everything into the street, even the cushions of my bed. I have seen it happen."

"What were they looking for?"

"Hashish, contraband, money, religious articles, who can say? Jasfar would not tell me."

The more he learned about Mike Winn the less Sam felt he knew. Kerribar stood outside the bedroom door and argued with the girl, telling her she had to leave. "The first wife says you must go. If you do not leave I will call the police."

"Go away," Malan shouted.

Sam was already framing shots in his mind: low angle, hysterical girl in foreground, grim-faced police pulling her from the building; high angle, girl in the courtyard below, arms wrapped around the ankles of a policeman; normal angle through the back window of the car as they push her inside from the opposite

side. All he had to do was stand aside, flick his forefinger at the right time. But it was Mike Winn he
wanted to know about, and the girl was the one who
could tell him.

"Let me talk to her, I'll get her to leave."

Kerribar shrugged. "As you wish. If she refuses, I
have many friends with the police. They will take her
away."

When he was gone, Sam knocked on the door
and called in Arabic, "Peace be with you, daughter of
the desert." There was no answer. "I greet you in the
name of your husband."

"Who are you?"

"A friend who wishes to find Mike. Will you help
me?"

"Do you have word of my husband?"

"I have a letter. Open the door so we can talk."

The door opened a crack and a somber brown eye
gazed out. "Where is the letter?"

"It's safe," Sam said. "Come out and tell me what
you know." Her eyes searched the room beyond. He
said, "The others are gone."

Malan hurried to retrieve her scarf from the floor.
She inspected it gravely, fingering the small rip in the
border. Her eyes were large and vulnerable beneath
long dark lashes. A child-woman, Sam thought. She
looked up and smiled. "I can mend it."

"How old are you, Malan?"

"I have fifteen years." She went to the window
and peered out. Satisfied that the others were occupied, she gestured to the couch. "Will you have tea?"

"Let's talk first. Tell me about Mike, the last time
you saw him."

If anything, the girl seemed to know less than

Tracy about Mike's business. The first she heard of his disappearance was when the police came to the apartment five days after he left. They confiscated his camera equipment and photo albums and broke some of what she called "the old things."

"What kind of old things?"

"From the old cities. I will show you."

She brought out a cardboard box and pulled out artifacts from the Roman era. There were engraved ivory cylinders meant to be rolled across ink pads and used as seals, small statues of Roman deities, amulets, ankle bracelets and coins, worn thin by time, that still bore a ghost of Caesar's likeness. One of Mike's sidelines, the illegal exporting of antiquities.

"When the police came, did they see these?"

"Yes."

"But they didn't take them?"

"No, only his camera and photographic books."

"What was in the photo books?"

"Pictures of the old cities, of oasis," she hesitated, "and pictures of me when we make the clouds and rain."

"When you're in bed?"

She giggled. "He has the camera which makes pictures out the back."

"A Polaroid camera?"

"Yes, they took that camera, too."

"Do you know why?" She shook her head. "But there was something else they were looking for."

Malan's look of quick surprise confirmed what Kerribar had told him. "I don't know."

"What was it?"

She put on an expression of false innocence. "Nothing else."

"Malan, if you want Mike back you must tell me everything you know. What else did the police want?"

"You are not Mike's brother?"

"No."

"Then I cannot tell."

"He could die, you know that? Imad Tayib might kill Mike. Is that what you want to happen?"

Tears welled up. "I promised not."

"What about Tracy, didn't you promise to obey his wife? His first wife?"

She nodded slowly.

"Will you tell her?"

"She hates me."

"She doesn't hate you, she was surprised. In America a man can have only one wife, and Mike didn't tell her about you."

"But I have seen her picture."

"Listen, Malan, if Tracy asks you, will you tell her what you know?"

She nodded.

"Good, you wait right here."

He went downstairs and found Tracy sitting in the car. Her shoes were off and she had her feet propped against the dashboard. "Is she gone?"

"She wants to talk to you."

"She can talk to my foot if she doesn't get out of that apartment."

"She knows something about Mike and you're the only one she'll talk to."

"Why me?"

"You're the first wife, a part of the family."

"Stop saying that."

"She's seen your picture. She trusts you, it doesn't matter why. Just go talk to her."

"She's a little liar. I know her kind."

"She could be the Wicked Witch of the West, but she knows what was going on with Mike. You want to find out or sit out here and sulk?"

Tracy gave him a look. "I pity your mother, with a shithead for a son."

They returned to the apartment, where Malan had prepared tea. Tracy sat with compressed lips and allowed the girl to pour her a glass, which she pointedly didn't touch. Sam sipped his tea and, when Malan sat down, he said to Tracy, "You want to ask or can I go ahead?"

"Go ahead."

"The wife of your husband asks what else you might know of Mike."

Malan smiled gratefully at Tracy. "The week before he left, Mike was very worried. I don't know the cause, but he watched many times from the window and was careful to lock the door. He showed me a way to greet the door." She reached to the wall and demonstrated three quick raps, a pause, then two more.

"What's that all about?" Tracy asked.

Sam told her and Malan continued, "Before Mike left, we drove to the tent of my father and he had the silver box. Mike spoke with my father and, when we returned, the box was left behind. When I reminded him, he told me to forget the box and tell no one where it is. When the police came, I was scared but I said nothing."

"When the police came, did they know about the box?"

"I don't think so."

"What was in it?"

"Papers I saw once. A notebook."

"What are you two talking about?" Tracy demanded.

"She says Mike had a silver box with papers in it. Sound familiar?"

"Like a jewelry box?"

Malan used her hands to indicate a small case.

Sam said, "Briefcase maybe. You remember Mike carrying anything like that?"

"No. Where is it?"

"Mike left it with her father."

"Oh, great. All this for nothing."

Sam turned to Malan. "The wife of your husband would like to see the box. Can you get it for us?"

"My father's tent is near Mayadin. If you have a car, I can take you there."

Tracy listened to Sam's translation and frowned. "Okay," she said finally, "we'll take her there and leave her there. Let her marry some little camel-humper her own age."

Sam and Tracy went to the Ragdan Hotel, recommended by Kerribar. It was a two-star establishment with a doorless elevator and shuttered rooms that shared a hallway toilet. "I've stayed in worse," was Tracy's only comment when she saw her room. At dinner she picked at her food and went immediately to bed. Sam sat on the porch overlooking the street, his mind filled with speculation about Mike Winn and the contents of the silver case.

NINETEEN

Tracy did not budge from the front seat when they stopped to pick up Malan in the morning. The Arab girl carried an overnight bag emblazoned with a Dallas Cowboys emblem. Tracy's mouth tightened when she saw it. "I hope she's got everything because she's not coming back here."

"She knows that."

Malan got into the back seat, and as soon as they were on the highway offered them sunflower seeds from a paper sack. Sam took a handful, Tracy declined. "I don't eat chipmunk food for breakfast."

They drove the wide alluvial Euphrates valley where fertile fields stretched in a patchwork of green and yellow toward clay cliffs that rose abruptly to the desert floor above. Herdsmen drove sheep along the roadside, and the land was dotted by small homes of adobe or concrete enclosed by low mud walls. A girl Malan's age dressed in multicolored *galabiya* rode a donkey burdened with huge sacks of produce.

Sam pointed to a distant smokestack where a tongue of orange flame danced against a hazy blue sky. "Is that where Mike works?"

"That's a processing plant. He works the rigs."

"Where are they?"

"Do I look like I memorized the concession map?"

Sam wanted to know more about Mike's working conditions but clearly Tracy had other things on her mind. After a moment he said, "There are advantages, you know."

"To what?"

"The newest wife has to do the laundry, cook the meals, take out the trash. It's like having a free servant."

"Don't start on me this morning. I'm not in the mood."

"Just so you understand, Mike may not be perfect but he's practical. This is a Muslim society where the second date is a proposal of marriage, and if you screw around without the ceremony, it dishonors the whole family and the woman's father and brothers are obligated to kill you. No, I'm serious. Family honor is no joke here."

"What about the woman's honor?"

"They sometimes kill her, too."

"Come on."

"You think I'm kidding? There was a British guy, Evan Higgins, ran a desk in Beirut. He started an affair with a divorced woman, not such a problem in a cosmopolitan city, except her father was a mullah and her brother was a devout Muslim. When things got a little too public, the brother ambushed him. Eight bullet holes in the car and Evan went home with a collapsed lung and a large intestine about a foot shorter than when he arrived. If he'd married the girl, all he'd have had to do later was say *'I divorce you'* three times, she goes home to daddy and everybody's happy."

"You mean the men are happy."

"Works both ways. Nobody's forced to stay married out here."

"You mean this girl could divorce Mike just by saying it three times?"

"Saying it to him."

Tracy turned to look at Malan. The girl offered the sunflower seeds but Tracy sat back and stared out the window, thinking hard.

Mayadin had the same unfinished look as most Syrian towns, but Malan pressed her face eagerly against the window as they drove down the main street, where shop owners were raising metal shutters in preparation for the day's business. They turned east and followed a side road until the first Bedouin tents came into view. Clearly excited now, Malan fumbled for a handle to roll down the window. She let out a squeal of delight when Sam did it electrically from the front seat.

The Bedouin camp was less a cohesive unit than a few common acres inhabited by whoever happened to be living there at the moment. Trucks had replaced camels as the principal method of transportation, but the people still followed the seasons, moving from place to place as weather and whim dictated. Most of the tents looked the same to Sam. The sides were made up of half a dozen rectangular fabrics, while the roof was the traditional black camel's hair. Waving and calling to friends, Malan guided them to her father's tent, where the car was quickly surrounded by women and children.

"These her sisters or mothers?" muttered Tracy as they stepped out of the car. Malan's father, a lean man named Achmed Hajjar, spoke to his daughter and approached with a smile. He wore a white *galabiya* and checkered headscarf that flowed over his shoulders and across his forehead at a slightly canted angle. After an elaborate exchange of greetings, he invited them to the tent.

"What'd he say," Tracy asked.

"May my beard grow long."

"Your beard?"

"Shhh."

They followed Achmed to the shaded side of the tent, where an oriental rug and cushions provided a place to sit. Achmed gave Sam the position of honor and adjusted the pillow to his back. He nodded politely to Tracy as she sat, and then issued instructions to one of the women to make tea. Half a dozen children, some in *galabiyas* and others wearing shorts and stained T-shirts, formed a perimeter, where they watched with open curiosity.

"Are these your children?" Sam asked.

"Only some of them. The older ones are with the goats and at the watering place. I have nine strong sons and many daughters."

"May your daughters bear sons as strong as their grandfather."

"Inshallah."

Tracy was watching two of the women who had returned to work sewing new panels for the tent. The panels were laid out on the ground, corners tied to stakes. The women wore black *galabiyas* over more colorful robes. They regarded Tracy with frank curiosity, their bronze skin decorated with black tattoos: on one a series of diamonds that ran from the corner of her mouth to her chin, on the other a single black tear hung beneath her lower lip.

Achmed turned his attention to Sam. "My daughter says that Michael has disappeared. It is true?"

Sam explained that Mike was taken hostage and that Tracy had come to rescue him. Achmed looked at her closely for the first time. "Does she speak the language of the Prophet?"

"She is not so blessed."

His expression turned crafty. "She is wealthy, yes?"

"Not really, she has a friend who is loaning her some money."

Tracy said, "What are you talking about?"

"You."

"Did you tell him we want that box?"

"Not yet."

"Do it and let's get out of here. I feel like a guppy in a goldfish bowl."

"Relax. One of his wives is making tea."

"That's the tradition out here? Two wives?"

"He's got four wives."

"Oh, great. Well, you tell him he's not going to marry off his daughter to my husband. She's home to stay. You tell him that."

Sam put it more politely. He explained that the American custom was to wed only a single wife and that Malan would be unable to return with Mike to the United States.

"But Malan is young and strong," Achmed said. "When the first wife is tired, she will massage her back. When her feet burn from walking, she will bathe them in cool water. When she is pregnant, Malan will make the clouds and rain to keep the fires of desire from inflaming Michael's mind. You tell her."

They were all watching him expectantly. Sam hesitated, aware that there was no way this was going to be a meeting of the minds.

"Well?" Tracy demanded.

"The father says he's sorry to lose a son but happy to have his daughter back."

"Good. Now call her over here."

"Why?"

Tracy frowned. "Malan!" The girl was playing with a child, tickling its nose with a crow's feather. Tracy waved to her and, when the girl approached, she pulled a piece of paper and a pencil from her purse. "Tell her to write 'I divorce you' three times on this paper. Put his name, too. 'I divorce you Mike Winn,'—have her write that."

"She has to say it to his face."

"She's never going to see his face. This'll work just fine. Go ahead, tell her."

Tracy pushed the paper and pen to Malan. Thinking it was a gift, the girl inspected the pen with a delighted smile.

"Why don't we wait on this?"

"Just tell her what I said."

Tracy was in one of her stubborn moods, but this wasn't the time or place to argue the matter. Sam turned to Malan. "The first wife wishes you to write a promise. A promise to obey Michael. You will write it three times so she knows your heart is true." Both

Malan and Achmed looked puzzled. "A custom in the United States."

"She cannot write," Achmed said.

"My name I can."

Tracy said, "She won't do it?"

Sam explained and Tracy shook her head. "Can't write? You mean she's ignorant as well as loose?"

Achmed called to one of the older boys, "Get Riyad, get the scribe."

The fourth wife brought tea. She handed the tray to Achmed, who placed it with great ceremony before his guests. The elongated teapot was made of brass, tarnished and dented, its base black from the flames. Three glasses slightly larger than shot glasses were arranged around it. Achmed poured the tea and waited.

"Drink," Sam said.

"I'm not thirsty."

"You don't have to be thirsty, just be polite."

"I don't happen to want these people's tea or anything else they have."

Alerted by the tone of her voice, Achmed and the others paused. Keeping his voice light, Sam said, "If you don't drink his tea, then you insult the man and, if you insult the man, he's not going to have his daughter sign the divorce paper. So you want to fix things up or fuck things up, it's up to you?"

All eyes were on her. Tracy picked up the glass and sipped the tea. She smiled and said between clenched teeth, "There, how's that?"

Sam turned to them. "The wife of Michael says the tea is delicious."

A collective sigh of satisfaction and smiles bloomed. Sam and Achmed spoke of the weather and the drive from Damascus and the merits of Achmed's truck until the scribe arrived. He was a frail man with few teeth and rheumy eyes, who carried his paper and writing instruments in a worn wood box. While Malan watched from over his shoulder, the scribe carefully wrote the declaration of obedience which Sam dictated. When he was finished, she wrote her name proudly at the bottom. Sam handed the paper to Tracy, whose smile was genuine for the first time since they'd arrived. "How do you say 'thank you' in their language?"

"*Shukran.*"

Tracy repeated it awkwardly to the delight of the children. Then she said to Sam, "Can we get the box and get out of here?"

Achmed sent the oldest boy, who returned with an aluminum briefcase with a combination lock. The son gave it to his father, who presented it to Sam.

"Ever seen it before?" he asked Tracy.

"No."

He tried the latch but it was locked. "Any idea what the combination would be?"

"Not unless it's his birthday or something." She took the case and began to line up numbers. Sam asked Achmed and Malan but neither of them knew the combination.

"It's not his birthday or my birthday either," Tracy announced.

"We must break it open," Sam told Achmed.

"I cannot allow it. Michael has left the box in my keeping and no harm must come to it."

"Achmed Hajjar, the husband of your daughter did not know he would be kidnapped when he left the box. The contents may help us free him. His first wife gives permission to open it. Will you not give your blessing that Malan's unborn children may see their grandfather in the face?"

The dual appeal to family and vanity convinced him. Achmed sent for a chisel and hammer and after repeated blows the clasp gave way and the case opened. Word of what was happening had spread, and a large group gathered to view the mysterious contents of the silver box. Sam lifted out a spiral notebook and a manila envelope.

"That's it?" Tracy said. Her disappointment was reflected in the faces of the onlookers. She took the case and pulled open the divider to make sure there was nothing else, while Sam slid the contents of the manila envelope onto the rug. There was a short article clipped from a newspaper about a train wreck and a series of photographs, apparently of the same wreck. He paged through the notebook. Most of the pages were blank, but in the beginning were scrawled notes: proper names, a heading called Irskenian I-E with an arrow to a set of numbers too long to be a date. Nothing was organized, no headings or columns, just names and numbers and cryptic abbreviations spread helter-skelter across the page.

"What's it mean?" Tracy asked. She was looking over his shoulder.

"You tell me." He handed her the notebook and turned to Achmed. "We will take these things with your blessing and perhaps they will help us find and free Michael."

Achmed was reluctant to let the box go, but he agreed when Sam suggested an official receipt. Again the scribe came. This time both Sam and Tracy signed

and with due solemnity handed it to Achmed. By the
time they left, everybody had a different impression
of what had happened, and Sam felt like Alice in
Wonderland.

TWENTY

ZENOBIA. KATHERINE REPEATED THE WORD TO HERSELF. IT WAS all part of Doug Livingston's cloak-and-dagger routine. First a code word, now a pass word. She half suspected he used them simply to impress her. Once again she felt like a character in a movie as the cab took her to the largest marketplace in Damascus, the Hamadieh Souk. A vaulted metal roof over the street created a perpetual twilight and provided an excuse for the garish neon illumination favored by Syrian shopkeepers. The taxi crept through the crowd at a snail's pace, horn beeping, the intrusion barely noted by people who ambled to one side to let it pass. A group of camera-laden Europeans moved shoulder-to-shoulder past off-duty United Nations soldiers going one way and Shi'ite women, invisible behind their black veils, going the other. Katherine was glad to leave the chaos of the street for the tranquility of Nadoub & Sons.

"Good afternoon, madame," the shopkeeper

greeted her in English. He was a thin stooped man with a reddish tinge to his hair and pale blue eyes. Feeling awkward and self-conscious, Katherine said, "Do you sell Roman coins?"

"For which period are you looking?"

"The reign of Zenobia."

"Of course, madame. If you will follow me." Two men playing backgammon behind the counter glanced up as she climbed a flight of narrow, worn stairs. Her host ushered her into an office and offered her a couch. "Your friend will be here shortly."

He left her. The place smelled of incense. There were shelves crammed with goods, a massive desk, and against one wall a highly polished safe with a fancy dial. Livingston arrived a few minutes later. He carried a leather satchel and closed the door as if he owned the place.

"Excuse the secrecy, but in deference to our staff I didn't want to meet at the embassy." He moved behind the desk and pulled out a stack of eight-by-ten photographs and a map. "Your friends went to Dier Ezzur. How did you manage that?"

"How did you know that's where they went?"

"You think these young men at the rental car companies work there for the twenty dollars a month they get in salary? The Mukhabarat pays them, we pay them, everybody pays them for information."

"What's the Mukhabarat?"

"Secret police. Why are they going to Dier Ezzur?"

Katherine told him and he nodded approvingly. "That's good. If you weren't so well-heeled, I'd offer you a job. You've got the qualities to make a successful intelligence officer." He smiled to show it was a joke. "Have you got a hair dryer?"

"Yes."

"Dump it and carry this one." He brought out a brown hair dryer. "Looks like the real thing, doesn't it?"

"Is that the explosive?"

"A miracle of modern technology. You wouldn't believe the scramble to get this thing here in time. They say the Japanese are clever, look at this." With a half-turn he took off the cap through which the power cord entered the handle. He pulled and the cord became thicker as it unwound from a spool inside the housing. "Looks like an electrical cord but it's composed of C-4 explosive. This stuff will cut through steel cable like scissors through spaghetti. Just wrap it tight around the power cable and put the plug in here." He stuck the connector into a receptacle camouflaged in the air vents. "There's a timer and detonator inside. Turn on the switch and, if it's plugged in like this, it'll blow at seven twenty-five in the evening." He unplugged the cord and let it wind back inside.

"Does the dryer work?"

"That's the one sacrifice we had to make to get batteries into the thing. But don't worry, Tayib's men aren't very sophisticated. Most of them are peasants, still got manure between the toes." He handed the dryer to her. "Here, you try it."

"It's too heavy."

"Won't matter. For all they pretend to hate the West, these people are in awe of technology. You tell them the Japanese have invented a perpetual motion machine, and they'd believe it."

"What about airport security?"

"For flights within the country, it's a joke. Check it through in baggage and you'll do fine." He indicated the map and photos. "Let's go over the terrain and I'll show you the step-up transformer. The quality of some of these shots isn't great but, considering Tayib's men shoot anyone caught taking pictures, it's not bad."

The photographs showed a narrow promontory of land that dropped off on three sides to a rugged canyon. At its tip was the castle protected by stone walls. The fourth side was separated from the adjoining town by a deep cut excavated into the hill. The only entry to the castle lay across a narrow suspension bridge that spanned the gap. Livingston pointed out a footpath that began at the bridge opposite the castle and wound its way upward to the step-up transformer.

"There's a guard here at the bridge. He can see the footpath so you'll have to find a way to avoid him. After that you're home free."

"I can't do anything until Mike Winn is safe."

Livingston shook his head. "No, no. Forget about it. Tayib doesn't have him."

"What?"

"He hasn't got Mike Winn."

"He *admitted* it."

"Sure he did. A week after Winn disappeared, because nobody else took credit. I'll tell you something. Mike Winn is no angel. He was involved in a few questionable deals over here and more likely one of them went sour. But whoever got him it wasn't Tayib."

"How can you be so sure?"

"Because our agent was there when Tayib heard about the kidnapping. Surprised the hell out of him. Believe me, Tayib doesn't have Mike Winn."

Katherine felt off balance, like trying to go through a door during an earthquake. "Then there's no reason to go to Raqba—"

"Yes there is—to sabotage the radar station. Don't you see? Tayib took credit to make himself look good but at the same time he's given you a reason to go to Raqba. It's poetic justice."

"I have to tell Tracy."

"You can't do that without telling her about me, and as soon as you do that you've got no reason to go to Raqba. Mike Winn is our Trojan horse."

She glanced up sharply. It was the same idea that had prompted her to contact Tracy, but from Livingston it sounded cynical. Yet he was right. Neither her original plan to kill Tayib nor the CIA plan to kidnap him stood any chance of success unless they invoked the cause of Mike Winn's freedom.

IN ALEPPO Sam told himself that the reason they were checking into the Baron Hotel was not because he had stayed here with Faye but because Mike had mentioned Irskenian Shipping in his notebook. Irskenian was an Armenian name and the owner of the hotel was Armenian. Mr. Mazlumian was a slow-moving bear of a man with white curly hair who wore a once-elegant Turkish vest now grown too small for him. When he saw Sam he touched a finger to his temple. "Wait. You are familiar." His eyes closed for a moment, then popped open. "Mr. Gaddis and—" he turned to Tracy and continued after a slight hesitation. "You have not been here before."

"You have a good memory, Mr. Mazlumian. This is Mrs. Winn."

"You are welcome, Mrs. Winn. Once a guest of the Baron, you are part of the family. The next time I shall know your name."

Like its owner, the Baron was rich in history but showed its age. The mahogany wainscotting was cracked, ceilings needed painting and the edge of the front desk was worn to the wood. Sam got them two rooms with private bathrooms. A wizened lady in a faded blue apron took them upstairs. Sam's room overlooked the street. It felt like the same room he and Faye once shared but he couldn't be sure. Tracy had the adjoining room. Sam found her lying on the bed, fully dressed, staring at the ceiling.

"How about dinner?"

"I'm not hungry." She had been in poor spirits ever since leaving Achmed's camp.

"You'll feel worse if you don't eat."

"My stomach's got the heebie-jeebies."

"Saladin's revenge. I'll have Mazlumian send up some Lomotil and a bottle of mineral water."

She curled into a fetal position and closed her eyes. Sam lifted a blue blanket from the end of the bed and covered her with it. The blanket had an embroidered *B* next to a burned spot made by a cigarette. Tracy shoved the blanket aside. "Don't, that makes me feel smothered."

Mike's briefcase was on the floor. Sam picked it up and left quietly. He ate dinner in the hotel dining room, where the chipped Limoges china outclassed the mediocre food. The other guests were all Europeans or Turks; the Baron was too far past its prime to attract the wealthy Arabs who stayed in the new five-star hotels.

After dinner Sam found a sagging chair next to a player piano in the lounge, ordered a Scotch and soda, lit a cigarette and reviewed the contents of the silver case. The newspaper article seemed straightforward enough: a train had derailed, a guard was crushed, some drill stems were damaged and two hundred gallons of drilling mud lost. He went to the photos and flipped through them. Apparently Mike had come across the accident and—

Something about the photo of the victim caught his attention. The man lay on his back, left hand lying free, right hand gripping the collar of the shirt. His tongue bulged and the face was swollen. Sam went back to the text of the article: "Although the engine crew was unhurt, one guard was crushed to death."

"Ooops," Sam said. The guard looked bloated, not crushed. Of course, it could have been a broken neck or the kind of major internal injuries that wouldn't show. But if someone had taken him from beneath an overturned freight car, why arrange the body in such a strange position? No, Sam had seen too many similar poses during the Iran-Iraq war, too many victims with dried blood etched into their chests from fingernails clawing for oxygen, not to recognize the symptoms.

A voice at his side boomed, "Faye!" Mr. Mazlumian stood beaming down at him. "She is the one you came with last time. Your wife. Her name, Faye."

"You've got the best memory in the business."

Mazlumian hung his head in mock shame. "I

confess I looked it up. Your new woman confused me. She looks very healthy, very delightful, so I gave you rooms with the same door, did you notice?"

"Thanks, but she's just a business associate."

"And what is a man's business but to enjoy the gifts of Allah? And what is a woman but the greatest of such gifts? Praise Allah and enjoy the woman."

"I've got a question for you, Mr. Mazlumian. Are you familiar with Irskenian Shipping?"

"With the family, of course. Another illustrious Armenian family almost as old as my own. We were here before the Turkish massacre, the Irskenians came after. My wife's cousin is the husband of Sarkis Irskenian's niece."

"What kind of goods do they ship?"

Mazlumian gestured helplessly. "I do not know the shipping business, my friend. You can talk to Sarkis. The other brother, Rabat, is in the construction business. Have you seen Tartous? The new development?"

He was referring to a coastal town to the south. Sam had never been there but this didn't matter to Mazlumian. "Go and relax. Take the woman. They have a new amusement park, summer homes and condominiums, a new hotel. Very nice, very popular with the people of Damascus. They drive two hours so the men can go fishing while the women read French novels on the beach."

Mazlumian would have talked all night. Finally Sam excused himself and went up to his room. He lay on the bed with the windows open, a latchless shutter squeaking whenever the occasional breeze tugged it. The story of Mike Winn might be bigger than he had thought. Here was a man who liked playing the angles, who shipped antiquities out of the country illegally, who had no qualms about marrying a fifteen-year-old Arab girl and keeping it secret from his wife. And now what? Was he also involved in shipping poison gas? Or had he stumbled across the wreck and decided to blackmail someone along the line?

Tracy picked herself a real winner, he thought. But Mike Winn's scam had been short-circuited by Imad Tayib's scam. Syria was a scammer's paradise. Sam used a bent coat hanger to lock the noisy shutter and finally fell asleep.

THE SCRATCH pad on the table bore the Presidential seal. The President of the United States wrote the words "Bright Justice" as he listened to the Director of the CIA describe the situation. There were three other members of the Security Council in the room—the Secretary of Defense, Secretary of State, and the National Security Advisor. Each man had a personal secretary who sat in a chair behind his boss. All but the CIA Director. The man who sat behind him was Bob Hatch.

The situation they faced was simple—to authorize a second attempt to capture Imad Tayib or to cancel the mission and bring the Delta team home empty-handed. The President wrote "empty" but didn't like the look of it. He crossed it out. Bob Hatch, sitting to one side, played a game, trying to figure out what the President wrote from the movement of the pen. Hatch was under no illusion about why the DCI had brought him. He was the lightning rod. If the new plan went sour, his superior could deflect the blame.

When the DCI finished his briefing, the President said, "Who's the new contact?"

"I'll let Mr. Hatch fill you in. It's his man."

A shuffle of chairs as the men turned toward him. "It's an unusual circumstance, Mr. President. The new agent has been developed by our Special Projects Officer in Damascus for a one-time function only: the sabotage of the radar station at Mount Kajar."

"What's the new agent's background?"

"I don't know. Our man agreed not to reveal the name or anything else. We either live with it or cancel the operation."

There was an audible murmur of dissatisfaction. The Secretary of State shifted his weight. "This man of yours still works for you, doesn't he? Order him to reveal the agent's name."

Hatch glanced at the DCI but got no help. "I tried that but the parameters are set. We can cajole, threaten or fire him, but I doubt if he'd yield and I don't think there's time."

In fact, Hatch had initially pressed for a name, but Livingston had told him, "You don't want to know," and Hatch believed him. In the world of cut-outs he understood that his protégé was offering him the protection of credible ignorance.

The Director said, "The new agent has a nine point five reliability."

"Nine five?" the Secretary of Defense said. "I'd be lucky to get that rating myself."

"According to who?"

"Again, our man in Damascus."

"If this is true," the Secretary of State said ponderously, "why did we first use a source with only a six rating?"

"When we began planning Bright Justice, LEG-HORN was the only man available. SCRIMSHAW is an emergency expedient."

"SCRIMSHAW? What does that mean?"

"It's a random code selection, computer-generated. It means nothing."

The President wrote the word "Scrimshaw." There was five minutes of discussion, during which Hatch studied the Chief Executive's face and found himself trying to imagine him in bed with his wife.

"All right," the President said, "let's make a decision." He turned to the Secretary of Defense. "Jim?"

"If we can knock out the radar station, I don't see that it matters who does it. I vote yes."

The Secretary of State looked dubious. "What kind of deniability factor do you give SCRIMSHAW?"

The DCI said, "Good to excellent."

"Based on your resident's assessment?"

"That's right."

The Secretary shook his head. "Too much depends on this one man. I vote to cancel the operation."

The National Security Advisor agreed. The President turned to the DCI, who answered carefully. "If Mr. Hatch's analysis is correct, we have a lot to gain if it works, and not much to lose if it fails."

"Is that a yes?"

"A qualified one."

The President frowned. "That's like being half pregnant. There's no yellow light here, it's either green or red. Let's have it."

The DCI knew he had no choice. It was his op. "I say let's go for it."

The President's pen moved; a simple word this

time: *Go.* He circled it. Bright Justice was a go. Hatch wondered if the President's decision would have been the same had he known that the explosives were hidden in a hair dryer.

TWENTY-ONE

KNOWING AS HE DID THAT THE SINGLE PHONE LINE THAT LINKED Raqba with the outside world was tapped, Imad Tayib relied on personal envoys for sensitive matters and used the phone only for more public information like that which reached him from Abu Shapour. The American wife of Mike Winn, accompanied by a reporter and a woman whose children died on Flight 67, was on her way to Raqba. She was prepared to pay a half-million American dollars in ransom.

Tayib had rebuffed the women every step of the way and still they came. Now he considered carefully whether Allah had a purpose in their visit. While he would not abase himself before Western currency, it occurred to him that the money could benefit those more worthy of it than the ones who owned it.

He had a young man who had grown up in Beirut brought to him. "Naguib Elyas, you speak the language of the English and Americans."

The chubby boy had arched lips and brown eyes,

luminous in the presence of his leader. "I renounce it, Imam, along with all false values of the West."

"Does not He Who Guides The Stars provide an adze for the shipwright? Before you renounce the tool Allah has placed in your hand look first to His purpose. Speak to me in the language of the infidel."

In English Naguib recited, " 'Tiger, tiger, burning bright, in the forests of the night; what immortal hand or eye, could frame thy fearful symmetry.' "

Tayib smiled. Speaking English himself, he told the young man what to do.

KATHERINE TOOK a morning flight from Damascus to Aleppo where Sam and Tracy met her at the airport. As the women greeted one another, Sam circled them with the camera to his eye. Tracy said, "He's been like this ever since we left. You better get used to it."

When they reached the car Tracy got in back and Katherine sat in front with Sam, who seemed more alert and not so volatile as he was in Damascus. When Katherine asked about Dier Ezzur he said to Tracy, "You want to tell her or shall I?"

"Do you have to make a big deal about every little thing?"

"It wasn't so little last night. You couldn't even eat dinner."

"Because we ate goat intestine or whatever it was that Miss Feet-In-The-Air's daddy fed us."

"Who?"

Tracy sat back and crossed her arms. "Mike had him a girlfriend, big deal."

"Spelled w-i-f-e."

"No, spelled s-e-x."

"Our boy Mike collects ancient artifacts and youthful wives."

Tracy kicked the back of the seat. "Just shut up."

A new familiarity had grown between them, Katherine saw. Two days ago she and Tracy had been a team and Sam the interloper. Now the experiences in Dier Ezzur had drawn them together, just as the knowledge that they would not find Mike Winn at Raqba set her apart.

They entered the coastal mountains where the land was green and the valleys rich in trees and foliage. It was ironic, Katherine thought, that the closer they got to Imad Tayib, the more idyllic the setting. They reached the mountain turn-off at five in the afternoon. The main road continued to the Turkish border but two others ascended the mountain, one to the radar station and the other to Imad Tayib's camp. As they turned into the dirt road Sam said, "Okay, Tracy, button up for Allah."

"What?"

"The blouse. You forgot a couple buttons this morning."

"That's some kind of religion that wants women to look like a sack of potatoes."

She had barely finished speaking when they turned a corner and found the road blocked by a long pole counterweighted with stones. Three men lounged in the shadow of an army tent. They wore khaki uniforms but their red-and-white-checked *kaffiyehs*, headscarves, declared them Palestinian, and the yellow arm bands identified them as Tayib's men. Boys with guns, Katherine thought. It was hard to believe these were the kind of people who had killed her children.

Sam greeted them in Arabic and after a quick discussion a decision was made. The leader ordered them out of the car while, one by one, each bag and suitcase was inspected. The soldier who opened Tracy's bag moved red lingerie aside and his eye traveled from the younger woman to Katherine and back.

"Tell him not to drool on it," Tracy said. "That's Mike's homecoming present."

The soldiers balked at letting Sam take photographs until he gave them cigarettes and the atmosphere became friendlier. They paid no attention to the hair dryer, but when one man saw the Mont Blanc among the contents of Katherine's purse he immediately picked it up. Katherine's stomach tightened. The man called to his friends, compared the pen with the cigarette and pretended to smoke it like a cigar. The soldiers laughed.

After personal belongings came the car: wheel wells, under the hood, beneath the seats. It was a half hour before they were ready to go again. At the last minute one of the soldiers decided to go with them and ordered Katherine into the back seat with Tracy. "Tell him he can ride in back," she said.

"You don't understand, you're the woman, he's the man. He can't ride in back."

"Then have him drive."

Sam thought for a moment, then said something that caused the soldier to step back. He opened the rear door but instead of getting in he stepped up and rode half in and half out of the car, elbows braced between the roof and door.

"What did you tell him?" Katherine asked as they pulled away.

"That the back seat made you car sick and you'd vomit down his neck."

The road wound upward away from the river and climbed steeply over a series of switchbacks. Every time they hit a rut, the soldier's rifle clanged on the roof. The castle came into view, its stone walls an extension of the steep-sided promontory.

"Holy shit," Tracy said. "It looks like Disneyland."

"Except here you pay to get out."

The adjoining village was surrounded by steep terraced fields tended by women and children. Sam honked to clear the road of a flock of sheep. The soldier directed them to a parking area at the edge of town, where they got out and waited five minutes until a young man in fatigues with a yellow arm band joined them. As he spoke, he tossed his head whenever a lock of hair slid across his brow.

"Hello. I am Naguib Elyas, sent by Imad Tayib. If you wish to see the Imam, you will leave the car and follow me."

Without moving, Sam said in Arabic, "Peace be with you."

Naguib blinked in surprise, then replied, "And upon you be peace."

"Do you offer us welcome in the name of Imad Tayib?"

"All that is done here is done in his name. Will you accept his hospitality?"

Damn right, Sam thought. A cup of coffee, the traditional stranger's welcome, made a host responsible for his guest's safety for forty-eight hours. They followed Naguib past makeshift homes of rock and mud, with tin roofs held in place by rocks. A group of veiled women with pails waited their turn at a communal water tap. They became silent as the Americans passed. When Naguib made a right turn away from the castle, Sam stopped.

"Where are we going?"

"The home of Abu Hamri. You will spend the night, and tomorrow you will see the Imam."

"We don't want to stay the night, we just want to see Imad Tayib."

"First you must eat a meal prepared by Palestinian hands. It will flush your system of pork and other unclean foods."

"We haven't eaten any pork," Tracy said. "In case you hadn't noticed, they don't serve it in this country."

"The Imam says that to spend a night in a refugee camp is to take the first step toward enlightenment."

"I got all the enlightenment I need. What I want is my husband."

Katherine said, "If we spend the night, then Imad Tayib will see us?"

"After morning prayers he will see you."

"We can do that."

The others looked at her as if she were crazy. Don't fight me on this, she wanted to say. By staying the night, she would have a perfect opportunity to plant the explosive.

"Fine," Tracy said, "but I'll sleep in the car."

"I am sorry," Naguib said. "Abu Hamri is your host. Spurn him and you spurn the man you come to see. This is the decision of Imad Tayib."

Sam said to Naguib, "Excuse us for a moment." He drew the women aside and spoke in a low voice.

"This isn't Tayib's house. We're not under his protection unless he's our host."

"What can he do to us later that he can't do to us now?" Tracy said.

"You heard him," Katherine added, "This is the only way we can see Imad Tayib."

"Just so you know the risks. And don't expect the Sheraton." He turned to Naguib. "We'll spend the night."

Like most of the houses, the home of Abu Hamri was made of rocks joined by sticks and mud. It was a two-room affair with a small enclosed patio in back, where cooking was done. Naguib introduced them to their host and left them, saying he would return in the morning to take them to the castle.

Abu Hamri was a reticent man whose smile became spontaneous only when he talked to his children. Boys and girls of varying ages peeked into the room where the adults sat on cushions and drank coffee. Overhearing their excited chatter from beyond the doorway, Sam told Tracy, "They've never seen yellow hair before. They wonder if it's real."

"As real as God and Clairol can make it." She turned to the kids and held out a strand. "You want to touch it?"

There was embarrassed chatter but finally one of the boys came forward. Abu Hamri watched as the boy reached out his hand and said something that made Abu Hamri smile.

"He says it's warm," Sam translated.

All the kids took a turn touching her hair. Tracy was in her element, as natural with them as if they were her own. She asked questions about them and then pointed to a photograph on the wall draped in black. "Who's that?"

Tears came to Abu Hamri's eyes as he spoke. Sam translated in quick bursts. "Oldest son. Beautiful and brave, he says. Died a martyr to the Yellow Wind." Sam's features stiffened. "Bastard," he said in a low voice.

"What?"

"Forget it."

Abu Hamri's final words were impassioned. He pointed to Katherine and then to the photograph, then clasped his hands and bowed his head a moment as if in prayer.

"Is he talking about me?" Katherine said.

"Son of a bitch," Sam whispered.

"Sam, what?"

"His son died on Flight 67."

Tracy said, "He got on that plane by mistake?"

Katherine turned pale. Sam was watching her. "What?" Tracy said. "What's wrong?"

Katherine stood up. "Tell Abu Hamri I have to get some things from the car."

"We don't have to stay—"

"It's all right," she said, her voice flat. "Just give me the keys."

"I can come with you."

"I'd rather be alone."

Abu Hamri watched her leave. The children had become silent. Tracy whispered, "What happened?"

"This man's son carried the bomb onto Flight 67."

"My God." Tracy closed her eyes. "Stupid me and my big mouth."

"Not you—Tayib."

Katherine was blind to the village and to the people who stopped to stare as she passed. When she reached the car she got inside and sat, trembling. Damn you, she thought. You did this deliberately, knowing the pain. It wasn't enough that you took my children, but you force me to sleep in the house of their murderer. *Your* murderer. She took the Mont Blanc from her purse and gripped it tightly. This is what I want, she thought. Not a courtroom, not a trial. I want you dead.

Slowly she regained control of herself. Despite her revulsion she dared not try to kill Tayib as long as Tracy and Sam were at risk. The only plan now was Bright Justice. Later, once Tayib was in America . . . she left the thought unfinished but in her heart she knew she could not go on living until that man was dead.

Katherine took her overnight bag out of the trunk, removed the cosmetics to make room for the hair dryer, and brought out a roll of toilet paper. What had seemed a clever way to camouflage the explosive now seemed stupid in view of the fact that the village had no electricity. Livingston should have known. Her anger included him as well as Tayib. She could count on no one but herself.

When she returned to Abu Hamri's home, Tracy tried to apologize but Katherine cut her off. She didn't want to talk about it. Dinner was served but the earlier mood was broken. The portrait of the dead boy cast a pall over the room and they ate largely in silence broken only by the hiss of the pressure lantern. The oldest daughter, a girl of twelve, brought each dish on its own tray, from which everyone ate with his fingers. Occasionally they heard Abu Hamri's wife giving orders to the children but they never saw her.

After dinner, the call to evening prayers, amplified from the mosque inside the castle walls, boomed over the valley. Tracy glanced at their host, who was licking sauce from his fingers.

"Doesn't he have to fall on his face now or something?"

"It's more relaxed than that. Like Catholics and confession, they go when it suits their needs."

"What would suit my needs is a bathroom right about now."

"I'll go with you," Katherine said. "I brought toilet paper."

Abu Hamri gave them directions. None of the homes had running water or bathroom facilities, but at the end of each block was a communal latrine housed in a squat, concrete building. Sam gave Katherine a flashlight from his camera bag. "Just keep it pointed at the ceiling," he warned.

The oval hole in the ground she expected, but the smell almost made her choke. Breathing through her mouth, she slid her slacks and panties to her knees, and managed to keep them off the damp concrete slab while balancing awkwardly in a squat. *I will not vomit,* she repeated mentally. Pointing the flashlight at the ceiling illuminated the cobwebs and beetles crawling along the edge of the corrugated roof.

Back outside, she rejoined Sam and gave Tracy the flashlight and toilet paper. Sam was smoking a cigarette. "I'm sorry about this," he said.

"You should have had children, Sam. The less appealing aspects of basic bodily functions wouldn't be such a novelty."

"I meant Abu Hamri."

She was silent. The prayers had ended and people returning from the mosque slowed to stare at them. Then the loudspeakers erupted again, this time with a strong, strident voice. "That's him," Sam said.

Tracy joined them. "That place could gag a maggot."

"Shhh." Katherine held up a hand.

"Now what, more prayers?"

"He's making his radio broadcast," Sam said. "That's Imad Tayib."

They turned toward the castle, where a lone electric light shone from a window in the radio room. Beyond it the silhouetted mountain peaks merged with the heavens as the last flush of cobalt blue turned to black.

TWENTY-TWO

THE SLEEPING ARRANGEMENTS WERE SIMPLE: ABU HAMRI SENT his wife and children to stay with relatives. He and Sam slept in the living room, while Katherine and Tracy shared a thin mattress in the bedroom. Tracy jerked reflexively as she dozed off but Katherine stayed wide awake. The bomb on the plane had not been directed at her, but staying in this house was. She could *feel* Tayib's presence like a force, almost as if he knew why she had come here.

In the other room Sam and Abu Hamri exchanged a few words in Arabic before they went to sleep. Except for the occasional bleat of a goat and voice from a nearby house, the night was silent. A patch of silvery moonlight slid in from the window and slowly worked its way across the room.

At one o'clock Katherine peeled back the blanket and rolled off the mattress. Tracy turned restlessly but didn't wake up. Katherine put on a jacket, picked up her bag with the hair dryer and moved through the

217

living room past the two bodies on the floor. Slowly she lifted the latch and inched the door open until she could slip out.

The house was one of five homes that shared a common area linked to the road by a narrow corridor. At her approach a shadowy form moved and a sleepy voice said something in Arabic. A soldier sat with his back against the wall, squinting up at her. Katherine remembered the guidebook phrase for the bathroom. *"Wayn twahlet?"* He grunted and pointed. *"Shukran,"* she said.

In case he was following her, Katherine went to the latrine and paused to look back. The street was empty. She made her way toward the castle. Some of the homes had walled enclosures, where animals moved about restlessly. At one point a dog barked, making her start.

This is madness, she thought. Her every move looked suspicious. All it would take was one person having a sleepless night, and she would be discovered. And if they searched her, how could she explain the stupid hair dryer?

Knowing there would be a guard at the suspension bridge, she worked her way down a ravine that smelled of garbage and stagnant water and continued more slowly until she spotted the man sitting on a five-gallon can, elbows on his knees, an AK-47 on the ground. He was motionless. Asleep, she wondered? A mosquito bit her neck but she didn't dare slap it. The guard stretched and shifted his position. Awake but not alert.

She considered the twenty feet of open terrain that separated her from the path. With the moonlight there was a good chance he would see her out of the corner of his eye. She glanced at the sky. A dark cloud rimmed in silver was drifting toward the moon. She waited until its shadow turned the gray landscape to charcoal, and in a crouch crossed the open area. Gravel shifted underfoot and she froze her position. Was he looking? She couldn't tell. She waited as long as she dared and continued until she gained the sanctuary of the trees.

No one followed. She moved with increasing assurance, no longer wincing at the rattle of every loose pebble. The incline became steep; by the time she reached the step-up transformer, housed in a windowless, concrete building, she was breathing heavily.

Tall poles linked the power line on its way to Mount Kajar. Katherine followed them, scrambling down a steep embankment to a place where the line spanned a deep gorge. Here a concrete block anchored the steel cable from which the power line hung suspended. She set to work, repeating the steps she had practiced in the hotel: remove the cap, unwind the detonation cord, wrap it and insert the plug. The entire operation took only a few moments.

Feeling calm and clearheaded, she stripped branches from trees to cover her work, then removed Allison's amethyst necklace and held it tight. She turned her eyes to the islands of stars caught between the ragged clouds and whispered to her children, "This is for you." She draped the necklace over the explosive. Praying that the timer had been set correctly, she gritted her teeth and flicked the switch *on*. It was done.

She took as an omen the moon slipping behind the mountain peaks. Darkness made the return easier.

She felt more confident with each step. Nothing could happen to them now. Whatever Tayib decided —to see them or send them away—it was done. Not even the light pouring from Abu Hamri's house or the voices raised in anger could shake her confidence.

She stepped inside and blinked at the harsh light. Sam and the guard were arguing, Abu Hamri sat crosslegged on the floor smoking a cigarette, and Tracy, sleepy and confused, stood in the doorway to the bedroom. When they saw her, conversation stopped.

"What's the problem?"

The guard unleashed a stream of Arabic. Sam said, "The problem is that Abdul here is supposed to keep track of us and he's having a shit fit because you disappeared."

"I went to the bathroom."

"For an hour?"

"Was it that long?"

As she passed him, the guard grabbed her overnight bag and pawed through the contents. He looked up and said something.

"He wants to know why you were gone so long."

"Tell him I got lost."

She grabbed the bag back, walked into the bedroom and flipped the curtain shut. Tracy whispered, "What happened?"

"I couldn't sleep so I went for a walk." She sat down and pulled off her shoes.

"That's all he's screaming about? Jesus."

In the other room the guard spoke harshly and the front door slammed. Sam came into the room and knelt beside Katherine. "Is there anything you want to tell daddy before you go to sleep?"

"Good night, Sam."

"Katherine, women of your class and social standing just don't go wandering refugee camps at two in the morning."

"You don't know anything about women of my class and social standing."

"Help me out. What's going on?"

Tracy said, "She went for a walk, what's the big deal?"

Sam picked up Katherine's shoes and sniffed. "In a garbage dump?"

"I slipped. I fell. It's late and I'd like to get some sleep." She pulled the blanket up and curled away from him. Sam sighed and stood up. "Oh, what a tangled web we weave . . ."

He left the room. Tracy lay down and adjusted the blanket. "I know why you did it."

Katherine's eyes blinked open. "What?"

"Went outside. I wouldn't want to stay in a house of some guy who killed my kids, either."

"Tracy?"

"Umm?"

"Whatever happens tomorrow, I won't give up until we get Mike. Just remember that." Feeling better than she had in months, Katherine fell asleep.

IN THE morning Naguib took them to the castle. Children followed as far as the footbridge, which swayed beneath their weight as they crossed it. A massive portcullis hung above the entrance, its rusted spokes aimed downward. A brick wall blocked the way to the inner grounds and forced them to make a sharp right turn, where four guards waited in an arched alcove. Naguib indicated a long wooden table. "Place your belongings there."

Katherine and Tracy were directed to a small room, where three Arab women in fatigues waited. Katherine stood stiff as a statue while the hands traveled over her body, beneath her arms, her breasts, the small of her back, up and down her legs. Were security precautions always this stringent or had her disappearance last night alarmed them?

When they returned to the alcove, they found all their belongings had disappeared. "They will be returned when you leave," Naguib told them. Sam argued unsuccessfully for his camera equipment. There would be no photographs inside the castle walls. Katherine was afraid to draw attention to the Mont Blanc, still in her purse, so she said nothing.

Naguib led them to the battlement on top of the castle wall. The feeder line that brought power to the castle hung suspended from a cable that draped in a shallow arc across the chasm. It was anchored in the same manner as the one Katherine had sabotaged. Sam, who had been watching her like a hawk, noted her interest and turned to look.

For God's sake, she thought, and deliberately turned her attention to the inner grounds. The buildings were made of stone except the more recent repairs of cement and cinderblock. A slender minaret topped by a crescent identified the mosque. Army tents pitched haphazardly at one end of an open field where thirty recruits wearing yellow arm bands practiced hand-to-hand combat.

They descended the battlement and entered the headquarters through two sets of huge doors. The bottom floor was a living area for Tayib's personal soldiers who stared with frank curiosity as Naguib led them up a narrow flight of stairs. A fierce elation came over Katherine. This was the home of the enemy. Here she would look death in the face, here she would know the murderer of her children.

They stepped into a large room with arched windows set into thick walls. Oriental carpets covered the floor and armed guards with automatic weapons lounged along the walls. Katherine's attention was drawn to the man sitting on a cushion at the far end of the room. Flanked by five young men in white, Imad Tayib appeared smaller than in the photograph, a slight, straight body dominated by an angular face with deepset green eyes framed between a dark beard and black turban. He wore an open black robe over a white *galabiya*.

Sam moved forward. *"Salaam aleikum."*

Tayib raised a hand and in English said, "The language of the Prophet is profane from the lips of an unbeliever. We will speak of corrupt matters in a corrupt tongue. Which is the woman whose husband steals the wealth from our land for benefit of the Western nations?"

Tracy stepped forward. "If you mean Mike, I'm his wife and he didn't steal anything from you or anybody else."

Tayib's gaze shifted to Katherine. "You are the one whose children died in the glorious crash of Flight 67."

"I'm the one—" Whose children you murdered. She stopped herself. Careful, careful.

Sam said quickly, "The last time we met you offered a stranger coffee."

Tayib turned to him. "When did we meet?"

"Beirut in 1985. You gave an interview and I took your picture."

A slight pause, then recognition. "It was a bad picture."

"Give me back my camera and I'll try again."

"Excuse me," Tracy said, "but we came to see about Mike. Ms. Cahill here is willing to pay a ransom if you let my husband go."

"Impatience is a virtue only in the West. I know why you are here. The *Rih Asfar* is a holy movement. Our Arab brothers provide what we need in funds. We do not grovel before Western currency."

"We're talking about a lot of Western currency. Something like—how much, Katherine?"

Staring at Tayib, Katherine heard nothing. Except the word *murderer* echoing in her head. You murdered my children—

"Katherine?"

"What?"

"You said how much to get Mike back?"

"Half a million dollars."

"There, see?"

Tayib stood up. "Does a hawk change its diet to grass if you double the size of the pasture? Offer the wealth of America and we would refuse it, but there are those who may benefit. In the name of Allah the merciful I will deliver your husband if you give half a million dollars to the Red Crescent."

"The what?"

Sam said, "The Muslim equivalent of our Red Cross."

"And you'll set Mike free if we do that?"

"As I have said it, so shall it be."

She turned to Katherine, still staring at Tayib. "Is that okay?"

"What proof do we have?"

"What?"

"How do we know he has Mike?"

"Well, he . . . what do you mean?"

Tayib said, "It is not for a woman to question the word of a man."

You're not a man, you're an animal. The words sprang from deep in Katherine's heart and it was all she could do to catch them in her throat. Control. I've got to maintain control. "Do you have Mike Winn?"

"I have said it."

"Then swear it. On the blood of the Prophet."

Naguib drew a quick breath. Tayib's eyes turned to ice.

What the fuck is this, Sam thought? He felt like the train had jumped the tracks and was careening down the mountain without an engine. In Arabic he said, "The women are unfamiliar with Arab custom. Let's speak privately, you and I."

Tayib ignored him. Keeping his eyes fixed on Katherine, he crossed the room followed by the five *shaheen* and stopped in front of her. "Woman, have you come with vengeance in your heart?"

"My heart died with my children."

"Children are only ornaments of this world. Your heart's death is the death of your pride. Praise Allah that he has shown you humility."

"They didn't die to teach me a lesson. They died because you put a bomb on the plane."

"Katherine," Sam said quickly, "why don't we finish with Mike first?"

Tayib raised a hand and, without looking at him,

continued to Katherine. "Your government kills thousands of Arab children every year, but where is your voice when they die? Where are your tears? You will cry for the death of a pet dog but for our children your eyes are dry."

"America doesn't kill Arab children."

"You can not separate the snake from its venom. Your bombs, your bullets, your blind support of the Zionist aggressors—your country has sown a generation of death and misery and your children pay the price. In their death they become the symbol of the war we are fighting, nothing more, nothing less—"

"My children are not *symbols!*" She pulled three photographs from her pocket. "*Look* at them. Look at their faces, if you've got the guts."

Tayib took them and glanced at each one. "Jeff," Katherine said, "eleven years old, he wanted to be a doctor. That's Allison playing the piano, she was nine. And Joey, he would have been seven next week. They weren't *symbols,* they were children who never did you any harm and you murdered them."

Tayib deliberately ripped the photographs in two and let them fall. "I would carve the child from your womb if it would move forward the liberation of Palestine by so much as an hour."

Hatred erupted like a volcano. Sam saw it coming and yelled her name. Too late. Without hesitation or warning she spit in Tayib's face. There was a gasp. Tayib's features darkened, his hand moved in a blur beneath his robe and emerged with a knife. Sam rushed forward but soldiers wrestled him back. Tracy was shouting, "Get your fucking hands off."

Two of the *shaheen* pinned Katherine's arms.

Tayib grabbed her hair, yanked her head back and brought the blade to her throat.

"No," Sam yelled. He rammed an elbow into one man's stomach, broke free and threw himself at Tayib. Something smashed the back of his head, jagged pinwheels of light, the room tilted and he was on his hands and knees. A drop of blood glistened and disappeared into the rug. Dead, he thought. We're all dead.

About to cut her throat like a sheep's, Tayib saw in Katherine's eyes something far beyond defiance—a glint of triumph. He hesitated. You want this, he thought. That is the real reason you came to Raqba, not freedom for this woman's husband but your own death.

The eyes of his soldiers were on the knife, but his *shaheen* watched their leader's face. They had never seen Imad Tayib out of control. Tayib forced himself to smile. He leaned close and whispered, "I know your heart."

He turned abruptly and left the room. Not until he was in the privacy of his own chamber did he wipe away the spittle and rinse his face. His hands shook as he began planning Katherine Cahill's fate.

TWENTY-THREE

KATHERINE WAS STILL SHAKING AS THEY ESCORTED HER OUT OF the building. She caught sight of Sam and Tracy amidst the phalanx of soldiers that moved like a tide across the courtyard to a row of metal doors set into the side of an overhanging buttress. One soldier drew aside a rusty bolt. The door swung open and they were shoved inside. The four short steps that led to the sunken floor of the cell were lost in gloom, and Katherine stumbled as the door clanged shut, cutting off all light except that from a narrow grate in the door.

Sam touched the spot behind his ear where he had been hit. It was sticky with blood. Tracy said, "Are you all right?" She reached toward him but Sam brushed her hand aside and took hold of Katherine by the shoulders. "You know what you've done here? Do you have any idea, even the faintest conception of what you've done?"

"I'm sorry—"

"Fuck *sorry.*" Sam released her.

"I don't blame her," Tracy said. "I'd do the same thing to a man who killed my children."

"Don't worry, you won't live long enough to have any."

"So she spit on him, big deal."

"It is a very big deal. You think this is Disneyland? You think we're wearing mouse ears and taking the Tayib Tower ride? This isn't America. It's not even Syria, for God's sake. The sun rises and sets on the whim of a man who bombs airplanes for breakfast and earns gold stars in heaven by killing Christians."

"You think he's going to keep us here?"

"If he doesn't kill us."

"Oh, come on."

Sam turned to Katherine. "She doesn't believe me. You tell her. You did research, you read books. Tell her what a joke it is over here when someone does what you just did."

"I didn't plan it, Sam. Something just . . . when he tore the pictures . . ."

Tracy's attention was still on Sam. "You're saying he'll kill us?"

With exaggerated patience Sam said, "Spitting on someone is a mortal insult. They kill men for doing it and they kill women for a whole lot less."

"It's just me, Sam," Katherine said. "You and Tracy didn't insult him—"

"Neither did your children."

The words chilled her. With her impetuous act she had put all their lives at risk.

"The government knows we're here," Tracy said. "The people at the embassy, they'll do something."

"Like they did for Mike?"

"Sam, they couldn't do anything for Mike because Tayib doesn't have him," Katherine said.

"How do you figure that?"

"I talked to Doug Livingston. He said—"

"Livingston? When?"

"Two days ago. He's sure that Imad Tayib doesn't have Mike. He said it was probably somebody Mike was doing business with, something illegal."

"Irskenian?"

"What?"

"Did he mention the name Irskenian?"

"No, why?"

"Never mind. Go on about Livingston. How'd you end up seeing him again?"

"That's the reason I stayed behind." She lowered her voice. "There's going to be an attack on this place. To kidnap Imad Tayib."

Sam cautioned her with a hand-wave. He went to the grate and looked out. In the courtyard a soldier was talking to the recruits in excited tones, probably telling those who hadn't witnessed it what had happened. He made sure no one was listening, then returned to the women. Katherine told them quietly about Bright Justice and her part in it. When she finished, Tracy said, "You knew all the time Mike wasn't here?"

"I thought it would be safer if you didn't know."

"What about me?" Sam said.

"Livingston said you were . . . well, unstable. After the way you acted when we arrived—"

"You know why I did that."

"I didn't know if it would happen again or how or why. All I knew was that we had a chance to get Tayib first and find Mike later." She turned to Tracy.

"I meant what I said last night. I won't give up until we find him."

"You planning on being reincarnated as a bloodhound?"

Tracy frowned. "Saying stuff like that isn't going to help us get out of here."

"I'm not the one who got us in here."

"Well, you know these people and how their minds work. You're supposed to guide us."

"I'm the photographer, remember? I'm supposed to be on the other side of that door taking pictures of people on this side." He lit a cigarette. They were silent for a moment.

"What about this?" Tracy said. "We tell Tayib there's something important he should know and we'll tell him if he lets us go."

"Sure, and he'll pull out our fingernails and stick pins in our eyes until we tell him and then he'll kill us. After that he'll turn off the electricity long enough to lure the choppers to come here so the missiles can shoot them down. *American assault repelled by valiant Yellow Wind soldiers*—great publicity."

Katherine had been only half-listening. Now she looked up. "Sam, I want to talk to Naguib. Can you tell the guards to get him?"

"What for?"

"If I can get you two out of here, you could call Livingston and let the Delta team know I'm here. Maybe they can get me out. Either way you'd be safe and I'd have a better chance than if we all just sit and wait."

"How are you going to get us out?"

She explained what she had in mind. At first they rejected the plan but finally Sam sent for Naguib.

Katherine stood on her toes at the grate and spoke to him. "Tell Imad Tayib I know he doesn't have Mike Winn. Tell him these people with me are innocent—they didn't know what I was going to do. Tell him I'll give him the money—make a donation, whatever he wants—if he frees Sam and Tracy immediately. I'll write out a will leaving my entire estate to the Red Crescent. That's over five million dollars if he frees these people."

"The Imam is at prayer, I will tell him when he is finished."

They waited in silence, aware that as the minutes ticked away the chances of reaching the Delta team diminished: it would take an hour to drive to a town with a phone; long distance lines were notoriously erratic; Livingston might not be at the office; it might not be possible to contact the Delta Force . . .

Naguib did not return until five o'clock, this time accompanied by soldiers. "Mr. Gaddis and Mrs. Winn will come with me. You must remain here."

Tracy embraced Katherine and whispered, "We'll get you out of here, I promise." The girl's eyes glistened and Katherine thought, This is how it would feel to have a grown daughter. Sam hesitated, then extended his hand. "I hate leaving you like this but I'd hate it worse if I stayed."

"You remember the number?"

"Yeah, yeah, 707 just like the airplane."

Katherine nodded. The call to Livingston was her only hope.

They were silhouetted for a moment in the wash of light at the door, then darkness. Exhausted, Katherine slid to the floor, her back against the cold rock wall. If the Delta attack failed she would die. Worse,

Tayib might torture her. She had read Amnesty International reports detailing horrors ranging from broken bones and lacerations to electric shocks and sexual abuse. She imagined herself screaming in pain while strangers watched with cold satisfaction. It wasn't the pain she feared so much as the ignominy of the body's reaction to it, the degrading loss of control . . .

Something tickled her wrist, started up her arm. With a cry she scrambled to her feet and stared at the floor, trying to pierce the gloom. A cockroach. She stepped back and stumbled. The irony of her situation struck her. With every likelihood of being killed, she was worrying about bugs crawling on her arm.

Footsteps outside, the clang of a bolt and light flooded the cell. Naguib and five soldiers stood in the doorway. "You will come with us."

Her stomach tightened. "Why?"

"Imad Tayib has said it."

The will, she thought, trying to calm herself. Nothing would happen until she had written the will. She blinked as she stepped into the light. Instead of the headquarters tower, they headed in the opposite direction. "Where are we going?"

"The Imam has sent for you."

"Where?"

"This way."

With Naguib leading the way, one guard at each arm and two behind, they left the castle and crossed the footbridge. Villagers watched somberly as they left the road and started up a hill pockmarked by hoofprints of goats. At its crest, backed by low gray clouds, Imad Tayib stood flanked by his five *shaheen*. The ominous figures filled her with dread.

As she came close she saw six armed soldiers waiting behind a stand of scrub pine. They're going to kill me, she thought. On this distant hill and miserable day this is where I'm going to die. She was so sure of it that when she saw Sam and Tracy, bound and gagged, standing five feet apart, it took a moment before she realized the two pits behind them were freshly dug graves.

Tayib stepped forward. "Do you still wish to spit in my face?"

"Why are they here—?"

"Your insult was great but greater still will be your remorse."

"They did *nothing.* I'm the one, for God's sake, let them go."

"Granting a favor is not a punishment. You wish to die, therefore you live. But one of these two will wash away your insult with his blood. It is for you to choose who will live and who will die."

"What?"

"Choose."

"You don't mean this, you can't—"

"Be grateful I do not execute you all."

She looked at Naguib. "Didn't you tell him?" And then to Tayib, "I'll give you everything, all my money, my estate, I'll make out a will, five million dollars, just let them go free."

"It is written that one will go free and one will this day join his God. That is your choice."

"No."

"Choose."

"I will *not.*"

"Then both will die on the count of five." Tayib's robe and the ones of the *shaheen* moved in unison before a gust of wind. He turned to Major Yazdi. "Kill them both."

"Five million dollars. You can give it to the Red Crescent, use it to feed your people, buy guns, anything you like . . ."

Yazdi called the men to attention. Three barrels pointed at Sam, three at Tracy. Katherine ran into the line of fire and turned, arms outspread. "Kill me, let them go."

Soldiers dragged her back, forcing her arms behind her back. When she struggled, Tayib hit her across the mouth. Her eyes watered and she tasted blood.

"If you do not choose, both of your friends will die. For the last time—"

"You killed my children, what more do you want?"

Tayib stepped away and nodded curtly toward Yazdi. He raised his hand and began to count in Arabic, *"Wahid. . . ."*

Sam Gaddis lifted his eyes, keenly aware of the sky, the blustery wind, the low-lying clouds, the intermittent sunlight's touch on a rocky peak. The months since Faye's death paraded before him, a time of dissipation and waste. He called forth her memory but saw only the specter of death and he realized with awful clarity that, like some dark star, Faye had pulled him into her orbit and consumed him.

". . . ithneen. . . ."

Tracy lifted her chin defiantly. *Kill me and let Sam go.* She wanted to say it but her life stretched before her and she couldn't speak. The smell of distant rain brought tears to her eyes. *I can't die. Not here, not now, not this way.*

"... *talata*...."

Beg, Katherine thought. You have to do *something*. Get down on your knees, beg, promise anything
... But she couldn't make herself do it. Not in front of the man who killed her children."

"... *arba'a*...."

"Wait." Katherine's voice cracked. "Wait, I'll choose."

Tayib raised a hand and the soldiers froze.

"Which will you save?"

She looked at Tracy. You're my responsibility, she thought. You're the one I brought here, the one I chose to give me a reason to reach Imad Tayib. I led you to this moment, it's my fault ...

She turned to Sam and saw in his eyes that he already knew her decision. Her lips formed the words soundlessly, I'm sorry. He nodded slightly, but his eyes were distant, his attention focused on some far personal horizon. She took a deep breath and said to Tayib, "It's you who kill an innocent man. Let Tracy live."

Tayib turned to Yazdi. "The girl lives. You have your orders."

Yazdi let his hand drop. "... *khamsa*."

A ragged volley cracked the chilly air. Fabric danced and blood blossomed across her chest as the impact carried Tracy backward into the grave. Time stopped. Sam stared at the empty spot next to him. The echoes of the gunshots were drowned by Katherine's anguished cry.

Imad Tayib smiled.

TWENTY-FOUR

KATHERINE RAN FORWARD. TRACY LAY CRUMPLED ON HER SIDE, legs slightly drawn up, one knee propped against the edge of the shallow grave. Blood darkened the earth beneath her.

"Tracy . . ." She climbed into the pit. The girl's body was warm, her arm heavy as Katherine felt for a pulse. There was none. "No," she whispered, "please, *no*." She placed two fingers against her neck searching for the heartbeat she knew was forever stilled.

"Now you must bury her." Naguib stood at the edge of the grave with a shovel.

Enraged, Katherine climbed out and faced him. The others had gone, leaving only Naguib and four soldiers who shifted uneasily as she turned to each, her bloody hand held up high. "Is this how you win your freedom? You think this makes you worthy of a homeland, because you can shoot a woman? Bomb an airplane? You're worthy of *nothing. Nothing—*"

They fell back as she came toward them. "Go ahead, you've got guns. Kill me, too. What's the matter? I'm a woman, I qualify. Or do you have to tie me first? You can't kill someone unless they're tied and gagged. Give me the gun, I'll show you how. Killing is easy, the easiest thing in the world, just pull the trigger."

She worked her way back to Naguib, who held his ground. "You." she said. "Her blood is on your head." She reached toward him but Naguib used his shovel as a shield.

"You must bury her."

"You do it, you killed her."

"She is an infidel; if you do not bury her she will remain as she is."

Katherine grabbed the shovel, closed her eyes against the horror of what she was about to do. *Forgive me.* Stones mixed with the earth grated against the metal blade. Focus, she thought, don't give in to grief . . . that's what he wants, that's why he did this. Tayib's malevolence was like a physical presence, disembodied, probing, searching for weakness—

Sam. God, she had almost forgotten him. Had they taken him back to the cell? She risked a glance at her watch. Five-thirty, less than two hours until the attack. She had failed Tracy, she could not fail Sam. I have to free him, but how? She slowed her pace while her mind raced. Naguib watched, bored, while the soldiers sat on their heels and shared a cigarette.

AT THE United States Signals Intercept Station in Urgazi, Turkey, Major Layton surveyed the sky. All day clouds had gathered and the forecast was for rain. Not a good omen. He and his Delta team had been here for two weeks, a time of clear nights and starlit skies. A few days ago D-day had been inexplicably postponed, but now they were scheduled for launch and it looked like rain.

He watched the flight crews remove the camouflage covering from the three Sikorsky HH60A Night Hawks. It was not the presence of the helicopters, so much as their modifications, that the army wanted to conceal, items that advertised a low-level night mission, like the periscope lens, part of the Lumina infrared night vision system, and the two scythe-like cable cutters outthrust above and below the cabin. Painted black and without insignia, their arched back and upswept tail reminded Layton of a leaping dolphin.

A man in a dark green flight suit stopped beside him. The flight leader, Captain Perez, was chewing gum. "Ready for fun and games?"

"We may get rain."

Perez contemplated the sky. "Birds fly in the rain and bats don't. The rain screws up their sonar. They get false reflections, think they're flying into trees when they're in the open, dodge out of the way and hit a barn. That's what my uncle told me once. I never found out if it was true."

"Which are we, bats or birds?"

Perez smiled at some private joke. "Death on wings."

He wandered off, leaving Layton irritated by the pilot's insouciance because it surpassed his own. He returned to the Ready Room, where men with blackened faces sat watching a video movie they had seen a dozen times since their arrival. Layton shut off the television and began a final equipment check.

KATHERINE WORKED as slowly as she dared. If she could keep from being locked up again, there was a chance she could somehow escape and free Sam in the confusion of the attack. But just before six o'clock Naguib called a halt. "That's sufficient."

"I'm not finished."

"Finish tomorrow. Imad Tayib is waiting."

They returned to the castle, where Naguib took her to a classroom lit by three buzzing fluorescent lights hung by chains from the ceiling. The room was filled with young men, recruits, sitting on benches at long tables. The boisterous chatter subsided and all eyes turned toward her as Naguib indicated a stool in front of a blackboard. "Sit, please."

She faced at least thirty recruits, men with shocks of black hair and luminous brown eyes who regarded her with silent curiosity. Their uniforms were a hodgepodge of heavy trousers and loose shirts, but identical arm bands proclaimed their allegiance to the Yellow Wind. A map on the wall showed Arab lands without an Israel. Cutaway models, crudely painted, of hand grenades, land mines and a rocket launcher sat on a shelf.

Imad Tayib entered, his black robe flowing behind him. The recruits jumped to their feet and greeted him. Tayib motioned for them to sit. In English he said to Katherine, "These are my followers, young men whose zeal for justice will force your countrymen from our land. Like raindrops that bring forth the invisible desert flower they will nourish the seeds of Arab nationalism and bring forth a united Arab nation—"

"You'll never live to see it." The flowery language struck her as obscene.

"Allah knows, man knows not. He has shown me a vision of the *Rih Asfar,* the burning wind from the east which will turn the earth to ash and rock to burned cotton. The Yellow Wind will seek out the unbeliever no matter if he hides beneath the mountain or behind the palace gates. His flesh will blacken and fall from the bone and only the faithful shall survive."

"Led by a killer who hides his lust for blood in piety."

Tayib's eyes narrowed. "You invite death to escape your own guilt, but you will live to know the full measure of remorse."

One of the *shaheen* entered with her purse. Katherine held her breath as Tayib emptied the contents onto the nearest table: wallet, guide book, pills, calculator, checkbook, address book—and the Mont Blanc pen. Tayib picked up a plastic canister and read the label. "Darvocet." He inspected a sheet of metal foil dappled with yellow pills in plastic bubbles. "Chlor-Trimeton." He looked at Katherine. "Your headaches are your refusal to hear the word of God."

She was surprised. Had he guessed about the headaches or was he familiar with the drugs?

Tayib held up the pills and spoke to the class in disparaging tones. He returned to Katherine. "Two medicines for a single headache when the children of Palestine have not enough sulfanilamide to prevent ringworm or enough tetracycline to cure them of typhus. This is the waste of the West. In the contents of your purse we see the indifference to the suffering of Arabs.''

And I see that you have a familiarity with Western medicine, she thought. What else could she learn about Tayib's past?

Tayib handed the bubbled metal foil to the *shaheen,* who took a hammer and nailed it to the wall. He picked up two sets of keys, one of them to the rental car. "How many cars do you have? Three? Four?''

"One.''

"An expensive car—a Mercedes-Benz? a Rolls-Royce?''

"None of your business." Her attention was on the Mont Blanc. One of the recruits had picked it up and was admiring it.

"The oil beneath Arab lands is none of *your* business, but you do not hesitate to exploit it." He waved the keys at the class, denounced them in Arabic and tossed them to the *shaheen,* who drove a nail into the wall and hung them on it.

My God, Katherine thought, it's some macabre version of Show and Tell.

Tayib opened her wallet and pulled out a business card. "Who is Coldwell Banker?" She said nothing. "It says here *real estate.* Do you buy and sell land? Is that how you make your fortune?''

"I sold my home because I no longer had a family." You son of a bitch.

"Palestinians lose homes and families within them to American-made bombs." Another denunciation in Arabic and the card was nailed in place beside the car keys. Tayib held up another card. "Who is Brian Cahill?" She stared at him. "Father? Brother?

His address is here. Greenwich, Connecticut. Perhaps he would pay a great deal of money for your safety." Tayib tucked the card inside the folds of his *galabiya.*

Katherine's attention was on the Mont Blanc. The recruit had unscrewed the cap and was testing the nib on the back of his hand. She reached for it. "May I have my pen, please?"

The recruit gave it to her but Tayib placed his hand over it. "Let me see." He twisted it from her fingers and inspected it. "How much did this cost?"

"I don't know." She reached but Tayib pulled it away.

"How much?"

She told him. He brought out his own pen, a cheap plastic one, held them both up and expounded in Arabic, brandishing first one and then the other. He turned to Katherine. "The cost of this pen could feed a refugee family for a year."

He tossed it to the *shaheen,* who drove a nail into the wall and hung the pen from it by its clip. "Use this," Tayib said, handing her the plastic one. "You will discover that it writes as well as one which steals meat from the table and milk from the baby's mouth."

She hesitated, her attention fixed on the weapon now dangling against the wall. She fantasized lunging at Tayib and firing it into his heart. A fantasy because, even if she could reach the pen, it would take valuable seconds to unscrew the top and cock the hammer. And there was Sam, who would pay the price for such an act. No, there had been enough death on her account.

Tayib removed Katherine's credit cards and spread them across the table. He picked up each in turn. "Bloomingdale's, Bergdorf Goodman, Harrods,

Saks Fifth Avenue. This is wasteful. You need only one card. Which is the best?"

"There is no best."

"This one, American Express. With a Roman gladiator pictured on it. You think of yourselves as conquerors, we see it here in your credit card. But when America comes to Arabia, we will break you." He bent the card in half and tossed it to her. "You can keep this one."

The Visa card was embossed with a hologram of an eagle. Tayib angled it back and forth. "See what your Western technology produces? Here is a vision of an eagle; tip the card and the eagle moves, you can see its wings stretch toward you, its eye is bright. This is the very image of an eagle but is it an eagle? No. Such is the deceit of the West."

He gave instructions to the *shaheen*, who, instead of nailing it to the wall, took a knife and cut out the hologram, then carved the remaining portion of the card into matching pieces. None of it made any sense, and Katherine had a growing feeling of unreality.

Tayib held up a blue-and-white card. "A Pan American World Pass. Your corporations reflect the arrogance of your culture. Do you think you own the world that you can purchase it with a ticket? A pass to the world that is not yours."

One by one he vilified all the cards and handed them to the *shaheen*, who proceeded to cut them into postage-stamp-size pieces. Katherine wanted to shout, *I don't have to take this,* but knew it was better to let him talk. Let him turn every article of her life into some sort of warped proof that the West had wronged him. As long as I'm not locked up when the attack comes, she thought, there's a chance I can find Sam and escape. She glanced at her watch. An hour until the explosion. Ignoring Tayib, she stared over the heads of the recruits and imagined their faces, Jeff, Allison, Joey . . .

THE DELTA team boarded the helicopters at six-thirty. They wore lightweight Kevlar body armor beneath black jumpsuits. Tiny speakers nestled in each man's ear would allow Layton to communicate with all of them simultaneously. They carried weapons suited to special tasks: Heckler & Koch submachine guns, an Armbrust shoulder-launched RPG with armor-piercing shells, flame throwers, automatic shotguns. On their belts, smoke grenades and concussion bombs, "flash-bangs," as well as the climbing equipment they would need for rappelling down the face of the building. One man in each team spoke Arabic. All of them carried a photograph of Imad Tayib.

There was a whine of jet engines, the heavy blades turned slowly then blurred as the first chopper shuddered, tilted forward and slid into the air. One by one the dark shapes disappeared into the gathering gloom and headed west along the Turkish border. The Night Hawks would reach their orbit point seventeen minutes before the detonation was scheduled. After that it was eleven minutes to Raqba, six minutes over the castle, then forty-one minutes back to Urgazi: total time to kidnap one Arab terrorist, one hundred and thirteen minutes.

If the rain didn't screw things up.

● ● ●

TAYIB WAS enjoying himself. Katherine Cahill's insult had created an unpardonable image in the minds of his soldiers and recruits. This was true even for those who were not on hand; all had heard about the incident. It was an image that now had to be usurped by one more vivid and memorable—an image of Katherine Cahill's humiliation.

Tayib opened her cosmetics bag and dumped out lipstick, rouge, eyeliner and mascara. He spoke in Arabic. "You see here before you a woman who has already spent more money on her hair, her eyes, her cheeks and lips than your father earned in all his life."

He handed Katherine the lipstick. "Apply your paint. Show them the artificial beauty of an American woman."

"No."

"Put on the lipstick."

She ignored him. Tayib's hand disappeared beneath his robe and reappeared with Brian's business card. "Greenwich, Connecticut. Is that a difficult city to find? A difficult address to discover? How long a flight to America? How hard would it be for my men to find Brian Cahill's house, his wife, his children?" Katherine paled. "Yes, our reach is long as the wind which knows no boundary. It sweeps across oceans and continents with equal ease and with such ease my men can go to America." He twirled the card in front of her. "In your obedience lies the safety of this family. Apply the lipstick."

If I buried Tracy, she thought, I can do this. Her hand shook as she removed the cap. The pale color was not the garish red Tayib would have preferred but this was a small matter. As the sand wears away the mountain in tiny increments, he thought, so will I strip away your illusions of superiority until you stand humbled and subservient before me.

"Now the eye makeup. Apply it."

He could feel her hatred. Good. They were approaching a critical point which required him to judge the limit of his control with care. If she should spit on him now he would have to break her teeth and force them down her throat. The greater skill was to break her will without bruising her body.

"And now the perfume."

The students followed her every move. She unscrewed the cap, tipped the bottle to her forefinger and touched her forehead, her chest, her left shoulder, her right: the unbeliever's sign of the cross. Tayib's face darkened with a rush of anger.

"Stand up," he said coldly. He turned to the group and spoke in Arabic. "This is how the woman of the West advertises her charms to the stranger on the street. Today she considers herself superior to our mothers, our wives, our daughters, but look at her: is her hair richer, her ear more gracefully turned, her breath sweeter, her lips as full, her breasts softer, or thighs more warm of welcome than those of a chaste Arab girl? Women like this your forefathers took as concubines and purchased at slave markets for their evening entertainment."

He turned to Katherine. "Open your mouth."

"Go to hell."

His voice was too soft. "Hear me now. As Allah is my witness the house in Greenwich will burn to the ground if you do not obey me. Open your mouth."

For a moment he was afraid she would refuse, but finally she parted her lips.

"Wider."

Her mouth opened. His finger stretched toward her, she pulled back. He paused, let his eyes communicate the threat, then reached forward. This time she held her position as his forefinger traced her lips. In Arabic he said, "You see how the Westerner can be tamed. The lips which only this morning spit insults now give us warm welcome." He slid a finger into her mouth. Katherine slapped his hand away and the recruits laughed.

Still speaking to the recruits, he said, "I make her a gift to you, a living example of how the Westerner can be brought to heel. Tonight she shall become the bride of the *Rih Asfar,* available to any who wish to taste a woman of the West. The ceremonial tent is now being prepared. Let the man who is to be her first groom be chosen."

The squares of the credit cards were dumped into a wicker basket, which was passed above the heads of the recruits. One by one they drew out a piece. Before they reached the last man, a thickset boy with a beard of black cornsilk whispered to his companions, who called out, "Mehdi has the eagle. He has it here."

Tayib said, "What is your name?"

"Mehdi Bakhtiar."

"Stand up."

Embarrassed by the lewd comments and laughter, Mehdi got to his feet.

Tayib turned to Katherine. "You have learned obedience, now you will learn humility. You are the bride of the *Rih Asfar* and this man will be your first husband. He will come to you after prayers this evening. As long as you please him or any of my followers the family of Mr. Brian Cahill in Greenwich, Connecticut, is safe. If you fail to arouse desire—if you fight and scratch a man's eye or lie dumb like the carcass of a sheep . . . on that day a man begins the journey to Greenwich and his name shall be Death."

He expected the fear, the revulsion, and the hatred that he saw in her eyes but beneath these he sensed something else. You still hide something, but I will find it. As the fox drives the pheasant from the grass I will drive the hidden secret from your heart and destroy you.

TWENTY-FIVE

SAM WAS IN A STATE OF EUPHORIA WHEN THEY MARCHED HIM back to the castle. He walked with a light step, his every sense alert, every impression fresh. The smell of wood smoke, the cry of a sparrow, the wind in his hair, the sight of silver-rimmed clouds tumbling against the mountain peak—he experienced all of them vividly, with a wonder he'd never known. Even after the door to the cell clanged shut it took a while before his perspective returned to normal. He'd had a reprieve, but for how long? No firing squad today, but tomorrow? One thing was certain: if he wanted to escape from this place he had to be outside the cell when the attack came. What could possibly induce his jailers to open the cell door?

He looked at his watch. The explosion was set for seven twenty-five. How long after that would the attack begin? He wished he had questioned Katherine in more detail. And where was she? The look on her face when she ran forward to the grave would be forever etched in his mind. Had they killed her? No, probably not. Tayib had plans for them, or they'd have died with Tracy.

Tayib's plans . . . why had he kept Sam alive? Ransom? Torture? Execution? Whatever the reason, the guards would be charged with his safekeeping. This gave him an idea. The hangman hated to be cheated of his victim—what would happen if they thought he was dying? If he could get out of the cell before the attack started Sam was sure that he could escape the castle in the resulting confusion. But timing was important. He sat down and waited as daylight faded and the gloomy cell became opaque. He heard the muezzin's call to prayer and waited impatiently for it to end. Finally Tayib's voice boomed out over the loudspeaker. Sam went to the grate and yelled until he attracted the attention of a soldier. Pretending disorientation and shortness of breath he said, "I'm a diabetic, need medicine, insulin. Call Naguib. Tell him to come quick."

"What are you talking about?"

"Diabetic shock. A medical condition. Get Naguib. Go, find him . . ."

Five minutes later, when the guard returned with Naguib, they found Sam face down on the floor breathing with the sound of gravel in his throat. Naguib called to him with rising concern but Sam remained motionless, his face pressed against the floor. Come on, come on, I'm a sick son of a bitch. Open the door.

They did. As soon as the bolt slid free, Sam leaped forward, slammed the door into Naguib's face, and lunged past the guard. Pools of light illuminated the grounds. Tayib's amplified voice in his nightly broadcast drowned Naguib's shouts as Sam ran toward the castle's entrance, where three soldiers moved out from the brightly lit doorway. He veered away—before they saw him, he hoped, and headed toward a low hill lost in darkness at the far end of the parade ground. Footsteps hard behind him. A look over his shoulder. The guard, running hard but without his weapon, was gaining on him, while, further back, Naguib had attracted the attention of more soldiers.

A place to hide . . . keep out of sight for half an hour and maybe I can get the hell out of here in the confusion of the attack. He slowed as he raced up the slope. At the top of the embankment he ran into a chicken-wire fence, invisible until the last moment. He fell, rolled free and was up and running across furrowed ground that threatened to twist his feet from under him. A garden of some kind? He could hear the guard's heavy breathing, then a grunt as the man tackled him.

They hit the ground together. Sam kicked at him but the man clawed his way on top of him. With their hands at each other's throats they rolled once, twice, and dropped into a dark pit. Sam's shoulder and feet struck opposite sides of a rock lip, then nothing—except terrible darkness. His attacker's cry of alarm ended abruptly as they plunged into black, icy water.

Darkness and the muted sound of bubbles but no sense of gravity, no up or down. Sam forced himself to stay immobile until his body's natural buoyancy could assert itself. He kicked upward, broke free and gulped the air. Lost in darkness, he heard the guard coughing and splashing. Faint squares of light from four holes far above him, one of them interrupted by black figures, shouting down, "Kemal, are you all right? Can you swim?"

"Enough, yes."

"Not if I drown you first," Sam called out. He was gratified by the sound of Kemal swimming frantically in the opposite direction. *What the hell is this place?* An easy side stroke brought him to a vertical wall. The stone face was chiseled flat—the cavern was man-made. *Which way?*

Bobbing flashlight beams illuminated the walls of a tunnel-like entrance near the top of an arched ceiling. He could see Kemal now, doing an awkward dog paddle, gasping for breath. Sam swam in the opposite direction. Flashlights appeared and shadows of men leaped, danced thirty feet high along the walls. He hoped the far shore would offer protection but, as the flashlight's beam swept the vast expanse, he realized he was trapped in a huge cavern. From the single entrance near the ceiling, stairs led to the water's edge where his pursuers had gathered. A ray of light bobbed toward him. Sam reduced his effort so that only his nose was above the water. Finally they spotted him and a shot rang out, ricocheted.

"Don't," someone shouted. "The walls curve and your bullets may hit us."

"Imad Tayib wants me alive," Sam yelled. A stunned pause. Echoed whispers. "He speaks Arabic—"

"Don't worry, he can't get away—"

"Help me," Kemal shouted. He was twenty feet from the stairs. One of the soldiers swam out to him; the noise of their efforts obscured the conversation of the others. Sam, at the far end of the cavern, kicked off his shoes and treaded water. The soldiers managed to pull Kemal to safety, and as they did a deep, hollow voice called, "Mr. Gaddis, come out. No one will harm you."

"Come and get me."

"You will drown."

With your head under my arm, he thought grimly.

"Mr. Gaddis?"

Still short of breath, Sam didn't respond. He reduced the energy of his strokes, gently swirling the water to conserve his energy. If only the choppers would get there . . .

THIS IS not happening, Katherine thought. Naguib had left her with a tiny woman named Hooda and four assistants. They were in a bath chamber where a yellow-and-blue tile tub the size of a fountain was surrounded by benches of varying heights. There was a fire in the hearth and suspended above it like an oversize gravy boat was a metal tank filled with water. As Katherine watched the water was spilled into a rock channel that emptied into the bath. The air was damp with steam and smelled of incense.

Hooda poked her arm and said something in Arabic. Katherine shook her head, "I don't understand." They gestured for her to take off her clothes.

"You're *women*," Katherine said, "why are you doing this?"

Hooda's bony nose and wispy gray hair showed from beneath her headscarf. She repeated her command impatiently. The younger women, all dressed in dark *galabiyas,* watched with open curiosity.

"No," Katherine said, shaking her head, talking

to herself. Hooda's hands sliced the air as she issued a string of commands. The other women circled warily around her, while Hooda advanced wielding a broom like a staff. Bright Justice was still half an hour away, Katherine thought. Let them have their stupid charade as long as it used up time.

"All *right*," she said. She unbuttoned her blouse and slipped it off, then stepped out of her slacks. Still in her underwear she stepped into the tiled fountain, where the hot water stung her ankles. Hooda gestured; she was to undress completely.

"Fine," she muttered to herself. She slipped off her bra and panties, which the women passed among themselves, fingering the French lace. Katherine sank into the water as far as she could. Naked, surrounded by strangers, she felt more vulnerable than she would have facing Tayib's firing squad. Two of the women hitched up their robes and stepped into the water with her. One filled a dented pot and lifted it, but Katherine drew back. The woman mimicked washing her hair.

"*I'll* do it," Katherine said. The second woman scooped a thick highly scented shampoo from a jar, but again Katherine insisted on doing it herself. While she lathered her hair, the first woman tried to wash her back with a cloth. Katherine grabbed it from her. "I *said* I'll do it."

The woman complained but Hooda waved her silent. They went through the same routine after the bath when Katherine stepped out and two women tried to dry her. She took the towels and dried herself, then brushed her hair and applied the heavy perfume they insisted she wear. She accepted help only when they fitted her with the *galabiya*, first the pale under-robe, followed by an embroidered black one. Last was a black headscarf embroidered in gold.

Hooda gave her a glass of water that smelled faintly of roses. Katherine took a small swallow and the women burst out laughing. Hooda held up the glass and demonstrated: she took a mouthful, sloshed it noisily between her teeth and spit it out. A mouthwash, not a drink. Katherine followed her example and they seemed satisfied.

Because her watch had been removed before the bath, it wasn't until Tayib's voice rang out over the loudspeakers that Katherine knew prayers were over. The soldiers escorted her across a courtyard to a large tent with pale translucent walls. God, I need the attack to begin now, she thought.

A soldier pulled back the flap and motioned her inside. Katherine was seized with the terrible foreboding that if she entered the tent she would never come out alive. A rough hand on the small of her back. Before she could turn or protest he shoved her inside and closed the flap.

HIGH ABOVE the clouds that obscured the Syrian border a Sentry E-3B surveillance plane monitored the radar emissions from Mount Kajar. When the radar signature disappeared at seven twenty-five the signals officer on board relayed the information to the assault team.

"Candy Units this is Big Store. You are Go for Bright Justice. Repeat you are Go for Bright Justice."

As they turned toward the Syrian border the helicopters descended into a broad valley where they would be hidden below the mountain peaks. The copilot flipped down the night-vision goggles and the advancing terrain popped out at him on a monochrome green-and-black video screen. They bounced up briefly to clear a ridge and then headed down another valley. A horizontal shadow on the video screen, a slap on the window, the quick scrape and tang of metal as the chopper jerked and recovered.

Major Layton leaned into the cockpit. "Problem?"

The pilot said nothing; his eyes raced over the instruments: temperature, pressures, rpm's—all looked normal. The copilot said, "Cable strike."

The entire area was mapped, how could they hit an unknown cable? Layton wanted more information but the pilots were preoccupied. Apparently the scythe-like cutter had done its job, but if the rotor was decapitated they'd drop like a rock. He turned around and faced the cabin. In the dim red light his men stared at him, tension evident beneath their face-black camouflage. This was the worst part, Layton decided. For all his team's skill at assault, scaling buildings, rescuing hostages and dropping terrorists, here in a helicopter flying two miles a minute up a quick-twisting canyon, they were just so much human baggage.

WHEN KATHERINE stumbled into the tent, Mehdi Bakhtiar, eyes glistening with anticipation, looked up at her. He sat on a low couch and had exchanged his fatigues for a white *galabiya* with an embroidered collar and sleeves. Katherine's attention was drawn to the opposite side of the tent, to a bed covered by rose-colored damask and surrounded by flower petals, which lent the air a sweet fragrance. Amber light from a half-dozen kerosene lamps suffused the tent. Mehdi said something in Arabic and pointed to a spot beside him.

"No, thank you." It sounded stupid under such circumstances.

A pot of tea sat on a charcoal brazier next to the couch. Mehdi poured tea into two small cups without handles, lifted one and held it toward her. She was about to refuse and then thought, Why not? Anything to waste time until the attack.

"All right." She came forward, her feet sinking into the thickly carpeted floor, and accepted the cup. Mehdi waited for her to drink first. Drugged, she wondered? She took a sip. Mehdi smiled and slurped his tea noisily. A bulky young man with heavy yellow teeth hidden behind lips as delicately shaped as a girl's, he patted the couch again and said something in Arabic.

"Your name is Mehdi?" Katherine said.

He beamed and nodded, pointing to himself and repeating his name.

"I'm Katherine."

He repeated it and she nodded. "That's right, *Katherine.*" I have a *name,* I'm a person . . . Listen, Mehdi, do you speak any English?"

His response included only one recognizable word—*arabee.* Mehdi spoke only Arabic. He stood up and motioned her to sit. Okay, she thought, we'll share some tea and maybe there's a way to humanize the situation. She sat down and he joined her eagerly.

"Mehdi, you're Muslim, aren't you? Islam. I read about your religion and it's not right what you're doing. Whatever Imad Tayib said, don't let his words fool you. Don't let them destroy who I am, who *you* are. Whatever you've heard about America, our differences, I'm still a human being. Whatever he's told you about me is not true, I'm a woman like your mother or sister or the girl you want to marry." She knew it was crazy, talking in a language he probably couldn't understand a word of, but she had to try. Maybe the tone . . .

His eyes ran down her body and he held up his cup, grinned and drank.

"Mehdi, I don't want to be here, I don't belong here do you . . . understand? I don't want this . . ." She pointed to herself, then to the tent, and shook her head. He nodded happily and also pointed. She turned to look but it was her hair he was indicating, and now reached to touch it. She moved off. "Don't do that."

His expression soured. "Here," she said, trying to distract him, "have more tea." Her arm was outstretched and she was leaning forward when he grabbed her breast. She dropped the pot and jumped up. *"Stop* it."

Mehdi reached for her leg but she dodged his hand and crossed quickly to the door. He called out and two guards appeared. Katherine tried to step between them, but one man wrapped his arms around her from behind and shoved his pelvis against her buttocks. With his face pressed against her neck, he made thrusting motions and bleated like a goat in her ear—*naa, naa, naa.* The guard in the doorway laughed and shouted encouragement. Katherine twisted free and stumbled back. Mehdi elbowed the guard away and spoke angrily. Maybe they would fight each other and leave her alone, but with a lewd gesture the guard went back outside. And Mehdi pointed at the bed. She didn't understand the words but she got the meaning loud and clear.

"La," she said, Arabic for no. She'd learned that much.

From inside his robe he brought out Brian's business card and waved it at her. She grabbed it, he took her arm and they struggled. She dropped the card, but Mehdi kept his fingers locked in hers, bent her arms back, forcing her to her knees to keep her wrists from breaking. He leaned down to kiss her, and when she turned her face from side to side he wrenched her hands back, then with a sudden movement stepped forward, pushed her onto her back and sat on her stomach. Grinning, he tried to pin her arms—

"It's not a damn game—"

He trapped one arm beneath his knee and used his free hand to tug open her robe, exposing her breasts. Somehow, she managed to free her arm and hit him in the face. For a moment they flailed at one another before his fingers closed around her wrists. He leaned down, outspreading her arms, brought his lips to her breast. His mouth was hot and his moustache moved like a caterpillar against her skin. She could smell the cologne in his hair while his tongue dodged insistently at her nipple.

Enraged, Katherine bucked and pitched him onto his side. She scrambled to her feet—but Mehdi caught her robe and used it to pull himself up. He embraced her and they careened awkwardly across the room, sending a tea cup flying against the tent wall. She was caught in a bear hug now, his arms locked around her chest. He began to squeeze.

"Stop it, I can't breathe—"

With an abrupt motion he locked his fingers and tightened his grip. Katherine felt as if a thousand-pound weight were lying on her chest; she had to take a deep breath . . . He pulled tighter and the room began to spin . . . Going to kill me . . . a scream, more a ragged hiccup, as the last bit of air was cut off, and she blacked out.

SAM SHIVERED in the icy water and prayed for the attack to begin. His pursuers still stood at the landing, blocking the only way out. Someone kept a flashlight trained on him, but they had given up trying to persuade him to come out of the water. What time was it? What was going on out there? *And where was the damn Delta team?*

Commotion and voices from the stairs as a new group arrived. Naked men in silhouette. Someone called out, "Ali, are you ready?"

The answer came from an opening in the roof. "Go ahead."

Five splashes as the men leaped one after the other into the water. Great, Sam thought. These guys are fresh while my arms feel like stone. What if they're armed? Have knives? What if Tayib has given the order to kill me?

In the unsteady gleam of the flashlight, a rope snaked its way from the opening in the ceiling, a noose spinning slowly. One of the swimmers grabbed the loop as he passed. When they got to Sam, who had his back against the wall, they formed a half-circle around him. The sounds were close now of men breathing and the slosh of water. Come on, mother-fuckers, Sam thought desperately, I'll drown you all.

At the leader's command they converged on him. Sam ducked below the surface, pushed off the wall and swam under the water until he surfaced fifteen feet away. He headed for the far wall but three of the men were excellent swimmers and caught up with him. Again he was encircled.

This time when they came at him he didn't dive deep enough. His shoulders brushed the feet of a swimmer who kicked him in the back. Air bubbled and water trickled down his throat. He swam as fast as he could to the surface, and then they were on him, hands grabbing, a fist in the side of the head, a knee in the stomach. He felt the rope over his shoulders and flung it aside. Someone gripped his head from behind, forcing him beneath the surface. In the struggle he forgot about the rope until he felt it beneath his arms.

"Pull," someone screamed in Arabic, "pull *now*."

The noose tightened around his chest. He tried to slip out of it but managed only to catch his thumb beneath the tightening loop. The soldiers fell away and water swirled as he swung pendulum-like to a spot directly beneath the opening. Gravel and dirt splattered the water, the rope tightened and his feet were free, kicking air. He rotated slowly as they hauled him up in short abrupt motions. His head banged on the underside of the cavern as they dragged him over the lip where eager hands pulled him out. They removed the rope and yanked him to his feet. He was exhausted and still gasping for breath when Major Yazdi punched him in the stomach.

Time, Sam thought, as they hustled him across the courtyard. A few more minutes, a few more seconds, the attack had to begin. When they reached the cell he grabbed the wall and braced himself until they nearly broke his fingers prying him loose. Someone lifted his feet and they carried him struggling and kicking into the cell. The door slammed, the bolt slid shut. He was still on the floor, panting for breath when the first explosion lit the rectangular grate in a blaze of white light. More explosions. Sam was on his feet, shoved his face against the grate.

"Ten seconds, you fuckers. You're ten seconds too late . . ."

TWENTY-SIX

KATHERINE HEARD THE DISTANT THUNDER OF APPROACHING helicopters moments before the first explosion. She had regained consciousness within moments to find Mehdi kneeling over her with a worried expression that cleared as soon as she opened her eyes. He said something she understood to be reassuring and shoveled his arms beneath her. She tried to protest but it was no use, she was still trying to recover her breath. Mehdi lifted her and staggered to the bed, where he put her on her back and stood up to strip off his clothes. He was tugging his underwear free of an erection when the first explosion shook the tent and lit up the walls.

Mehdi did a half-turn, and then, as the battle outside erupted, ran to the couch, retrieved his rifle and disappeared out the door. Katherine got to her feet. Overlapping explosions tore the night, men shouted, a woman screamed. She crossed quickly to the entrance and peered outside. The guards were gone. She started running.

The low clouds flickered with each explosion that rimmed the buildings in orange. A dark shape thundered overhead as tracers sliced across the court-yard and fingered the tent, which buckled, danced and disintegrated. She went to the classroom, telling herself that she wanted the Mont Blanc for a weapon but knowing the real reason was to take back the ele-ments of her life Tayib had stolen and ridiculed.

The room was unlocked and empty. Her belong-ings, including her purse, were still fixed to the wall like butterflies pinned in a collection. She grabbed the Mont Blanc first and tucked it toward a pocket. Except the *galabiya* had none. She broke a fingernail yanking her purse free, grabbed the rest of her posses-sions and threw them inside it. It took some fifteen seconds, but by the time she had moved outside she realized that she had misjudged the ferocity, and at-tendant chaos, of the attack. Thick white smoke bil-lowed from the headquarters building, threatening to isolate her on the wrong side of the castle.

Lifting her robe out of the way, she ran toward the prison cell. Down-wash from still-invisible heli-copters tugged at the *galabiya*. An explosion near the mosque illuminated a guard thrown high in the air. A stream of flame spewed from the sky, igniting the tents of the recruits. Running figures engulfed by thick white smoke turned into half-seen shadows. A high-pitched explosion sent fiery objects crazily spin-ning across the ground, giving forth high-pitched shrieks. Clouds of white smoke roiled forward, envel-oping her; the world shrank to a luminous white fog that ended five feet away.

A straight line, she thought, try to follow a straight line. A brilliant white flash, and a wall of hot air slammed her to the ground. Dazed, a ringing in her ears, she got to her knees and fumbled for her purse. A red orb danced in front of her eyes. Someone collided with her and went sprawling. When she turned to look, the red orb followed. Only her peripheral vision seemed intact. I'm blind, she thought. My God, how can I get out of here, I'm blind . . .

MAJOR LAYTON was in the first helicopter, Candy One. Candy One and Two carried the assault teams; Candy Three was an armored gunship whose mission was to create havoc among the defenders with concussion grenades, napalm, smoke bombs and "sizzlers," which exploded into a half-dozen self-propelled shrieking fireballs that spun madly across the ground.

An M262 illumination warhead provided one-million candlepower for the first fifteen seconds of the attack. After the roof was swept by a withering 2,000-rounds-per-minute, Delta team members slid like spiders down ropes and secured the top of the building. The first two helicopters angled away and took up protected positions in the shelter of the canyon while Candy Three continued disrupting and disorienting the soldiers in the courtyard.

Team Alpha attacked the stairway while Teams Bravo and Charlie rappelled down the face of the building into a layer of white smoke. Confusion reigned around them as they blew the main door with an Armbrust antitank projectile. Two grenades and two flash-bangs chucked inside, take cover, wait for the blast and rush the room. The battle was swift. Of

the fifteen Arab soldiers on the ground floor, three
were badly wounded by grenades and six temporarily
blinded. The rest made it to the stairs where two of
them opened fire. One member of Team Bravo was hit
in the leg before their opponents were killed. The remaining soldiers surrendered and Tayib's soldiers
were disarmed and forced against the wall. Each man
was quickly checked and identified—Imad Tayib was
not among them.

Team Bravo forced its way upstairs and linked up
with Team Alpha, entering from the roof. Together
they cleared Tayib's living quarters and massed outside the radio room. A solid wood door separated
them from their target. The heavy-weapons man fitted
the Armbrust RPG over his shoulder and braced himself. Layton signaled the go-ahead. A deafening blast,
the door shattered. Two men nearest the smoking
opening tossed flash-bangs inside, waited for the explosions, then rushed the room. One of the *shaheen,*
temporarily blinded, fired wildly. A shotgun blast
spun him against the wall. He slid to the floor, where
his white robe turned a slow, bright red.

Layton swept the room with his pistol: a radio
console, table, chairs, notebook, faded portrait of the
Ayatollah Khomeini and photograph of the Grand
Mosque in Mecca, a basket of fruit . . . .

There was no one else in the room. Tayib had
disappeared.

Impossible. The target had been broadcasting
when they attacked. No way he could have escaped
the building. Layton radioed the assault team: "Negative Yellowfox. Repeat, negative Yellowfox. Double
ID all hostiles."

As he finished speaking, two of Tayib's men

stumbled into the room followed by a Delta member with a shotgun. "Found them trying to squeeze out a window."

Layton glanced at his watch: four minutes ten seconds since the first shot and less than two minutes before extraction. He put a gun to the first man's head and said to his interpreter, "Ask him where Tayib is."

The prisoner's answer was to hunch his shoulders and keep silent. His companion, a young man wounded in the arm, smiled uneasily. Layton pointed at him. "You, you'll be next." He dropped the gun to the first man's crotch, and pulled the trigger. The prisoner collapsed, screaming in pain. Layton turned to the second man, pointed the gun at his face, then slowly lowered it. "Now ask this one: Where's Tayib?"

The prisoner, beginning to shake, moved to cover himself with his hands. But before the question could be put, a soldier rushed into the room. "Found him."

"Where?"

"A tunnel."

In Tayib's sleeping quarters a chest had been pulled aside revealing an opening in the stone floor. Circular stairs no wider than a man's shoulders led steeply downward. A member of Team Alpha was holding a flashlight. "Goes through that arched column on the first floor and into the mountain."

"How far?"

"Can't tell."

Layton knelt, took off a glove, and held his hand over the opening. Cool air blew upward. He stood up. "Flame the tunnel and blow it. Blow the whole fucking place."

• • •

KATHERINE'S EARS were ringing but at least the red orb had faded and she could see again. It was a vision of hell. Smoke swirled and glowed orange with obscured flames, jagged bursts of light electrified the air, shadowy figures flickered in and out of view while hissing fiery objects skittered across the ground and seared the flesh when they struck exposed arms or legs. A man stumbled toward her, his chin gaping and bloody. She jumped aside and ran blindly until she found the castle wall.

Which way? She chose a direction but moments later recognized the mosque and knew she was going the wrong way. As she hurried back, needles attacked her eyes and nose. Tear gas. She coughed and covered her mouth. Tayib's recruits, running in the opposite direction, ignored her. Tears came, she could barely see. She felt as though she had glass in her eyes and lungs, but she forced herself to keep going. Her fingers found metal—she was at the cell door where something dangled from the grate. A belt. Sam was trying to swing it, loop it over the bolt.

She opened the door and Sam lunged past. She had to grab his arm to stop him and he almost hit her before he recognized her. They were both coughing so badly they couldn't speak. But they climbed together to the battlement where gusts of fresh air allowed them to breathe. They ran along the parapet, heading for the entrance, until a spray of bullets forced them to take cover in a rounded turret.

"You okay?" Sam yelled. She nodded. He indicated the *galabiya*. "What's all that?"

"Why are you wet?"

"Later."

The fusillade had stopped. They emerged cautiously, then ran in a crouch until they turned a corner and saw the bridge, jammed with men escaping the tear gas and the castle.

"Never make it," Sam said. He turned and stared at the helicopters that moved like black ghosts above the tower. "If they knew we were here . . ."

Katherine grabbed his arm and pointed to the spot where the power line reached the castle. A moment's confusion and then he understood. He ran to the anchor point and inspected it. The cable was looped through an iron bolt and clamped tight. It stretched across the chasm, a downward arc to a concrete block scarcely visible on the far hillside. "It's steep," he said. "Can you do it?"

"Will it hold?"

"I'll let you know."

He stripped off his shirt and in response to her questioning look said, "Protect my hands." He sat on the parapet, swung his legs over the edge, leaned out and layered the shirt over the cable. It was drizzling now and the cable was slippery. He glanced back. Katherine looked calm enough. Thanks, he almost said, then remembered Tracy and couldn't. He turned around, got a good grip and launched himself into space . . .

The cable sagged and became steeper. Dangling in the darkness, he slid quickly at first and then more slowly until he stopped at the bottom of a loop just ten feet from safety. He tried to make his way hand over hand. The shirt caught around his left wrist and he almost lost his grip. The moisture that aided his progress now made it difficult as the braided cable slipped through his fingers. He tightened his grip and ignored a broken strand of wire that punctured his palm. His feet touched loose earth, and he scrambled onto the block of cement. Kneeling, he waved with stiff fingers and shouted, *"Go."*

Katherine could barely see Sam but the cable had stopped jerking and she knew she had to follow. The thunder of helicopter blades beat more loudly and began to fade. She wrapped the headscarf over the cable, leaned forward and pushed into the void. As she fell, a massive explosion sounded behind her and the mountains were bathed in orange light. A whoosh of warm air momentarily billowed the folds of her robe like a parachute.

She slowed to a stop. The low point in the cable left her dangling helplessly ten feet from the concrete block, now bathed in a pale Halloween light. Where was Sam? She tried to move hand-over-hand but her fingers lacked strength and she almost slipped. Not strong enough, she thought. Legs, get your legs up . . .

She twisted to face the castle and tried to hook her knees over the cable. The folds of the *galabiya* got in the way but finally she managed. As she inched her way upward she heard Sam yelling encouragement. A steady drizzle, she blinked to clear her eyes. Wasn't she there yet? Had to be. Her fingers were stiff, her arms aching. And then she felt it, the cable moving like a greased pole as she slid backward with every pull forward. The purse tugged at her neck and the *galabiya* hung wet and heavy, dragging her down, forcing her fingers free. I'm not going to make it. Something tickled her cheek. A stick? A tree limb? Sam was poking at her, trying to push her away—

"Grab the branch!"

And then she understood. Summoning up her last reserves of strength, she embraced the branch as well as the cable and held tight. Sam began to pull. Smaller branches moved up her chest and caught beneath her arms. She used her legs to help. Someone was shaking the cable. No, her own arms, trembling with fatigue.

"Come *on*," Sam yelled.

I'm trying, damn it . . . Sam pulled harder, and the branch threatened to tear free.

A hand on her wrist. "Got you."

She reached for him and fell against the rocky precipice. Sam dragged her to the top of the concrete block, where the two of them flopped down, trying to catch their breath as the rain increased its tempo. Beyond the ravine, flames leaped from the roof of Tayib's headquarters and flickered behind its arched windows.

"You think they captured him?" Katherine said.

"I hope not," Sam said. "I hope they killed the bastard."

TWENTY-SEVEN

KATHERINE AND SAM WORKED THEIR WAY AROUND THE PERIMETER of the village. At one point they came on a man and his family hiding in a ravine. Both groups were startled and the father put a protective arm around his children. Sam said something low in Arabic and they hurried on.

"What did you tell them?"

"To be very quiet because there were men with guns behind us."

Distant shouts reached them; soldiers were calling villagers to help put out the fire. In the darkness and rain they almost missed finding the car. Sam approached cautiously but no one was guarding it. Shivering now, they got their bags from the trunk and tossed them into the back seat. Sam put on a dry shirt and a sweater. As they pulled onto the road, he slowed for one last look at the tongue of flame fingering the night sky. "My kingdom for a camera."

"Go, *please*."

The castle was lost to view as Sam turned his attention to the muddy road beyond the rainswept windshield. Beneath the *galabiya* Katherine pulled on dry slacks and a blouse, then threw the robe out the window. "What'd you do, convert to Islam?" Sam said.

She told him about the humiliation of the classroom, the mock bridal preparations and Mehdi's aborted seduction. "I tried talking to him but he didn't understand; nothing I said made any difference."

They were approaching the roadblock. "Better put your shoulder harness on. I don't feel like stopping."

The pole loomed ahead. Apparently the soldiers hadn't heard about the attack. One of them emerged from the tent, visible in the sweep of the headlights, his rifle looped casually over his shoulder. Sam slowed until they were close, then stepped on the gas. The wheels spun and the car surged forward. Katherine had a good look at the man's face, mouth open, sliding past her window. A crash, the log splintered and hit the windshield, which erupted in a spiderweb pattern. Then they were past the barricade, speeding into the night. The stutter of the automatic rifle made Katherine flinch as the Mercedes fishtailed around a muddy curve and they were on their way.

Sam pounded the steering wheel. "Eat my dust, you fuckers!" He turned to her. "Who was it who said there's nothing like imminent death to focus a man's mind? The guy must have spent a few minutes staring down the business end of half a dozen rifles."

"I'm sorry, Sam, I had to choose someone—"

"Don't apologize. You did what you had to do."

She shook her head. "You don't understand. I used Tracy to reach Imad Tayib. I was going to kill him."

"You mean kidnap him."

"No, kill him." She explained her original plan, the gun hidden in the Mont Blanc, the offer to Tracy as a way of meeting Tayib. She was prepared for his anger, his outrage, his condemnation, but after she finished Sam remained silent. When he finally spoke, it was not about Tracy.

"What about me? Why'd you show up on my doorstep?"

"I was trying to find out more about Imad Tayib."

"You weren't trying to get me to come along?"

"Is that what you think?"

"You're like one of those Chinese boxes—open one up and there's another inside. What else are you hiding?"

"I'm not hiding anything."

"Except a gun in a Mont Blanc pen. Let me see it."

She took it out of her purse. Sam turned on the dome light and divided his attention between the pen and the road. "This thing fires bullets?"

"One bullet."

"And you were going to use this on Tayib?"

"I wish I had."

She felt drained, empty. After putting the pen back in her purse, she rested her forehead against the darkened window. One of the headlights, canted upward from the impact, lit the underside of passing trees. The heat was on and the warm, moist air made her drowsy. Sam strained to reach something from his bag in the back seat. The car swerved.

"What do you want? I'll get it."

"Sweater in my bag."

Katherine found it but, when she offered it to Sam, he said, "Thought you could use it for a pillow."

"Thank you." She rolled it up and tucked it against the side window. The sweater smelled faintly of cigarette smoke. Katherine dozed then to the sound of drumming rain and the heartbeat rhythm of windshield wipers.

DOUG LIVINGSTON, listening in Damascus to Tayib's broadcast, felt like cheering. Precisely eleven minutes after the scheduled detonation, he heard the first explosion followed by Tayib's stop in mid-sentence and the muted din of the attack before the microphone was switched off.

"Yes," Livingston whispered, and slammed his fist into his palm. The interpreter, Nancy Aziz, looked up, puzzled. "He went off the air . . ."

Permanently, Livingston thought. The bastard thought he was a media star with his nightly broadcasts. Same time, same station, same geographical location. And while he was filling the airways with messianic bullshit, the Delta Team knew exactly where he was.

He returned to his office, wearing a smile. The difficult we do immediately, the impossible takes a little longer. Right on. He imagined the kudos waiting for him in Washington. He might even be in line for one of the CIA's confidential citations that could never be publicly acknowledged but was all the more coveted for the distinction.

He popped a breath mint into his mouth and wished that Ursula, his SwissAir stewardess, was in town; victory made him horny. He called a secretary at the Egyptian embassy, a canny little fuck-bunny who hoped to trade bedroom expertise for a marriage proposal, and invited himself to her apartment. He watched the clock and waited. Word of the outcome would be flashed to Bob Hatch in Washington while the assault force was still airborne.

An hour went by. He heard nothing. He went to the Signals Room and sent a coded message to his mentor Hatch: *Request information.* Hatch would know what he meant. Five minutes later the code clerk handed him a reply: *No joy no details.*

Shaken, Livingston returned to his office and slammed the door. The goddamn army could fuck up a wet dream. Hadn't he given them Tayib on a silver platter? Time, date, place—what did he have to do, nail the guy's feet to the floor?

Thoughts of a citation faded. In Washington they would be tossing blame like hand grenades. He began to plan how he would separate his part of the operation from the army's. *He* had been successful. *His* agent—which was how he thought of Katherine—had done her part, done it damn near perfectly. He was right about her. The woman had brass balls. At least he could look forward to debriefing her.

KATHERINE SLEPT fitfully during the drive from the mountains to the Mediterranean coast. At one point she woke to wind tugging her hair. Sam had his hand out the window, parallel with the slipstream, tilting it up and down, the way children do. Another time the car swerved violently and Sam yelled "G.I.R."

"What's wrong?"

"Goat in the road. Go back to sleep."

Sleep was a needed balm, and Katherine dozed until, just before midnight, they stopped at Tartous, a tiny coastal town three hours from Damascus. Along the narrow strip of beach they found a hotel misnamed The Grand that faced the ocean with a uniform display of stubby concrete balconies overlooking a dismal water fountain illuminated by red, blue and amber lights.

They were given two adjoining rooms decorated in an unsuccessful blend of garish Arab furniture and luxurious French bathroom appointments, which included a bidet and Jacuzzi. While Sam went to find something to eat, Katherine settled into a hot bath and surprised herself by falling asleep. She woke up to lukewarm water and Sam knocking on the door to the adjoining room. She wrapped herself in a thick robe of cheap synthetic terrycloth that seemed to repel the water rather than soak it up.

"Dinner at the Maison Grande," Sam said, indicating with a sweep of his hand a tray on wheels in the center of his room. *"Poulet Syrienne,* also known as chicken sandwiches and champagne."

Katherine stared at him. "Aren't you tired?"

"Aren't you hungry?"

"No."

"Then keep me company while I eat." He moved behind her, took her by the shoulders and guided her to a chair.

"I fell asleep in the bathtub."

"Here." He gave her a chipped water glass filled with champagne.

"There's nothing to celebrate."

"Tayib's capture."

But all she could think of was Tracy's death. She forced herself to join Sam in a toast. On an empty stomach the champagne went quickly to her head, and her tension ebbed as she listened to Sam's account of his escape and recapture. Finished with his sandwich, he sat back and balanced the glass of champagne on his knee.

"I think I misjudged you. When I saw your place in Greenwich I thought here was a spoiled daughter of wealth and privilege right out of the social register. I could have written your biography, which probably would have been all wrong."

"What would you have written?"

He raised the glass and squinted at her through it. "Grandpa left you a trust fund, you got a horse for your twelfth birthday, went to Paris to have a dress designed for your coming-out party, never dated a boy whose car didn't have leather upholstery, got a degree in one of the three A's, married a man enough of a rebel to attract you but not enough of one for daddy to disown you, then came kids, community, good works, golf, tennis, aerobics, Christmas party flirtations, maybe a near-miss affair that made you feel noble or something consummated that made you feel tragic, a divorce postponed a couple of times on account of the kids and messiness of it all . . ." He tilted his head from behind the glass. "How'm I doing?"

"Fifty-fifty."

"Which fifty?"

"What are the three A's?"

"Archeology, Architecture, or Anthropology."

She shook her head. "MBA. Dad hoped both Brian and I would join the business."

"Harvard?"

"Stanford."

"You rebel, you."

He reached to refill her glass but she pulled it back. "I can hardly keep my eyes open." She stood up woozily.

"I'll walk you to your door." She didn't say no when he took her arm. At the door she turned. "Well, thank you for the . . . beautiful evening." It sounded silly, and she smiled.

"I'll escort you to your bed."

"Sam . . . Okay, okay, here's the bed."

He was staring at her, his brown eyes intense. "Do you have any idea how beautiful you look right now?"

"Don't say that."

"It's true." He cupped her face in his hands, his lips brushed hers, and she felt—and responded to— the warmth of his body. She pulled back. "Don't, Sam . . ."

"Shhh." He leaned toward her but she twisted away. "Sam, for God's sake, she's *dead*. Doesn't that mean anything to you?"

"It means everything."

"You're acting like that damned Mehdi."

She drew the robe close and crossed her arms. Sam regarded her silently, turned and walked back to his room.

"I didn't mean—" she began, then stopped. It's my fault . . . leave me alone, don't leave me alone.

She closed her eyes, took a deep breath. Too much champagne, not enough food.

Sam was back, holding a photograph of Tracy and Mike.

"Look at her, goddamn it. I should have died today but this girl died in my place. Not to sound pompous, but that's a gift of life and I'm not going to waste it. Good innocent people get ripped off, and innocent people live full and rich lives. Murderers are punished, and murderers laugh with their buddies and die in their sleep on their hundredth birthday. I'll be the first one to testify at the trial and I'll be there the day they lead Imad Tayib to the gas chamber or electric chair but if I don't live my life then Tracy's was stupidly wasted. I'm alive, I'm glad I didn't die out there on that hill today—"

"I wish I had."

"No, you don't."

"I do, Sam. It should have been me. I'm the one he hates."

He put Tracy's photograph on a table and took her hand. "I want to show you something."

"Sam . . ."

"Come here, come on."

He opened the sliding glass door and led her out onto the balcony. Below was the parking lot, the garish fountain, the black ocean with the lights of boats at anchor, the strip of beach across the road with darkened figures walking along it. "Fall from here and you'd die real quick. You want to die, Katherine, *do* it. Go ahead and jump. I won't grab you this time."

"Sam—"

"You want to die? Here's your chance."

"You proved your point." She tried to step past him but he moved close. "Please move."

"Say it: *I want to live.*"

"I don't."

"Then jump. Do it, Katherine. Your children are dead, Tracy's dead, go ahead and join the ones you're mourning. Two seconds, it'll all be over. Go ahead." He pushed her. *"Jump. Do it."*

She pulled back instinctively, staring at him with horror. "Stop it."

"Say what's in your heart. Admit you want to live."

"Why are you doing this?"

"Say it."

"I can't."

"I want to live."

"No."

"Liar. And Tracy knows it."

He turned away but Katherine had grabbed his arm. Her lips quivered, her eyes filled. "I want to live," she whispered.

"Again."

"You heard me."

He took her by the shoulders. "Say it again."

"I want to live, are you satisfied?"

"Louder."

"I want to live."

"What?"

"I want to live."

They were close now, eyes on one another, hers blazing in affirmation, his bright with desire. Their lips met, hard and demanding, shifting in their excitement, greedy and eager to know, to feel one another. Stumbling, touching, kissing, they made their way back into the room. She felt his hardness and fumbled at his belt. Sam slid the robe over her shoulders, ran his hands down her back and cupped her breast. His fingers traced a spiral pattern to her nipple, which stiffened at his touch. The robe fell to the floor, Sam stepped out of his clothes and lowered Katherine to the bed.

His lips brushed her cheek, slid behind an ear and danced down her neck. He worked his way down her body, fingers preparing the way, his breath warm, lips alive with gentle kisses. His face drifted across her stomach and nestled in her pubic hair, his unshaved cheek lightly scratched her inner thigh, then lowered further.

No, she thought, not there, and her legs stiffened momentarily before she gave in to the quick discovery that sent tremors through her body. She tangled her fingers in his hair as tremors of delight rocked her body. Sam moved above her, braced himself, and entered her slowly, drawing out every movement, texture, sensation. She caught her breath and saw him shiver as her own ardor was mirrored in his eyes. Slowly, pause, slowly, pause—she locked her legs around his waist, he slid forward and they came together. Her head arched, she ran her hands down his back, felt the muscles and the shape and movement of him as they found the rhythm of love.

TWENTY-EIGHT

THE ESCAPE ROUTE FROM THE CASTLE LED TO A TUNNEL DEEP IN the limestone heart of the mountain. The stairs had been carved at the time of the Crusades, but during the next thousand years a portion of the tunnel collapsed and the entrance in the tower was sealed underneath a tiled floor. Workmen installing the radio transmitter discovered the stairway, and Tayib renovated it. Because he distrusted the Syrian Army, ostensibly his protector but whose orders were the whim of the country's leader, he kept the escape route a closely guarded secret.

In the first moments of the attack it quickly became apparent that a defense could not be sustained. Leaving one of the *shaheen* to close the entrance behind them, Tayib and four other martyrs made their way into the narrow passage, where the sound of gunfire faded, to be replaced by labored breathing and sandals slapping rock steps. They reached the tunnel and ran in a crouch preceded by multiple shadows.

An inflatable raft was stored at the mouth of the tunnel. With two men on each side, they moved the boat down a rocky path to the water's edge. The sounds of battle echoed off the rock cliffs as the *shaheen* paddled toward the swift mid-stream current—an explosion from the tower produced a fireball that threw a helicopter into high relief, caught among a thousand descending drops of rain as it climbed away. Tayib pointed an accusing finger at it. A machine of the West, like a *shaitan,* one of the black devils that came at night to snatch men's souls. Only these men were not devils but Western assassins . . .

One of the *shaheen* raised a rifle and fired. Tayib grabbed his arm. "Foolish is the fox without a lair who tempts the eye of the eagle."

The raft pitched and rolled as it swept downstream. The men swayed with the rhythm of their work, while Tayib stared into the darkening water, where reflected flames looked like fissures of hell blurred in the river's bed. And now the rain began in earnest, shrouding from view the burning castle.

Tayib appeared calm but inwardly seethed. How could enemy helicopters have penetrated the missile defenses unless the Syrian government had been party to the attack? Reports had reached him of the government's growing animosity, but Tayib, knowing his support among the people, had felt secure. Had President Assad turned his tongue to the American palm now that the Soviet hand was empty? Or had the Americans acted alone?

He recalled the explosive device of Fawzi Ashraf; had it been intended as part of the attack? If so, to what purpose? The destruction of a building? Or an assassination device intended to kill Tayib himself?

Fawzi said he was working for the Americans. Was it possible that Sam Gaddis had accomplished what Fawzi Ashraf had not? And the two women, were they a distraction whose true purpose he had misjudged? Why would the Cahill woman offer him such an insult? Too much was unknown. He would have to hold his hand until he learned which of his enemies wielded the knife.

It took an hour before the river emerged from the canyon, slowing as it entered a broad plain. They paddled to shore and walked to the home of Abu Farras, a farmer who tilled the fields bordering the river. A dog barked at their approach and a rangy man with a dirty *kaffiyeh* appeared in the doorway. Abu Farras brought his hands together and bobbed his head as he welcomed them. *"Ahlan wasahlan."*

"Is your family well, Abu Farras?"

"As the mice breed in the field so does my family increase."

"The rewards of Allah are great for the faithful."

"Come inside, sit, have coffee."

"In a moment, Abu Farras. Were you listening to my broadcast tonight?"

"The batteries in my radio are dead. When I go to the souk I will buy new ones."

"You have heard nothing of the attack on Raqba?"

"Allah forbid it!"

"Inshallah. What is the condition of your vehicle?"

"It uses more oil than gas."

"Then it shall grow fat on oil. We must have your truck, Abu Farras."

"Tomorrow I need the truck to go to the souk."

"Did you not hear my words? There has been an attack by Westerners and Zionists on a home of the faithful. You have been chosen by Allah to offer your aid. Be grateful that you have a chance to earn merit in His eyes."

"Yes, of course, I mention it only to earn merit in your own. When do you wish the truck?"

"Immediately."

Abu Farras went to get his keys. From the other room they could hear his wife's querulous voice raised in complaint: they needed the truck, there was not enough food in the house, the men could bring trouble. Tayib and his men pretended not to hear.

"Rashid, you will return to Raqba. Tell no one where I am but bring me a report. There will be rumors concerning the attack. Listen to them and try to discover the truth. Let no one know if I am alive or dead. Say only that the faithful should recite the ninety-nine names of Allah each day and, if Allah is willing, on the ninety-ninth hour after the attack I shall return and raise my voice in humble praise of He Who Made The Sun and righteous anger at those who seek to destroy His disciples."

Ninety-nine hours was just over four days. That, Tayib figured, would give him enough time to confound his enemies, unsure if he was alive or dead, and sow the seeds of jubilation in his followers. Four days to find a radio transmitter to astound the multitudes with news of his invincibility. And ninety-nine hours to discover those responsible for this attempt on his life, and to destroy them.

● ● ●

IN THE morning Katherine lay still in Sam's arms. Comforted by his rhythmic breathing, lulled by the warmth of his body curled around hers, she felt almost newborn. This was the first day of a world without Tracy. Yesterday she had felt as if she couldn't go on living. Now, sheltered in the arms of the man she had condemned to death, she made her farewell to Tracy. *I never meant it to happen*, she whispered silently, *you must know that now* . . .

Sam jerked away, his body tense. He stared at her, then relaxed. His eyes traveled over her body and stopped at her breasts. "You're looking perky this morning."

She lifted the sheet. "So are you."

They made love slowly, taking time for tenderness, for new explorations, for whispered words of encouragement and pleasure. Afterward, Katherine sat on the edge of the bathtub wrapped in a towel and watched Sam shave. He used a brush and a cup of shaving cream and a straight razor with a mother-of-pearl handle.

"Sam, yesterday when I told you Tayib didn't have Mike you mentioned someone's name. Someone who might have a reason to kidnap him."

"Sarkis Irskenian. He's a ship owner whose name is all over the packing crates in Mike's photos."

"You think he has Mike?"

"A good possibility."

"I won't ask you to help me, but I have to see Irskenian."

"Look out the window and tell me what you see."

She went to the bedroom and pulled the heavy velvet drapes aside. Light flooded the room. The storm had passed leaving a bright blue sky dappled with quick-moving white clouds. A fishing boat rounding a jetty sent a silver plume of spray high in the air. Behind her Sam wrapped his arms around her waist. "What do you see?"

"People, cars, the beach."

"What else?"

"Ships, boats." He nuzzled her neck. "Sam . . ."

"Keep going."

"I can't think when you do that."

"The island. Say *the island.*"

"What about the it?"

"It's called Arwad. It's where Sarkis Irskenian lives."

She turned to face him. "How did you know I wanted to go there?"

"I didn't. But I knew *I* did."

TAYIB DREAMED of the horseman riding toward him across a wind-scalloped desert. Unlike his earlier vision, in this dream the horse was not white, but black, and its rider wore black robes which trailed after it like dark smoke. He knew that this was a *shaitan,* the devil, come to take his soul. The hoofbeats were loud, the earth trembled and the horseman lowered his lance, the tip pointed at Tayib's heart. Only faith could shield him from this supernatural foe, so he stood and bared his chest. At the last moment he saw sand flying from the horse's hooves and in an agony of sudden doubt, he cried out—

He woke up, heart pounding. Outside the window the first flush of dawn paled the eastern horizon. Stepping over the sleeping soldiers, he left the house and walked to the river's edge. The weather had cleared and the earth was patterned in rivulets from last night's rain. The rooster's crow joined the chirp of crickets and the first faint morning breeze carried the smell of embers from yesterday's fire. On such mornings as a child, he had gone to milk the goats and begin the endless tending of sheep. Now Tayib considered the meaning of the dream. Surely the *shaitan* was meant to symbolize his enemies and the sand beneath the horse's hooves meant the threat was material, not spiritual. So the culprit was America. Allah's message was clear: Sam Gaddis and Katherine Cahill were somehow responsible for the attack.

The morning clouds were turning a pale coral when Rashid returned in Abu Farras's green Volkswagen pickup. Major Yazdi was in front and Naguib, with four soldiers, rode in the back. While Abu Farras served a breakfast of cheese, hummus, *khobz* and olives, Tayib took Yazdi aside and listened to his report. Five men had died and sixteen were wounded. The top two floors of the tower, including the transmitter, were destroyed. Half the recruits' tents burned and many buildings were pocked by bullets.

"How did he neutralize the radar station?" Tayib asked.

"Who?"

"The American, Sam Gaddis."

"Not Gaddis. It was the Cahill woman. She planted an explosive at the transformer that cut power to Mount Kajar."

Tayib hid his surprise. "How do you know it was the woman?"

"Abu Hamri said she disappeared for an hour the night she stayed at his house."

"Where was the guard?"

"It was beneath his dignity to follow a woman to the bathroom so he let her go alone. By the time he sent someone to look for her she had disappeared."

"I should have been told."

"The guard told no one. It was only after the attack that I discovered it."

Imad Tayib kept his features neutral but his neck burned. Not a man but a *woman* was his adversary? And her insult was double: personal and political—when she spat in his face she had already sabotaged the power line.

"How did they escape?"

"By car." Yazdi described how the Mercedes had smashed the roadblock. He thought Tayib would be angry but the leader seemed almost pleased.

"The eagle without wings is prey for the fox. Allah has confined our enemies to the ground that we may overtake and destroy them. We will call Abu Shapour and tell him to watch the hotels where the Americans stay. Then you will return to Raqba and take charge during my absence. Naguib and Rashid will come with me. Abu Farras will drive us to Aleppo to catch the morning flight to Damascus. Before the ninety-nine hours passes we will return to Raqba with the hearts torn from the bodies of Sam Gaddis and Katherine Cahill."

TWENTY-NINE

LEAVING THE HOTEL, SAM SHOWED AN ENERGY AND SENSE OF purpose Katherine had not seen in Damascus. For the first time she sensed what she never had before—that Sam Gaddis might be very good at his job. He had a plan but wouldn't give details and for the moment she was content to let him take the lead. They drove to a small shop where he bought a box of Band-Aids.

"Have you got a cut?"

"I wanted tape but this was all they had. It's like shopping in Moscow."

They drove to an abandoned amusement park bordering the sea. Three men were fishing from a rotting pier that extended from the gravel parking lot where they left the Mercedes. A taxi took them to the ferry dock, where a rocky breakwater formed a sheltering arm for the small harbor. In contrast to the drab Arab buildings, the boats were brightly painted in white, blue and yellow. They stepped aboard and joined a crowd of people, many with plastic net shopping bags, who stood inside the cabin or sat on a swaybacked bow. The boat chugged out of the harbor and a gentle swell lifted them.

Sam brought out the Band-Aids and cut the tape from the padding. He made a series of loops with the sticky side out, flattened them and pressed them onto an empty Winston box.

"What's *that* for?"

"A Stafford special. Little trick I learned from one of the reporters at the *Herald*."

"Tape on a cigarette box?"

"Let's say you're a burglar and you just heisted the crown jewels. You hide them in the garage in a can of paint. I suspect you've got the jewels but can't prove it so what do I do? I walk into your house and tell you the jewels were returned to their owner in a brown unmarked package. What's the first thing you do when I leave?"

"Look in the paint can."

Sam grinned and held up the Winston box, one side now sticky with Band-Aids. He slid the Pearl-corder into it. "We name our crown jewels 'Mike Winn'."

The island, low and white, was ringed by ships lying at anchor. The engine raced and water roiled from beneath the hull as they backed stern-first into a narrow space at a pier crowded with fishing boats. They stepped ashore and made their way beneath billowing canopies past outdoor tables piled high with cheap souvenirs to a group of fishermen mending their nets. Sam spoke to one man in a faded red shirt who nodded enthusiastically and pocketed the one hundred Syrian pounds Sam gave him.

"What's that for?" Katherine asked.

"He's taking us back to the mainland."

"Why can't we take the ferry?"

"With any luck the ferry will be too dangerous."

Most buildings on Arwad had a tumbled-together look but not the Irskenian Shipping office, which sat in solitary splendor thrust out over the water. A forty-foot cruiser, glistening white with polished brass fittings, was tied to a private dock, and a small flower garden bordered the front walk. Chimes sounded as Sam and Katherine pushed open a heavy glass door. Speaking in Arabic, Sam told an attractive black-eyed secretary they wanted to see Sarkis Irskenian.

"Does he expect you?"

"He doesn't expect us and he doesn't know us, but tell him we have business in regard to Mike Winn and I think he will see us."

The secretary spoke into an intercom and then said, "One minute. Mr. Antun is coming."

Sam nodded and turned to Katherine. "Mr. Antun is coming."

"Who's he?"

Sam turned to the secretary. "Who's Mr. Antun?"

A door opened and the secretary's eyes slid past his shoulder. "Mr. Irskenian's private secretary."

Antun looked less like a private secretary than a bodyguard. He was just under six feet tall and wore a pale cotton shirt stretched tight beneath his armpits. With a weight-lifter's strut, Antun led them down a carpeted hallway lined with photographs of Irskenian ships. Sam said to Katherine in a low voice, "Types a hundred words a minute with his knuckles."

Sarkis Irskenian stood up to greet them. He was a short, stocky man with a flat ridge of black hair and heavy-lidded eyes. A brass telescope mounted on a tripod stood before a picture window overlooking the harbor. As Sam made introductions in Arabic he noticed an *International Herald* on the desk. "Ms. Cahill doesn't speak Arabic. You don't mind if we speak English."

"As you wish. How can I help you?"

Sam pulled his chair close to the desk. "We're trying to locate an American who disappeared last month, a man by the name of Mike Winn. We believe he came here."

Irskenian's eyelids lowered slightly. He pursed his lips and made a show of thinking. "Winn . . . no, I don't recognize the name. Are you friends of his?"

"He said you were the best shipping agent in Syria."

"It is a reputation I hope is fairly earned."

"He said you were an expert at handling dangerous materials. Things like nerve gas and mustard gas. Is that so?"

A long moment. When Irskenian spoke, his mouth moved as if he were chewing leather. "That type of material is under strict international control. We do *not* handle such materials."

Sam placed a photo of Mike on the desk. "Maybe he was using another name. You're sure this man didn't stop here?"

"I'm positive."

"Aren't you going to look at the picture?"

Irskenian gave it a glance, his eyes hidden beneath the heavy lids. "I have never seen the man. If you have no further business—"

"How about this man?" Sam tossed him the picture of the dead train guard. While Irskenian inspected it, Sam leaned forward and slid his hand beneath his chair. Irskenian looked up. "Where did you get this?"

"Postcard from Mike Winn. He took it at the train wreck where one of your shipments of poison gas got into the wrong lungs."

Irskenian shoved a stubby finger onto the intercom button. "Tell Antun our visitors are leaving."

Sam stood up. "Don't bother, we know the way." As they left the office, Sam said in a low voice, "Faint when we get to the reception area."

"I'm not the type—"

"Then get *sick,* ask for water, anything to stall for time." He rushed his last words as a scowling Antun stood aside for them to pass, then followed them down the hall. At the reception desk the secretary looked up as Katherine grabbed Sam's arm. "Wait, Sam . . ."

"Are you all right, honey?"

"A little dizzy." She turned to the secretary. "Maybe some water?"

Sam repeated the request in Arabic but Antun interrupted. "No, you must leave."

Katherine gasped, her knees buckled and Sam helped her to a chair.

"Water," Sam said. "Get her some water."

The secretary ran down the hall. Sam turned to Antun. "Do you have any aspirin?" Without waiting for an answer, he went after the secretary. "We need some aspirin," he called, but, instead of following her, he dodged down the hall to Irskenian's office and entered without knocking. Irskenian sat hunched forward, the phone to his ear. He looked up, surprised, as Sam crossed to the desk.

"Think I left my cigarettes," Sam said. He reached beneath the chair, pulled the Winston box free, and held it up. "Yeah, here they are. Sorry to interrupt."

As he left, he tucked the box into his pocket. Antun grabbed him in the hallway and hustled him back to the reception area, where the secretary was holding a glass of water for Katherine.

"Out, both of you," Antun ordered.

As soon as they were in the street, Katherine said, "Why did I faint?"

"So I could get this." He showed her the box with the tape recorder still running. He took it out and turned it off. Katherine reached for it but Sam held it back. "Let's get off the island first."

The fisherman was waiting with his son, a boy about thirteen years old, who cast off the lines and then sat with his arms around his knees, somberly watching the Americans. After they were underway, Sam told the captain that their destination was not the main harbor but the old pier at the amusement park. The man shrugged, all the same to him.

The wind had come up and the trip back took longer than the ride out. Occasionally the boat slammed into a wave, sending a sheet of spray over the bow. At one point Sam tapped Katherine's shoulder and pointed toward the island. Irskenian's white cruiser rounded the jetty, rose high in the water and headed like an arrow for the mainland. Sam cupped his hand to her ear. "I told you the ferry would be too dangerous."

"You think they're coming after us?"

"You think Antun ran out of typewriter ribbon?"

For a moment it looked as if the cruiser was following them but slowly its course diverged and it headed for the main harbor.

At the amusement park pier, broken concrete pilings made docking difficult, so Sam and Katherine stood on the bow and jumped ashore. Once back in the car Sam rewound the tape and jockeyed it back and forth until he found the spot where they had walked out of Irskenian's office. The recorder was between them, and their heads touched. "The crown jewels have been recovered," Sam said in a low voice. "What's the first thing he's going to do?"

There was the sound of the door shutting, a pause, and then a phone dialing. A moment later Irskenian's voice, thin and tense and barely audible. "Is Victor there?" Sam raised an eyebrow—Irskenian was speaking in English. A pause, then in a more confidential tone, "Listen, we have a problem." His voice dropped and the words became momentarily unintelligible. Then with rising agitation, "Yes, yes. A few minutes ago. He came with a woman. (Pause) No. Katherine Cahill. First they said they were looking for—"

The sound of a door opening and Sam's voice, brash but distant. "I think I forgot my cigarettes." The next phrase was drowned by an amplified sound of tape pulling free and the too-close wrinkle of cigarette carton. Sam frowned and flipped off the recorder. "Know anybody named Victor?"

Katherine shook her head. "Is it a first name or last?"

"One way to find out. Call him."

"How do we get the number?"

"Thanks to a Stone Age telephone system we already have it." He rewound the tape. "Rotary dial telephones click off each digit as they go back to zero. I'll count the clicks, you write down the numbers."

"You're kidding."

"O ye of little faith." He switched the Pearlcorder to slow, turned up the volume, and replayed the portion of the tape in which Irskenian dialed the number. Each ratchet was dimly audible and each set of clicks was another digit. First a group of three, then two, then four . . .

"Damascus exchange," Sam murmured.

"How do you—?"

"Shhh." His lips moved slightly as he counted the next set. "Seven." A long sequence. "Zero." And the last set—He sat bolt upright.

"What is it?"

His eyes were hard and distant. "Son of a bitch."

"What are you talking—?"

"Seven, that's the last digit."

"I know."

"Just like the airplane, isn't that what Livingston said?"

She stared at the number: 324 707. Ask for Adam, he'd said, not Doug Livingston.

THIRTY

ABU SHAPOUR CAME FROM THE YELLOW WIND OFFICE TO MEET Imad Tayib at the airport. Along with Major Yazdi, Shapour had been with the Yellow Wind since its inception. Together they formed a triumvirate led by Imad Tayib, with Yazdi in charge of military operations and Shapour responsible for keeping up the urban infrastructure.

Shapour had not seen Tayib in over a year but he felt his presence even before he saw him. Tayib marched through the terminal, looking neither right nor left, his pale eyes framed by coal black beard and black turban. He was accompanied by two men, who glanced uneasily at the soldiers who were part of the normal security force. The two friends embraced in the Arab fashion.

"You honor us with your presence, Imam."

"Your eyes do not share the joy of your words, Abu Shapour. What divides your spirit?"

"Bad news travels more swiftly than good. Major

Yazdi called half an hour ago. The Syrian Army has used last night's attack to march on Raqba. They have established a military control zone, calling it a 'protective measure.' Our soldiers have been disarmed, except those who escaped with Yazdi."

"How many escaped?"

"I don't know. Yazdi has told them to gather at the house of Abu Farras, where they await your instructions."

"Allah never closes one door but opens another." They walked to the parking lot. "What about the Americans? Have you posted men at the hotels?"

The change of subject surprised Shapour. What about our soldiers? he wanted to ask. But he had learned long ago that his leader's reactions were unpredictable. "The Cahill woman never checked out of the Sheraton. She maintains a suite on the top floor."

"Someone watches for her arrival?"

"A man called Hegazi."

They got into the car, a Peugeot station wagon with prayer beads dangling from the rear view mirror. Shapour asked about the attack on Raqba. When he heard that the Cahill woman was responsible, he was filled with misgivings. Recruits went to Raqba to be trained in military matters and infused with a sense of mission, but now he sensed that Tayib's zeal had turned from the larger cause to the two Americans.

They entered the old city, with its crooked streets crowded by sagging buildings with overhanging balconies. A young man wearing a vest over his *galabiya* ran out waving his arms. Shapour braked quickly. The man, whose cheeks were pockmarked beneath a thin beard, came to the window. "Excuse me, Abu

Shapour, but you cannot go into the office. The police have posted guards and are watching the street."

"For what purpose?"

"They say it is for our protection but the rumor is that they are looking for Imad Tayib." His attention shifted to Tayib. "Forgive my manners, Imam. I am called Ibrahim."

"May Allah grant you many years, Ibrahim."

"May your own be twice as many, Hope of Our People."

The truck behind them began honking its horn. Ibrahim motioned for it to back up so they could turn around. Shapour maneuvered with difficulty while onlookers called advice. They drove to the welding shop of a Yellow Wind partisan, where Tayib abbreviated the greetings in his haste to discover if the Americans had appeared at the hotel.

This is madness, Shapour thought, as he had his man paged at the Sheraton. Shapour still walked with a limp, a result of the many bones broken in his feet during interrogation by the Mukhabarat, Syria's secret police. If the army and police had turned against them, they should get out of the country, but Tayib seemed unaware of the danger.

"No one has arrived yet," he reported. "But I gave Hegazi the phone number here."

Tayib sat on a cushion in their host's office, surrounded by followers, who, in deference to their leader, sat on the floor and ignored two empty chairs pushed against a wall.

"We will need weapons. Do you keep them at the office?"

"The office is too often searched. They are hidden in homes of our friends."

"Bring guns for five men and two knives, thin and strong, made for stabbing."

"Imam, what do these Americans matter? You must escape the country before the police discover you."

"From the mountains a man sees danger before his enemy's dust becomes visible to one sheltered by the oasis. The Western armies prepare to invade Kuwait. When that happens, the support of the faithful will turn against corrupt governments. As the Ayatollah Khomeini deposed the Shah of Iran, so shall we raise a revolution and sweep aside President Assad."

"Forgive me, Imam, but we have not yet sufficient strength to mount an uprising."

"How much strength does the spark require to raise a wall of fire in the tall grass? You have been in the city too long, Abu Shapour, and are too easily impressed by the tools of repression."

No, Shapour thought sadly, you have been in the mountains for too long. With growing uneasiness he dispatched one man to gather the weapons, another to bring a barber and a third to find the articles of clothing Tayib wanted.

IT WAS Thanksgiving. Doug Livingston was in his apartment unwrapping a new Ralph Lauren shirt he had saved to wear to the annual Embassy picnic when the phone call came. Since the attack on Raqba he had been waiting to hear from Katherine Cahill while he tried to pierce the rumors surrounding Tayib's disappearance. If Tayib were dead, the *Rih Asfar* disciples would be parading his body up and down the streets, whipping themselves into a frenzy of vengeance. But if Tayib were alive, he'd be trumpeting his victory over the infidels and threatening a thousand kinds of retaliation.

Sarkis Irskenian's phone call, routed through the Embassy 707 switchboard, erased all thought of Tayib. Sam Gaddis and Katherine Cahill had discovered the poison gas shipment. How? And how much did they know? More important, could Irskenian stop them from leaving Arwad? Livingston felt a prickling sensation run down his spine. Everything was coming apart, unraveling. He waited anxiously until Irskenian's second phone call brought more bad news. "They escaped."

"It's an island, how can they escape?"

"They avoided the ferry and hired a private fishing boat. I think it is up to you, now. They are Americans, they are your people and your problem. You must find a solution."

Eat shit, Livingston thought. Aloud he said, "Did they arrange for the boat before or after they came to see you?"

Irskenian paused. "Before. Does that make a difference?"

"Think about it," he said and hung up.

Yes, it made a difference. It meant they knew enough about the shipment before going to Irskenian to realize they were in danger. Livingston wondered if they had linked him to the shipment yet? The Cahill woman might keep her mouth shut if he appealed to her patriotism, but not Sam. Like a bloodhound he would follow the trail until he was sniffing at Livingston's feet.

Okay, he thought, you want to play hardball, let's do it. Livingston picked up the phone and made a series of calls, blanketing the city with people eager to earn a few dollars by bringing him word of Sam's return. Fuck you, Gaddis, he thought. I'm a spider and my web is Damascus. You set foot in this city and I'll know exactly where you are.

"IRAQ," SAM said with finality. They had left the green coastal region and were driving Highway 5 through the arid plains that led to Damascus. On the seat between them a plastic bag was almost empty of almonds and nuts. From time to time Sam grabbed a handful and popped them into his mouth.

Katherine said, "You're jumping to conclusions."

"Who else? Saddam Hussein loves poison gas like a dog loves dead fish."

"I mean Livingston. We don't know how he's involved."

"Remember the Iran-Contra scandal? The U.S. sells missiles to Iran in exchange for the release of American hostages and enough extra profit to buy guns for our Contra buddies fighting for truth, beauty, and justice down in Central America? Livingston was a shadow warrior in that little deal. Faye was tracking him in Lebanon, that's how she met him."

"Was Livingston making money on the side?"

"All the spooks make money. They develop underground channels to serve the government and pretty soon they're serving themselves."

"Sam, you don't know that."

"When you find the cesspool you know you're at the end of the sewage line."

Katherine remembered the sincerity of Livingston's congratulations when she agreed to sabotage the radar station. No, she thought, I don't think he's doing this for money. But it was pointless to talk to Sam, whose animosity toward the CIA agent blinded him to any other speculation.

Sam said, "Any more water?"

Katherine emptied the last of the bottled water into a cup. As Sam reached for it the back of his hand brushed her breast. "Sorry," he said automatically.

The word hung in the air. They hadn't discussed it but Katherine realized now what she sensed when they left the hotel, that their lovemaking was a unique event, a commemoration of life more than a foundation for the future.

"Sam, about last night . . ."

"Shhh." Sam's hand went to the radio and turned up the volume to listen to an Arab newscast.

"What is it?"

"Tayib." He stiffened. "Shit, they don't know where he is."

"They didn't get him?"

"It sounds like he disappeared. The Syrians are making protests, our government has no comment, and the Yellow Wind is calling the faithful to pray for a miracle."

It never ends, Katherine thought bitterly. Tayib's capture, his escape, nothing would bring back her children or turn back the clock for Tracy.

When they got to Damascus, Sam dropped her at the Sheraton. "I'll be right back. See if you can set up a meeting with Livingston."

"Where are you going?"

"To leave Mike's photos with a friend of mine. Call it an insurance policy, in case things get rough."

Get rough? Livingston was an agent of the U.S.

government. Was he capable of violence or was Sam's caution exaggerated because of his hatred for the CIA man?

Preoccupied with such thoughts, she didn't notice the Arab in the lobby, who sat with a book on his lap and a pot of tea beside a shortbread cookie on a low table. When he spotted Katherine, he slid back the sleeve of his *galabiya* and looked at the photograph from a newsmagazine taped to the back of his arm. He compared it to Katherine, and as soon as she disappeared into the elevator he stood up, brushed the crumbs from his lap and went to call Abu Shapour.

THE BARBER, who was fat, stood behind Imad Tayib and cut his hair. Tayib could feel the man's stomach moving against his head. Devout Muslims did not cut their hair, but in times of special danger there was a practice known as *taqiya*, concealment, by which a man was allowed to adapt his appearance to an otherwise threatening environment. Tayib was practicing *taqiya* now, but as each clump of black hair landed on the cement floor, he renewed his hatred of the woman who had made such sacrilege necessary.

While the barber worked, Tayib reviewed his plan. He would carry two stiletto knives, one for each of the Americans. He would knock on the door of their hotel rooms, and offer a copy of the English-speaking *Syria Times,* compliments of the Sheraton. When the enemy reached for the paper Tayib would slide the blade into his heart. If they were both in the same room he would have to work quickly. To protect his clothes from the spray of blood, he had two knives, one for each victim. He would leave them embedded in their hearts.

The barber finished and Tayib put on the tight-fitting garments of the West—slacks, shirt, sportcoat and the suffocating thick shoes. He slid a knife into each pocket of the coat, the lining of which had been slit to accommodate the blades, then moved into the outer room, where his followers were deep in heated discussions about the army's move on Raqba. A hush fell over them. Tayib spread his arms. "Behold the Father of Palestine walks in Western clothes to slay the Western enemy."

THE DESK clerk at the Meridien was named Cyril. His father was French, his mother Arab, and he was particularly sensitive to the type of insult he had endured three nights earlier from the drunken American, Sam Gaddis. Later that night, when Gaddis created a disturbance, he had been happy to call the police. Now, as the American approached him, he wondered if he would remember him.

"Which room is Skip Robinson?"

Find it yourself, Cyril thought as he checked the register. It was just as well the man didn't recognize him. "Room 406, sir."

Gaddis was smoking a cigarette. As he turned away an ash fell to the polished counter. Cyril flicked it away in disgust and kept an eye on the American, who carried a briefcase and seemed distracted. Gaddis made a call from the house phone. When there was no answer he got a piece of hotel stationery from the concierge and wrote a note, then returned to Cyril and lifted the briefcase to the desk.

"I want to leave this for Mr. Skip Robinson. And put this in his box." He handed him the envelope embossed with the hotel logo.

"Of course, sir." *Your mother fucks donkeys.*

As soon as the American left, Cyril made certain that the other clerk was busy with a guest, then slipped the envelope into the briefcase. He made a phone call. Fifteen minutes later an Arab in Western clothes arrived. "Mr. Sam Gaddis left a case for me?"

"Yes, sir, here it is."

Cyril exchanged the briefcase for a brown envelope. He then went to the bathroom and, inside a marble stall with a gurgling Western-style toilet he counted out one hundred American dollars, three months salary. *I wonder what was in the briefcase,* he thought. *I hope it was important. I hope it causes much trouble for the American who insults a man's family and forgets his face.*

TAYIB CHOSE his ambush team: Rashid whose nerves were iron, Naguib because he knew English, Ibrahim who had taken the initiative and warned them about the police, and Abu Shapour as his driver. They carried three Soviet AKS-74 automatic rifles, each with five thirty-round magazines, and two Helwan 9mm. automatic pistols.

He had forgotten the noise and dirt of the city. Some women wore Western dress covered only by a white headscarf or, sometimes, no head covering at all. They passed a statue of President Assad, hands spread benevolently over the chaotic traffic.

"There is a measure of the nation's weakness,"

Tayib said pointing at the statue. "The bird behind the peacock's feathers is not a hawk."

Ibrahim grinned at the rarely voiced irreverence for the country's leader, but Shapour looked uneasy. He's an old man, Tayib thought irritably. I should not have chosen him for this operation.

At the hotel they parked at a spot that commanded a view of the entrance. If a hasty escape were necessary, the ambush team could cut down any pursuers. Tayib left his pistol in the car and carried only the two knives. He looked every bit the businessman in his dark blue suit, green-and-blue striped tie, white shirt and sunglasses. An obsequious doorman in a gaudy uniform opened the oversize carved door.

That's right, Tayib thought, scrape and bow before the rich guest. I'm just another corrupt businessman here to drink whiskey and fuck beautiful young whores, and cut the hearts out of two traitors.

"DID YOU find your friend?" Katherine asked when Sam returned from the Meridien. They were in her room. While Sam was gone, she had changed from travel clothes to a skirt and blouse.

"He wasn't there, so I left a note. Whatever happens those pictures will make it to the *Herald*. Did you set up a meeting with Livingston?"

"He's not at the Embassy. It's a holiday and there's only a skeleton staff."

"What holiday?"

"Thanksgiving." A time of family gatherings that Katherine had deliberately pushed from her mind. "Did you get his home number?"

"I didn't need to. The secretary said he was at an

annual picnic they have at the American School. I think we'll have better luck if we take him by surprise."

"We'll have better luck if we take him at gunpoint." He lifted the Mont Blanc from the table. Katherine took it from him and put it in her purse.

"No more guns, Sam."

"You think he's going to take us to Mike because you blew up the power line for him?"

"No, he's going to take us to Mike because if he doesn't do it you'll publish a transcript of his conversation with Sarkis Irskenian."

"We don't have a transcript. All we have is a one-sided partial conversation."

"He doesn't know that."

A slow smile spread across his face. "They'll be recruiting you next."

There was a knock at the door. Katherine crossed the room while Sam went to the balcony to light a cigarette.

"Yes?"

"Room service."

She opened the door and a porter brought in two bottles of Perrier and a canister of ice. Katherine signed a chit and the porter left. She took an aspirin from the purse and felt a chill of apprehension; the last person who had held the canister was Imad Tayib. She shrugged the feeling aside and filled the glass.

TAYIB HAD never been inside the Sheraton. He noted the *nargileh* and brass coffee pot sitting on the brazier tended by a man in turban and *galabiya,* the traditions of a culture turned to toys and games for Westerners. Abu Shapour had told him that no one would question him, and he had been right.

He stepped into the elevator, lined with brass so highly polished he could see his reflection, an alien one with its short hair neatly parted down one side, prominent nose and full upper lip no longer hidden by a moustache. He pushed the button to the top floor and stepped back as three other guests stepped in. They made two stops at intermediate floors, and then he was alone once again. Inside the jacket pocket he fingered a knife as the elevator bumped to a stop for the last time. The doors opened. Katherine Cahill and Sam Gaddis stared at him.

THIRTY-ONE

TAYIB BRACED HIMSELF FOR THEIR REACTION. SAM AND Katherine, in the middle of a conversation, waited for him to step out of the elevator . . . And then he realized—the haircut, the clothes—they didn't recognize him. Unwilling to risk speaking, he pretended confusion and pushed the button to the lobby. The Americans stepped into the car and turned their backs. The doors shut.

"No," the woman was saying, "let me talk to him."

"I know him best."

"You'll lose your temper—"

"No, no, look at my hand, I'm steady as a rock."

Tayib stared at them through darkened lenses. Twenty-four hours earlier they had stood bound and helpless in front of him, their lives hanging on a single movement of his hand. Kill them, instinct urged, kill them now. He pushed the button to the second floor, and his hand found the stiletto inside the jacket pocket. If no one was in the corridor when the doors opened, he would stab them and take the stairs to the lobby. By the time the hotel staff realized what had happened . . .

The car stopped on the sixth floor and four Arabs wearing richly textured *galabiyas* and silk outer robes joined them. Saudi oil shieks, smelling of Western cologne, laughing and talking loudly. One of them gestured broadly and his hand struck the hidden knife point in Tayib's pocket. The man let out a yelp and stared at the back of his hand as a bead of blood formed.

"You cut yourself, Auda?"

"I felt something . . ."

They turned to Tayib, who glanced about innocently. On the wall was a brass frame around a playbill advertising a nightclub act. Tayib rubbed a finger along its corner, testing the edge.

"Is it sharp?"

Tayib shrugged. The man leaned to touch it while Auda sucked his wound. Sam looked briefly over his shoulder and returned to his conversation with Katherine. The elevator bumped to a stop on the second floor. Tayib pushed past and walked down the hall until he heard the doors shut. He took the stairs to the lobby and followed the Americans to the parking lot, where he watched as they got into a Mercedes with a dented grill and cracked windshield. He crossed quickly to the Peugeot and slid into the front seat next to Abu Shapour.

"Follow them."

● ● ●

THE AMERICAN School was located on Chaoky Street not far from the embassy. While Sam waited in the car Katherine showed her passport to the guard and followed a group of newcomers to an open grassy area where picnic tables were draped in orange-and-brown tablecloths that fluttered gently in the wind. The feast was over and the skeletal remains of chickens lay heaped in plastic trash bins. Adults stood chatting while children, some dressed as Indians or Pilgrims, played volleyball. A six-year-old boy came running around the corner and bumped into Katherine. Behind him came his mother, a large woman in a billowing dress and straw hat. "Randy," she called, "you apologize to the lady."

"I'm sorry," the boy said in a low voice, then darted off. With an apologetic smile his mother went after him.

Katherine weaved her way among the tables until she spotted Livingston. He was talking with a dark-haired woman wearing a cowboy hat adorned with a tiny American flag. His hand touched her upper arm in a gesture both protective and intimate. Katherine approached and said loudly, "Mr. Livingston, can I speak to you a moment?"

He looked up.

"Or is your name Adam today?"

Livingston rose smoothly, made an excuse to the girl, who watched reproachfully as he moved around the table to Katherine. "That was foolish of you."

"Was it?"

"We need to talk but not here." He reached for her elbow but she pulled back.

"Sam's waiting outside."

As he followed her across the school grounds his

eyes roamed the crowd but he wore a patronizing smile. "I assume from your tone that Sam has convinced you I'm some kind of ogre."

"Sarkis Irskenian did that."

Livingston blinked. "Who?"

"The man who calls you Victor."

His smile died abruptly. "Don't jump to too many conclusions, Ms. Cahill."

"What happened to Imad Tayib?"

"He might have escaped, he might have died in the attack, we don't know yet."

Outside the gate Sam was leaning against the car. "Hello, spook. How's the betrayal business?" Before Livingston could answer he raised a camera and took a picture. Livingston reflexively raised a hand.

"No photos."

"I'll need one to go with the transcripts. Did Katherine tell you? We've got your conversation with Irskenian right here." He held up a microcassette.

"I don't know what you're talking about."

"Now, *Victor,* your memory can't be that bad."

Livingston kept his tone even. "How did you get that tape?"

"Do you think you're the only ones who know how to bribe a secretary or tap a phone line?" Sam opened the driver's door. "Get in."

"And if I don't?"

"Better take out a subscription to the *Herald.* We're planning a great new series: CIA disasters around the world."

Katherine said, "The arrangement is this, Mr. Livingston . . . you take us to Mike Winn and we'll give you the tape."

"How do I know you haven't made a copy?"

"You have my word, there's no copy of this tape."

Livingston looked from one to the other, shook his head. "Whatever you people think you're doing, you are *way* out of your league."

"Tracy Winn is dead," Katherine said. "I promised her I'd free her husband and I'll do whatever I have to do to keep that promise."

"Dead? How?"

"We'll tell you on the way to get Mike," Sam said. "You drive."

Livingston got into the car. Katherine joined the CIA man in front while Sam got in back. As they left the school Sam said, "So where's Mike Winn?"

"Bludan."

"I knew it." He flicked Livingston's ear with his finger.

"Where's Bludan?" Katherine asked. "Mr. Livingston?"

"A mountain resort twenty minutes away—"

"He's a real equal opportunity scumbag, steals husbands as well as wives."

"Some wives I don't need to steal."

Sam flicked his ear again but Livingston grabbed his hand. The car swerved and Katherine shoved her arm between the two men. "He's baiting you, Sam, can't you see that?"

"I see a man who's selling American lives for a Swiss bank account. How much do you want to bet Washington knows zilch about Mike Winn and the gas shipments to Iraq?"

Livingston glanced at him in the rear-view mirror. "Stick to taking pictures, Sam. You don't have the brains for this."

"It doesn't take brains to know that anybody selling poison gas to the Iraqis is a traitor."

"Read the newspapers you work for. You'd find out the Iraqis make their own chemical agents, they don't need to buy from us."

"Then who's getting it, the Iranians?"

"You're such amateurs, the both of you."

"The Syrians," Katherine said, sensing the answer.

"Now you know why I picked you instead of Sam to sabotage the radar station."

"You run an auction?" Sam said. "Sell to the highest bidder?"

"Not selling, giving. And not me, the U.S. government. *Your* government, Sam. A part of it, anyway. People who aren't afraid to take tough steps that will safeguard the future of our country. People who put careers and reputations on the line and do it not for money or glory or a byline in the *Herald* but for the future of America—"

"Just a humble public servant named God."

"I stand for something, you stand for nothing. You spend your life second-guessing people with guts enough to make decisions and trashing policies you can't begin to understand—"

"Why *are* we doing it?" Katherine broke in. "Why are we giving them poison gas?"

"So they'll give *us* support for the coalition against Saddam Hussein. The Syrians wanted their own poison gas to counter Iraq's. We were destroying stockpiles of the stuff in Western Europe so it made sense to divert it where it would do some good."

"Through third party middlemen like Sarkis Irskenian so it couldn't be traced to the United States."

"There's hope for you yet, Sam."

"None for you, though. Your career is over, I'll make sure of it."

"What about Bright Justice?" Katherine said hurriedly. "If Syria's cooperation is so important, why would we jeopardize it with an attack on Raqba?"

"Remember the line in *Casablanca*—*Round up the usual suspects*? That's what this is—*Make the usual protests.* You think we'd cross their border without a nod and a wink from the Syrians? They've been looking for a way to get rid of Tayib ever since Flight 67, but they couldn't grab him or risk a civil uprising."

"They know about Bright Justice?"

"No names, no dates, no details, just the general intent. They'll scream bloody murder, but you won't see them pulling out of the multinational force in Saudi Arabia."

"But what about Mike Winn?" Katherine said. "How long did you intend to keep him a hostage?"

"Until Kuwait is liberated."

Sam said, "And then he'd charge you half a million dollars and let you think you'd paid off somebody like Imad Tayib."

"Sam's sense of responsibility doesn't extend beyond the lens of his camera, Ms. Cahill. You're an intelligent, sophisticated woman. Maybe you should consider how something like this will affect Congress. They'll blow it up like the Iran-Contra affair, maybe even vote to pull our troops out of the Middle East. You know the precedent that would set in this part of the world? Every street Arab would make Saddam Hussein his personal hero, and every pro-Western Arab government would fall. And what about our allies? How would they feel if we went home and left their troops eating dust in the desert after pressuring them to send men over here? Our children will pay the price for years if we fail in our duty today—"

"Not your children," Sam said, flicking Livingston's ear, "Unless they're illegitimate."

The CIA man grabbed Sam's wrist. They struggled and the Mercedes swerved toward an oncoming car. Katherine grabbed the wheel as Livingston wrenched it to the right and braked abruptly. The car skidded across its own lane, turned slowly ninety degrees and slammed to a stop against a concrete abutment.

"Keep your fucking hands—"

"Want to get out?"

"—haven't a clue what's going on—"

"Stop it," Katherine shouted. "We're here to get Mike Winn, not wreck the car."

"Tell him to keep his hands off."

"Sit back, Sam. Sit behind me."

"I hate the view."

"What?"

"I can see him in the mirror."

"Fine, there." She twisted the rear-view mirror up to the roof of the car. "He can't see you, don't you touch him. If either of you talks, talk to me. Can we go now?"

A Peugeot passed them and slowed to a stop. The left side of the Mercedes scraped as they backed away from the abutment and regained the road. The Peugeot was backing up now. Livingston gave it a cursory wave but apparently they hadn't stopped to help since all the occupants were looking out the opposite window.

• • •

IMAD TAYIB and his men had not seen the accident. The Americans were momentarily out of sight and it took Tayib by surprise when they came around the corner and saw the Mercedes jammed against a concrete railing, dust drifting away from it. Shapour braked but Tayib said, *"No,* keep going."

An accident, or had the Americans spotted them? Or had Allah chosen this spot for their enemies to die? Once past the Mercedes he had Shapour pull to the side of the road. "Back up slowly. Get the weapons ready."

The men were still fitting the clips into their rifles when the Mercedes began to move. At the same time a bus came into view.

"Never mind," Tayib said quickly. "Let them pass ahead of us. Don't look at them."

Shapour's expression was uncertain. Major Yazdi should be here, Tayib thought. He would know better how to execute such an operation. They continued following the Mercedes but the incident put the men on edge. To restore their confidence Tayib recited lines from the Koran: "Warfare is ordained for you although it is hateful to you; but it may be that you hate a thing that is good for you and yet love a thing that is bad for you; Allah knoweth and you know not."

The road wound upward, and they caught glimpses of the Mercedes at intervals. As they approached Bludan, the Americans turned onto a gravel road where summer homes sat well back, hidden among the pines. When the Mercedes turned down one driveway Tayib and his men continued until they were hidden from view, then stopped.

"Allah has delivered our enemies," Tayib said. "The house is isolated and ideal for our purpose. Make your weapons ready."

Shapour said, "Shouldn't we send someone to find out how many are in the house?"

Yes, Tayib realized, but he was unwilling to admit the lapse of judgment. "It doesn't matter. Who shelters the thief shall share his punishment; who aids the enemy is himself condemned."

"They may be armed . . ."

"So are we armed, and not only with weapons but with our faith."

As they got out of the car Shapour's robe tangled with the seatbelt. Still rankled by his friend's reluctance, Tayib pretended to misunderstand the delay. "If you wish to stay in the car, Abu Shapour, deliver your pistol to me."

"Whose arm fells one enemy, mine shall kill two," Shapour said angrily as he got out.

Good, thought Tayib. In your anger lies resolve and resolve was what they needed now.

"IT'S THE wrong house," Livingston said. There were no cars in the driveway and the place looked deserted.

"You forgot where you put him?" Sam asked. Katherine gave him a warning look. She had kept the two men from speaking during the remainder of the trip and didn't want Sam starting any new arguments.

"I've never seen the place in daylight," Livingston said as they turned around. Returning to the road, they drove back the way they had come and turned into another drive which led to a white house with a red tile roof. It sat on a sloping hill with light angling through the trees, a bucolic setting reminiscent of a summer camp.

An Arab wearing a dark turtleneck and sportcoat came out to meet them. He had a thick moustache and an unfriendly expression that changed to a smile when Livingston stepped out of the car.

"My friend." He grasped Livingston's hand and touched cheeks in the Arab style.

"How is our guest, Jamal?"

"He is fine. Everything is good."

"Where are the others?"

"Salah is making coffee and Mustafa is repairing the hot-water tank. Always the flame is going out, perhaps the burner."

"It's a tough job," Sam said, "holding hostages without a hot shower."

Jamal's smile was puzzled. Livingston said, "This is Sam Gaddis and Katherine Cahill."

"Two friends are twice welcome."

So polite and so unreal, Katherine thought as they entered the house. The living room was messy; a jacket draped over a chair, magazines in piles next to the couch, a cigarette butt on the parquet floor. The television sat in a nest of video tapes and there was an unfinished backgammon game on the black tile hearth in front of the fireplace.

"Sit, please." Jamal gestured to the couch. "Salah will bring coffee." On a small table with a mosaic top a circle of tiny coffee cups was arranged around a bowl of brown sugar.

"Where's Mike?" Katherine said.

Livingston sent Jamal to get him.

"Just a little hostage cottage," Sam said, "courtesy of the United States government."

"Consider yourself lucky it's the United States. If we were Russian you'd be carving toothpicks in Siberia or buried in some nameless grave."

"You were born in the wrong country, Livingston. You're really a KGB type without the double chin. I can just see you up there on the podium with a red star on your chest watching the People's Army march past."

"You people take it all for granted. I'm protecting the country *from* people like you *for* people like you."

"Yeah, that's the burden of omnipotence."

Something bothered Katherine about the coffee cups. They weren't symmetrical. Only seven cups, the eighth missing or broken or . . . the half-formed thought was lost as Jamal returned with Mike, and Sam began taking pictures. Mike Winn was shorter than Katherine had expected, a stocky good-looking man squinting in the unaccustomed light. He was in handcuffs, his clothes wrinkled, hair unkempt, in need of a shave.

"Mr. Winn, my name is Doug Livingston. I work for the American government—"

"About time you guys got here." He pushed Jamal aside. "Fucking raghead."

"Great stuff," Sam said from behind the camera. "Do it again."

Mike grinned and tried to repeat the performance but Jamal grabbed him and slammed him against the wall.

"Enough," Livingston called out. Mike gasped for breath. "Who the hell *are* you people?"

"I'm Katherine Cahill, and this is Sam Gaddis. We're friends of Tracy's . . ."

His face brightened. "Is she here?"

She hesitated, then turned to Livingston. "Take the handcuffs off him."

Mike's expression changed to alarm as the third man, Mustafa, came in carrying two Uzi submachine guns. "Watch it, that one's got a gun—"

"Just relax and cooperate," Livingston said. "Any harm that comes to you will be strictly your own fault." He took one of the guns, chambered a round, and turned it on Sam. "I'll take the tape now."

Katherine said, "What do you think you're doing, Mr. Livingston?"

"To borrow a phrase from Saddam Hussein, you two are guests until the Kuwait problem is solved. The tape, Sam. Or shall I have Jamal take it from you?"

Sam tossed it to him. "Don't cream your jeans, it's blank."

"You think I believe you?" Livingston dropped it to the floor, then crushed it beneath his heel.

"It's true," Katherine said. "The original is with the photographs of the train wreck. If we don't get back to the hotel the transcript of your conversation, along with Mike's photographs, will appear on the front page of the *Washington Herald*."

Mike turned to her. "My photos?"

"No," Livingston said. "My photos." And from his jacket he took out Mike's pictures and tossed them to the table. "You people are such amateurs. Did you really think you could go to any hotel in Damascus without my knowing it? Did you think you were scaring me into coming up here? All you did was save me the trouble of getting you here."

Now Katherine realized the significance of the seven coffee cups. It wasn't that one was broken or missing—only seven had been laid out in expectation of their arrival. Was the seventh cup for Tracy or for Mike? Either way, Livingston must have phoned his men even before she got to the picnic. He had been one step ahead of them all along.

THIRTY-TWO

TAYIB FELT THE WIND ON HIS FACE AND FELT STRANGELY unprotected as they approached the house. He and Abu Shapour could conceal their pistols, but the rifles carried by Naguib, Rashid and Ibrahim made their intentions very apparent. They approached the house from the side. It looked deserted.

"Is there a guard?"

"I see no one."

"Where's the car?"

Tayib shook his head. If the Mercedes was there, it was in the garage. He sent Rashid to circle the place while he and the others moved close enough to look in a window. The furniture was Western but there were no lights, no noise, no sign of life.

"Should we break into the garage and see if the car is there?"

Before he could answer, Rashid poked his head around the corner and signaled to get their attention. He led them to a rear window, where Tayib peered cautiously inside. An old man, wearing the white embroidered skullcap of those who had been to Mecca, lay dozing on a sofa.

"Stay out of sight," Tayib said in a low voice. "I will talk to the old one."

He went to the front door and knocked loudly. An interminable wait, followed by the sound of shuffling feet. The door opened and the old man greeted him in a thin voice, "Peace upon you, stranger."

"And upon you be peace and many more years, *hadji.*" Tayib used the honorific title for those who had made the pilgrimage to Mecca.

"I would invite you inside but I am an employee and the owners gave strict instructions."

"The hospitable heart is valued no less than the open hearth. I rode with strangers who were coming to this area but I left my bag in their car. I do not know which home is theirs, but the car is a Mercedes with a broken windshield."

The old man nodded. "Such a car pulled into the driveway not ten minutes ago."

"Did you recognize them?"

"As I recognize all men as brothers, though none living who know me by that name."

Tayib hid his impatience. "Gray hair better fits a man's head than a crown, *hadji.* Did you *see* which way they went?"

"As man's years grow long so his eyesight grows short. Those you seek are hidden from my sight."

Tayib returned to his men. "Let us check the houses between here and the main road. When we find the Mercedes with the broken window we will surround the house, and destroy them."

"Inshallah," Shapour murmured, God willing. But Tayib had turned away and did not hear him.

"I DON'T get it," Mike Winn said. "We're all Americans, right? I mean . . . ?"

Livingston said, "Your new friends will fill you in on the details. All I can tell you is that you constitute a danger to the American effort to free Kuwait, and my assignment is to neutralize that danger. As soon as our armed forces return home, the three of you will be released. By that time I'll have resigned from government service and be living abroad."

"On some woman's money," Sam said.

Livingston moved toward him. "You created me, Sam, what do you expect? I'm a rogue agent, out on my butt no matter what I do. So before I resign, I'm going to make sure the job I was sent over here to do gets done. Meanwhile . . ."

Without warning he slammed the Uzi into Sam's chest and sent him stumbling back against the couch. Jamal hit him from behind, and he fell to his knees.

A thousand thoughts had been going through Katherine's mind. Now she moved forward to help, but the CIA man blocked her way. "He's okay. That was just a payback for the greeting he gave me at the embassy."

"Then what's my payback?" She slapped him, hard. Livingston jerked back, touched his bleeding lip. When he spoke, his voice was tight with anger. "I'm not the enemy, Ms. Cahill."

Sam was massaging his neck. "Sure you are. You're just too stupid to know it."

"Where's Tracy?" Mike asked. "Does she know I'm here?"

Sam glanced at Katherine, saw her turn away. "She's dead," he said. "A man named Imad Tayib killed her yesterday."

"Dead?"

"I'm sorry," Katherine said softly. From the kitchen Salah entered with a pot of coffee.

"Why? How?"

"She came here to find you. We were—"

A shot rang out. Salah let out a cry, pitched forward and the coffee splashed on Katherine's legs. Bullets from outside the house shattered the living room window. Mustafa dropped his Uzi and grabbed his throat, blood pulsing through his fingers. The front door burst open and an Arab entered in a crouch, shooting without aiming, spraying the area. Livingston turned, fired, hit the man in the arm. A new attacker came out of the kitchen and fired a burst at Livingston. The CIA man collapsed and the last kidnapper, Jamal, dropped his rifle and held his hands high.

Silence.

A third man stood in the door, his rifle pointed at Sam, who crouched near the fireplace. "Stand up, Mr. Gaddis. And lift your hands." He flicked his head to toss back an unruly lock of hair. It was Naguib, their guide from Raqba.

Katherine knelt beside Livingston. His stomach and chest were bloody, his teeth gritted in pain.

A chillingly familiar voice said, "You cannot outrun the wind that burns the hearts of the unbeliever."

Katherine looked up. A macabre version of Imad Tayib, cheeks hollow and skin pale, stood in the doorway like some vengeful scarecrow in Western dress. "The wind of faith is invisible but it uproots the strongest tree. Did you think the machines of the West could kill one chosen by Allah?"

Katherine stood as Tayib approached her. "He's badly hurt," she said. Tayib glanced down at Livingston, now trying to reach the Uzi. He kicked the gun aside, shoved a toe beneath Livingston's chest and flipped him onto his back. When Katherine tried to stop him, Abu Shapour, eyes filled with hate, pushed in front of her.

"He will die," Tayib said calmly.

"I recognize him," Shapour said. "He is a CIA man from the American Embassy."

Tayib's lips tightened. "You sent a *woman* to kill me?" He put his shoe on Livingston's face, rocked it back and forth, crushing his nose.

"Stop it." Katherine tried to push past Abu Shapour, who grabbed her by the hair and yanked her backward onto the couch. Sam took a step forward but Naguib fired a shot at his feet. "The next bullet finds your heart."

"Jesus . . ." Mike said in a low voice. Tayib turned his gun on Katherine. "You have one minute to purge your mind of impure thoughts and prepare your soul for freedom."

Never point a gun . . . Her father's words echoed in her memory as her eye registered the details . . . the pistol was a clone of the Beretta Model 951, its safety off, the hammer cocked, the gun ready to fire. The gun that would kill her.

"You were right, Katherine," Sam said loudly. "I told you Imad Tayib was a man of his word and you said he was a liar."

"Be quiet," Naguib said.

"You said he would never release Mike Winn even if you *gave him* the half million dollars . . ." He was staring at her with an imperative look. "Even though he *promised* if you made a donation to the Red Crescent society. . . ."

His eyes went to her purse and suddenly she understood. The Mont Blanc. But there was only a single bullet. Even if she could kill Tayib, what about the rest of them? She scanned the room. One of Tayib's men had lost the use of his right arm. His face was white and he leaned against the wall, his rifle cradled awkwardly in his left arm. The others had positioned themselves close to their captives. A fierce-looking man stood near the kitchen guarding Jamal, the kidnapper who had surrendered. Sam and Naguib were near the fireplace. Mike stood at the other end of the couch, with Abu Shapour between them. Five guns against a single bullet? Impossible. But if they were going to die anyway . . .

Katherine turned to Tayib. "This is Mike Winn. He's done nothing to you. You promised to release him for half a million dollars. I call on you to do it now or prove to the world and your own people you're a liar."

Tayib stiffened. "You exchange a bullet for your final prayer."

She pointed at Naguib. "You speak English. You heard your leader's promise at Raqba but now you see his words are worthless—"

Tayib raised his gun to her head. Katherine held his gaze. "Imad Tayib would rather kill an innocent man than contribute half a million dollars to the Red Crescent society."

Tayib's pallor was that of death. He wanted to pull the trigger, she could see it in his eyes, *feel* it in his look. "Where is the money?"

"In the bank, I can write you a check—"

"Your check will be no good."

"I came here to ransom Mike Winn. My check will be good, I guarantee it."

The gun lowered. "If you are lying, the family of Brian Cahill will die in flames." He watched her intently. Her eyes seemed opaque, revealing nothing. "Do you understand?"

Katherine reached into her purse—Tayib grabbed her arm.

"I need my checkbook."

He lifted the purse from her shoulder and tossed it to Shapour, who dumped the contents onto a chair: wallet, cosmetics, pills, guidebook, brush, the Mont Blanc pen . . .

"There." She pointed to the checkbook. He handed it to her and she pushed the coffee cups aside and placed it on the table. "And the pen."

Shapour handed her the Mont Blanc. She unscrewed the cap, willing her fingers not to tremble, resisting the urge to unscrew the base and cock the gun while Tayib's eyes were on her. She needed three seconds to arm the weapon. She looked at Sam. Do something . . .

Sam caught the look, understood. He turned to Mike. "You're going to live, Mike. You're going to live because of Tracy."

"What?" Mike looked up, confused.

Katherine printed the letters slowly and deliberately.

"Tracy died yesterday—this man killed her."

Mike's eyes cleared. *"Who* killed her?"

"He executed her yesterday."

"That's . . . ?"

"Imad Tayib."

With an anguished cry Mike started forward. Abu Shapour and Tayib both turned their weapons on him and he stopped short, face twisted in anger. *"Why?"*

Katherine gave the top a half turn and pulled it out until the trigger clicked into place. "Here," she said loudly as she detached the check and handed it to Tayib. He held it up triumphantly. "Allah is just. The wealth stolen from our country returns to aid the injured, to heal the sick, to bind the soldier's wounds and bathe the martyr's brow—"

Katherine's hand seemed to float upward, fingers shifting the pen, aiming at the spot behind Tayib's left ear, no hesitation, no reservation, a movement as practiced and natural as striking a match. Her thumb found the trigger, Tayib turning toward her, holding the check made out not to the Red Crescent but to Jeff, Allison, Joey, Tracy . . .

Tayib never saw the names. There was a blur near his cheek, the woman's hand exploding at his ear, searing heat bursting inside his head. *Kill her.* The command raced to his fingers, but muscles no longer obeyed, fingers slack, the pistol clattered to the floor and the room tilted crazily.

Sam, anticipating the shot, grabbed Naguib's rifle and they struggled, neither able to wrest control of the gun from the other. Naguib's finger caught the trigger and the whole magazine emptied into the ceiling, showering the room with chips of plaster, wood and glass.

Abu Shapour was dumbfounded . . . it was as if

the shot materialized out of thin air. And Tayib, lying there on the floor in a spreading stain of his own blood while the Cahill woman was scrambling for the pistol—

The pistol. He realized the threat, aimed his own gun at Katherine's back, but before he could pull the trigger, something struck him from behind. He fell to his hands and knees, glanced up as Mike Winn kicked the gun from his hand. It skidded across the floor and lodged under Livingston's hip. Livingston was still conscious . . . his hand moved slowly for the gun . . .

Jamal, the only kidnapper who hadn't been killed, bolted when the first shot rang out. From the corner of his eye the *shaheen* Rashid saw him coming and thought it was an attack. He turned, brought the gun to bear as Jamal disappeared into the kitchen. Gunfire erupted behind him. He had been needlessly distracted . . .

Ibrahim saw his leader fall and Mike Winn strike Abu Shapour. Ignoring the pain in his useless right arm, he raised the rifle with his left hand and pointed toward the center of the room as Mike kicked away Shapour's pistol. Ibrahim pressed the trigger. The barrel swiveled erratically, bullets pegged the carpet and caught Mike in the legs. He fell next to Livingston, who now held a pistol. Raising the pistol toward Ibrahim. No good, Ibrahim thought, as he tried to heft the rifle again. The handgun jumped in Livingston's hand. Ibrahim never felt the bullet that punctured his temple and shattered the left half of his skull . . .

Sam and Naguib were still wrestling for the rifle, now empty of ammunition. They stumbled against the fireplace, where Sam caught his leg on the hearth.

Still gripping the rifle, he sat down with a grunt. Naguib slammed a knee into his face and wrenched the gun free. Sam went after him but Naguib side-stepped, lowered the barrel to Sam's chest and pulled the trigger . . .

Rashid saw Naguib pull the trigger, saw nothing happen. Nothing? The clip was empty. Swiveling from the hip, Rashid sent a spray of bullets stitching their way across the wall toward Sam. An impact like an invisible foot kicked Rashid in the chest, then another. His rifle dropped, one hand pawed for support, and he collapsed.

Katherine knelt on the floor, arms outstretched, the pistol at the apex in a two-handed target grip. She shifted her target from Rashid to Naguib.

"Naguib," Katherine called out. His head floated above the white dot in her forward sight. "Drop the gun."

Naguib's eyes took in the room . . . Rashid and Ibrahim dead, Shapour kneeling beside Tayib . . . He let the weapon fall. As Sam bent to retrieve it there was a sharp crack. Naguib stumbled backward with a shocked expression. Livingston, crouched unsteadily, put two more bullets into Naguib's chest, then shifted his aim to Abu Shapour, who sat on the floor trying to shield Tayib. As if from a great distance he heard Katherine shouting, her words like whispers . . . "He's not armed, it's over . . ."

Livingston's eyes fluttered as he looked up at her. "I am not the enemy," he mumbled, blood trickling from his mouth. "Not the enemy, not . . ." He fell forward and lay still.

The world had grown silent for Imad Tayib. Abu Shapour's face hovered above him, detached, lips moving, but Tayib heard nothing, felt nothing. Blood, so much of it . . . a carotid artery, he thought vaguely.

Too late, Tayib saw the true meaning of the dream, not a mandate to kill the Americans, but a warning of death. He realized with a sense of wonder that Allah had warned him not once but three times today . . . at the hotel, on the road, and through the old man. He felt rather than heard the drumming of distant hoofbeats. Secure in his belief that He Who Sent Three Warnings would welcome him to Paradise, Imad Tayib died.

EPILOGUE

SAM ADJUSTED THE NEW GREEK FISHERMAN'S HAT SO THAT THE stiff sweatband didn't press against his temple. Sam stood in the airline terminal beside Jerry Riggs, the embassy official who had met them when they arrived in Damascus. Near the boarding gate Katherine helped Mike, whose leg was in a cast, find a seat. It was five days after the attack on the house.

"I heard something this morning that might interest you," Riggs said. "Abu Shapour just turned up in Baghdad. He says Doug Livingston didn't kill Imad Tayib."

Sam kept his expression neutral. After the attack he and Katherine had taken Mike to a hospital where, to avoid threat of retaliation, they told the authorities that Livingston killed Tayib before he was killed himself. By the time the police arrived at the house Abu Shapour had disappeared along with Imad Tayib's body. But if Shapour accused Katherine . . .

"What did he say?"

"That Tayib's not dead. That he wasn't killed at Raqba or shot by Livingston but is hiding until the day of liberation for Palestine. Meanwhile he's appointed Abu Shapour as his spokesman."

Sam relaxed. "Not unless Shapour is talking to ghosts."

"You're sure Tayib was dead when you left the house?"

"Was Kennedy dead when he left Dallas?"

Riggs glanced around uneasily. "Some people don't think we should be here. In Syria, I mean. But you know the saying, *Politics makes strange bedfellows*—that's what this is. We need this country in the coalition against Iraq *and* we need the support of the American people. Rightly or wrongly Doug Livingston was doing his job the best he knew how."

"Just don't go putting your boss in for any medals before you read next week's *Washington Herald*."

Sam thought of the film he was carrying, the photos and the story he would write that would jump-start his career and get him back in the game.

"I keep telling you he wasn't my boss."

"Your mouth says deputy public affairs officer but my eyes see a guy in dark glasses wearing a radio receiver in his ear. Funny how the mind plays tricks on you."

An airline representative announced preboarding for children and passengers needing assistance. Riggs faded into the background while Sam took pictures of Katherine and Mike saying farewell. A leggy Lufthansa stewardess escorted Mike through the boarding gate. Sam slid the camera back into the bag and approached Katherine.

"Informed sources tell me that Abu Shapour surfaced in Iraq. He's floating a story that Tayib wasn't killed, just waiting until the hour of liberation to lead the faithful back to Palestine."

Katherine nodded. "I told you he'd never admit that a woman killed Imad Tayib."

"I still think it's dangerous for you to stay."

"It won't be that long."

"There are more Middle East experts in Washington or New York than here in Damascus."

"But there are no Palestinian refugee camps in Washington."

"Anger and frustration, that's all you'll find there. The key to the Arab mind is hidden even from Arabs."

"I'm sure you're right."

"No, you're not. You're sure I'm wrong."

She returned his smile and said nothing, but there was a quiet certitude about her. She was wearing khaki slacks and a blue shirt and her hair no longer advertised a stylist's touch but was tucked back from her face, a few errant strands curled against her neck. The loudspeaker announced the boarding of Lufthansa Flight 133 to Frankfurt. Their eyes went to the boarding gate, then back to one another. Katherine moved forward and embraced him.

"Thank you, Sam," she whispered.

"Goes both ways," he said in a low voice.

They stepped apart. Sam hefted his bag. "Promise me one thing. If you're going to get yourself killed over here, give me twenty-four hours notice."

"So you can save me?"

"So I can have a camera ready."

Sam joined the other passengers. At the doorway he glanced back, touched his cap in a salute, then

stepped outside and walked briskly across the
tarmac. The smell of jet fuel hung in the air, a reminder of other assignments and other cities. He
looked south, toward Saudi Arabia. Somewhere over
the horizon troops were massing, an air base was being carved out of the desert, and columns of tanks
were snaking their way toward positions on the
Kuwaiti border. Sam mounted the boarding steps two
at a time. He was already marshaling the arguments
he would use to win an assignment from the *Herald*
to cover the next war.

KATHERINE STOOD on the observation deck and watched
the plane take off. Windows behind her rattled and
grew silent as the sound of the jet engines faded. In
her pocket she had a list of names the American consul had given her. Some were Westerners living in
Damascus, some were Syrians, some were Jews, and
some were Palestinians. Maybe they could help her
understand what kind of world had produced Imad
Tayib. And when she understood, maybe she could
do something . . .

As the Lufthansa jet turned across the morning
sun the name came to her: *Institute for Multi-Cultural
Understanding*. She shaded her eyes and saw the
faces of her children. This will be your legacy, she
thought. Killed by hatred you will live through me
and we will make a difference, you and I. Somewhere
in the world is another son or daughter, another husband or wife who is destined to die unless a ray of
understanding brings light to a mind darkened by
desperation or warms a heart frozen by hatred.

A gust of wind pushed a tendril of hair against

her cheek. Katherine left the observation deck and made her way outside the terminal past throngs of animated people greeting their relatives. A limousine with diplomatic plates pulled alongside. The darkened window rolled down and Jerry Riggs leaned out. "I'm going back to the city. Give you a lift?"

"No thanks," Katherine said. "We're not going the same way."

She turned aside, hailed a taxi, and stepped into a new life.

Richard Aellen served as a navy photo-intelligence specialist aboard the aircraft carrier U.S.S. Enterprise during the Vietnam War. He is a former professional pilot and instructor, and makes his home in New York City.

CAMPBELL ARMSTRONG

Agents of Darkness

Suspended from the LAPD, Charlie Galloway decides his life has no meaning. But when his Filipino housekeeper is murdered, Charlie finds a new purpose in tracking the killer. He never expects, though, to be drawn into a conspiracy that reaches from the Filipino jungles to the White House.

Mazurka

For Frank Pagan of Scotland Yard, it begins with the murder of a Russian at crowded Waverly Station, Edinburgh. From that moment on, Pagan's life becomes an ever-darkening nightmare as he finds himself trapped in a complex web of intrigue, treachery, and murder.

Mambo

Super-terrorist Gunther Ruhr has been captured. Scotland Yard's Frank Pagan must escort him to a maximum security prison, but with blinding swiftness and brutality, Ruhr escapes. Once again, Pagan must stalk Ruhr, this time into an earth-shattering secret conspiracy.

Brainfire

American John Rayner is a man on fire with grief and anger over the death of his powerful brother. Some say it was suicide, but Rayner suspects something more sinister. His suspicions prove correct as he becomes trapped in a Soviet-made maze of betrayal and terror.

Asterisk Destiny

Asterisk is America's most fragile and chilling secret. It waits somewhere in the Arizona desert to pave the way to world domination...or damnation. Two men, White House aide John Thorne and CIA agent Ted Hollander, race to crack the wall of silence surrounding Asterisk and tell the world of their terrifying discovery.